THE HIGHGATE PRIESTESS

Carmilla Voiez

THE HIGHGATE PRIESTESS

Book Cover by AOS Designs.

First edition 2024

Acknowledgements

With each book, I find myself in the enviable position of having more and more people to thank. My team of beta readers and critique partners for The Highgate Priestess has grown exponentially both in number and the advice I have been given.

I wish to thank Steven, Beth, Ann, Paul, Scott, Vanessa, Faith, the talented people of the OU Writers' Group, and my wonderful partner, Glen, who supports all my creative efforts; without them this book would have taken far longer to finish.

Thank you to my readers whose support and wonderful reviews never fail to humble me. Thank you to Jim (Ginger Nuts of Horror), Adam Nevill, Ramsey Cambell, Graham Masterton, and the Horror Community at X (a sometimes challenging but frequently supportive collective of writers, reviewers and fans).

I acknowledge a debt to all those writers of dark fiction who came before me, and the hand of friendship to those who follow.

Finally, thank you to my daughters who make me laugh, cry, see things from a new perspective, and make me want to be a better person.

THE HIGHGATE PRIESTESS

CHAPTER ONE

STEPH'S shout summoned me to our living room. 'Hey, Wanda. Come and watch this.' My beautiful partner was dressed for work but still trying to tame her strawberry-blonde waves into a bun. 'You have a new arrival.'

Towel wrapped around my crown, I sat beside her and leaned forward, staring at the television. An armoured bus waited outside the prison gates. Reflected sunlight glared from glass and metal, obscuring the camera's view of the interior until, in the shade of a passing cloud, I glimpsed a mass of long, almost-white, corkscrew-curls.

The prisoner's features were as delicate as the porcelain doll Mother gave me for my seventh birthday. She had wanted me to play with girl's toys, abhorring what she considered my boyishness. It wasn't long before I accidentally cracked the doll's face while helping her climb a tree. Too small to push the broken toy to the bottom of the refuse bin, and too naïve to find a more suitable hiding place, I failed to bury it properly, leaving its fragile fingers to reach accusingly from a shallow grave of single use plastics. When Mother uncovered my crime, she waved the evidence in my terrified face. Her narrowed eyes and trembling mouth filled my head until I shoved the memory away and focused my attention on the woman I loved.

After using a hairpin to imprison a stray curl Steph had missed, I planted a kiss where her pulse fluttered in her throat, inhaling the delicious scent of her.

'Who is it?' I asked, nodding at the television.

Steph gripped my thigh, clipped nails sinking into flesh. 'Melissa Powell, the Highgate Priestess.' Her mouth gaped as the gates inched open, and the bus climbed the hill towards the next checkpoint.

The self-satisfied sneer of a carefully groomed on-the-scene reporter filled the television screen. 'This morning, Melissa Powell arrived at Witchwood Prison to serve the remainder of her life sentence.' Video footage showed body bags on gurneys, wheeled from a Victorian town house, and accompanied by the reporter's account of the grisly discovery. 'Five years ago, in what appeared to be a Satanic ritual gone wrong, thirty-six mutilated bodies were discovered in a cellar in Highgate London. The sole survivor, thirteen-year-old Melissa Powell, was removed from the scene in a catatonic state.'

Another damn celebrity. Powell was infamous – a teenage mass murderer. Why hadn't the night shift been warned about her transfer to Witchwood Prison?

Steph would know every detail of Powell's history, but I was reluctant to ask. Much easier to deal with inmates without knowing the minutiae of their crimes. Most of my charges were victims of circumstance and despair, deserving of the same basic level of respect afforded to any human; approaching them from a position of prejudice made that more difficult.

People were complicated; if my job as a prison guard wasn't enough to convince me, my love life did the rest. Steph's freckled nose could frequently be seen between the pages of a dog-eared paperback, its cover invariably dominated by a lurid image of feminine evil: the shadowy features and shark-eyes of Myra Hindley, Rosemary West or another serial killer; exaggerated high-contrast photos which purported to reveal the monstrous depravity in their faces, reflecting a world without nuance, where people were devils or angels and physiognomy had never been debunked.

While I loved and admired my partner, Steph's fascination with true crime made me uncomfortable. As a student doctor, she spent fifty-to-sixty-hours each week saving people's lives, yet she wallowed in the gory details of vicious and grisly murders during her days off. It wasn't my place to judge her, but after spending my nights in the company of murderers, they were the last things I wanted to discuss during my downtime, and Steph's requests for titbits of information and anecdotes really dampened my libido. Was it selfish of me to want to escape such horror?

Working at the prison allowed me to support Steph financially. A means to an end. Although I hated my job and grumbled to myself every evening as I got ready for work, the routine helped me feel safe, prevented me from thinking too deeply and spiralling into paranoia or depression.

Steph and I were each other's support network, and it was a privilege to share life's journey with her. Our coupling kept me on track when my mood wobbled, my carriage tilted, or my wheels screeched to a halt beneath me. Many of the stations I'd steamed through as a child were too frightening to revisit, but the verdant beauty of the land ahead beckoned me ever onwards.

In a year, two at most, Steph would be fully qualified, and it would be my turn to follow my dreams, return to university and study to be a vet. A worthy ambition, and one worth waiting for, I believed – helping and caring for animals rather than keeping women in cages.

Steph checked her watch, kissed my cheek, and hurried out of our home. 'See you tomorrow,' she said before she closed the front door behind her.

A minute later, I sauntered to the kitchen, poured a mug of coffee, and stared out of the window at our fog-filled back garden, hoping Steph would drive safely. My arms trembled and dark drops of coffee added polka dots to the white towel wrapped around my torso. Melissa Powell's dainty features clung to my mind, as if some primal part of me sensed her arrival would change my life forever.

Clouds filled the sky and grazed the road, obscuring my vision as I headed to work an hour later. My headlights bounced off the tarmac, dazzling and disorientating. Demon-eyed fog lights shone, warning me of a vehicle ahead. My foot switched pedals, pressing firmly until my car shuddered to a stop. The pinch of a burgeoning migraine threatened to spread behind my eyes as I flicked on my hazard warning lights and turned off the engine. Stretching across to the back seat, I grabbed a bottle of water. Fingers trembling, I searched the glove compartment for my meds, and swallowed a Sumatriptan, hoping that by catching it early, the pain would be bearable.

The air was tainted blood-red by the lights of the vehicle in front. My door creaked as I pushed it open; its scream made my teeth ache. After checking for traffic, I clambered out and skirted my ageing Renault. Coils of fog danced on the warm bonnet, and within seconds, my clothes stuck to my skin. Mobile phone in my clenched fist and gritting my teeth, I checked the parked car – a sporty-looking black Audi, its engine still running. Peering through the passenger window, revealed empty seats.

When I turned my back on the vehicle, I saw more lights. Two red beams striped the sky, pointing upwards like bat signals from a car that had veered far off the road.

After locking the Renault, I headed toward what I assumed was a crash site. 'Is everyone okay?'

A dark silhouette appeared in the billowing grey. Huge, monstrous, looming towards me. It made me gasp and stop short. Muscles stretched as I craned my neck, trying to understand the strange shape above the broad shoulders, focusing next on the thing swinging at its side, imagining a bludgeon or a severed head.

Adrenaline pumped into my limbs. I squeezed my earlobe to curb the panic while balling my other hand into a fist in case I needed to fight. Five-metres away the darkness resolved into a man, well over six-foot-tall, with wavy hair and a thick beard that made it difficult to guess his age. The Audi driver, I told myself, not a ferocious bear, not a killer. The thing swinging beneath his arm wasn't the head of his victim or a murder weapon, but an ordinary carrier bag. Why was I so jumpy, making monsters in the mist?

His long stride rapidly consumed the ground between us. He barely glanced at me as he barged past. Plastic rustled as the carrier bag bounced against my elbow.

'What happened?' I asked.

No reply. He squelched across the wet grass to his car, shaking his head. Was he deaf, or incredibly rude? Either way, I would have to investigate even though it would make me late for work. Driving away, without checking whether someone needed my help, was unthinkable.

Despite the poor visibility, I knew the location well, having driven along this stretch of road at least ten times a week for the last six years. The edge of Witchwood forest stood thirty metres to my right, and ahead, below those tilted fog lights, a river raged.

Only when I drew close enough to hear the roaring water could I see the car – a silver Nissan, its chassis resting on the edge of the bluff, nose down and arse in the air. Both doors were open, but no one was inside. A familiar tune from the sixties played on the radio.

The windscreen was intact, no blood was visible, and the airbags hadn't inflated. Hopefully, the driver and passenger weren't injured. They probably abandoned the vehicle to wait somewhere safer, perhaps they had already phoned for help and were sheltering under trees. Unless they were joyriders; if the car had been stolen by thrill-seeking kids, they would be long gone by now.

'Hello?' I called.

No reply except the music and the ostentatious roar of the Audi pulling away.

The Nissan could lose its grip at any moment and plunge into the water, so I checked for damage from a safe distance, but couldn't see any dents to explain why the vehicle had veered so far from the road. Its headlamps illuminated a steep slope descending to the river, but no people. Nothing but dense silvery fog.

'Hello!' I shouted again, shivering from wet and cold. 'Is anyone hurt? Is anyone there?'

Only the radio replied. 'Don't bother trying to find her...'

Carefully, I backed away from the precipice and peered towards the treeline. Legends of witches and their executioners filled my head as I thought about that vast, untamed wilderness of gnarled and ancient trees which had somehow resisted the plans of modern land developers.

Steph and I had wandered there together once and got thoroughly lost. The thought of entering the forest in the dark, searching for people who were probably long gone, and arriving even later for my shift, did not appeal to me at all. My car waited on the grass verge, its blinking hazard lights painting the air with flashes of orange. Once inside the familiar sanctuary of that metal cage, I called the emergency services to report the accident.

My mouth felt dry; the only part of me that wasn't drenched. As I reached for the water bottle, I noticed a platinum-blonde thread stuck to my sleeve. I peeled it from my wet denim jacket. It looked and felt like a strand of hair, long enough to reach from scalp to waist even with the corkscrew curl. My hair was short, straight, and chestnut brown, and Steph's had a red tint, but this looked almost white. My thoughts raced to the face in the armoured bus – Melissa Powell. It couldn't be hers, but after Steph's excitement at the news of her arrival, I thought she might enjoy seeing and handling it. Instead of throwing it out of the window, I pushed the strand into a pocket.

)O(

By the time my Renault pulled up to the first checkpoint at the five-metre-high perimeter fence, the fog had lifted, replaced by sheets of rain that pounded the roof. One Operational Security Grade officer – OSG for short and colloquially referred to as grunt – checked my identification, while another led a sniffer dog around the chassis.

'Yer good to go,' the man with the dog informed me.

After a minute more of driving at a groaning ten miles per hour, I reached a second set of gates and stepped out of the car to open the boot. One of the two OSGs held a golfing umbrella above my head even though I was already soaked to the bone; and the second searched my boot, lifting a panel to reveal a bald tyre I should have replaced months ago. They checked my ID again and opened the gate.

The towering Victorian frontage of the prison greeted me. Seeing it always made me shudder. Something in the cold stare of those dark windows suggested an ancient evil had made its home within the red bricks. Two centuries ago, it was built as a hospital for lunatics and inconvenient daughters and wives. Concrete annexes were added at the rear in the 1970s – the cellblocks – and to this day, it warehoused the women society wished to hide. Sometimes, I thought I heard the voices of past inmates whispering in the corridors. Offices, solitary confinement cells, and the psych ward filled a third of the original building. The remaining rooms had been abandoned to dust.

After parking in the closest empty space to the entrance, I jogged towards the grim building, eager to remove my wet clothes. When I was dry and dressed in my uniform, I raked fingers through my hair. With a heavy set of keys secured to my belt, I made my way to the shift manager's office.

'Come in,' Sarah Reynolds called after I knocked on her door. She peered up from a stack of paperwork as I entered.

'Sorry I'm late, road traffic accident,' I explained.

She nodded and creased her brow. Reynolds wasn't easily flustered. She had earned her stripes as a guard before being promoted to supervising officer.

'What's up?' I asked.

'The new transfer. I've read an update from Smith. I suppose you saw the news.'

'Why weren't we told to expect her?' I asked.

'To avoid the tabloid sensationalism. Someone at Vinnie Green must have leaked it. It's nothing we can't handle, but Masterton, Wilson, and a few others have been, let's say, skittish.'

What skittish meant in this context was all too easy to imagine. Lily Masterton and Betty Wilson had shared celebrity status for years because of their high body-counts, and Melissa Powell was an unknown entity, one who could disrupt the dynamic.

Our prisoners, despite the system's best efforts, were not a homogeneous group. There were a few, including Masterton and Wilson, who maintained their power by dominating others on the block. These women were truly dangerous because they believed themselves superior beings ungoverned by the ethics of society. They felt victimised by the justice system and stalked their cages, rattled their bars, and attacked guards before we could subdue them.

However, most of our inmates found peace and safety in an environment where men were rarely encountered. Many had been sexually or physically assaulted and, for some, it was why they were here. Hodges in cell thirteen, a gentle and pleasant prisoner most of the time, was serving life for the murder of her husband, and she wasn't the only one whose story could elicit sympathy. Too often, I recognised aspects from my childhood in the wide eyes of inmates and had to pull back from my emotions and retreat inside my uniform to distance myself from their pain. Too much empathy was detrimental in my profession, and the women did not want my sympathy. They never forgot the prison's hierarchy even when I offered the hand of friendship. Them versus us. Any attempt to breach the divide made both sides vulnerable.

'Which cell is Powell in?'

'C forty-eight. I'd like you to monitor our new guest, Jones.'

Steph would cream herself with delight when I told her I was personally responsible for Melissa Powell. 'Of course, Ma'am.'

'Dawson's in the staff room. Join her there. She knows tonight's rota.' Reynolds bent her head and opened a file, effectively dismissing me.

Laney Dawson was my favourite colleague. Her intimidating size meant she could afford to be gentle and caring with the inmates, and she had an equally big heart. She was wiping down a table when I entered the staff room. Instead of helping her, I filled the kettle.

'Yuh alright?' she asked in her rich Caribbean accent.

I nodded. 'How was lock down?'

'Easier than expected.'

'Did you see her?'

'Only on TV. Me hate it when us get celebrities. The afternoon shift had to push through reporters.'

'Ghouls,' I said, then blushed when I recalled my partner's excitement.

Laney rinsed the cloth before joining me on the battered sofa. 'Yuh hair is wet.'

'A car veered off the road. I wanted to check everyone was okay.'

'Them alright?'

'It was empty.'

'Abandoned?'

'Radio and lights were still on. You know the Zombies track from the sixties: *She's Not There*?'

'Yea.'

'That was playing. Talk about synchronicity. Probably joyriders who panicked and scampered for the trees.'

'Makes sense,' Laney said. 'Ten minutes 'til us due at the cells. Me need to powder me nose.'

Allowing my eyes to close, I concentrated on the taste and warmth of the coffee. After a second helping, I swilled out my mug, and headed to the gate. It was one of four modern wings and purpose built with forty-eight cells on two levels plus toilets, shower blocks, library, and a computer room for inmates to study online. Our block could house seventy-two women, but some of the cells were only half-full. Humphreys and Clark were waiting outside the gated entrance.

'Whuz Dawson?' Humphreys asked in her familiar working-class Scouse.

'She'll be here soon. We still have three minutes before change over. How's it been?'

'Few whimpers.'

Had Humphreys caused any of those whimpers? I didn't ask because I didn't want to know. Some guards were nasty pieces of work who enjoyed psychologically and physically abusing the prisoners, and both Clark and Humphreys fell into that category. There was an unofficial blind-eye policy to abuses which did not require hospitalisation, making it pointless to involve management except in extreme cases. It made me anxious. If my life were on the line, a guard, who Laney or I had previously chewed out for misusing their power, might turn their own blind eye and walk away. Thankfully, I rarely felt threatened by the inmates. Respect went both ways.

'Why weren't you here at lock daahn?' Clark asked in her Yorkshire twang.

'Accident on the way in.'

Clark offered a sympathetic frown that put me on edge.

Like most of the prison staff, Clark was conservative, with both a big and a small c. We were not friends, not even close. Laney and I were outliers; Laney due to her exuberant joy and possibly her race, me because I was well-spoken and was considered a bleeding-heart liberal. They labelled me a middle-class snob without knowing I learnt to speak properly to appease my parents and survive my childhood. Humphreys' and Clark's amplified regional dialects probably came from a similar desire to fit in, signifying to all listeners that they belonged to a niche group of northern working-class women.

The thing I found most frustrating was my burning desire to be liked, even by people I hated. Steph warned me it was a symptom of undiagnosed c-PTSD.

'Ere she comes,' Humphreys said, smiling at Laney.

I fiddled with my keys, itching to reach the second floor and check our new arrival.

'Ready?' Laney asked after the others left.

We unlocked the gate to step into the communal space, an open area between walls of cells. Natural light flooded through the skylights during the day, but now they were black rectangles against an off-white ceiling. Nets hung like giant spiderwebs, ready to catch jumpers or women pushed over the chest-high barriers that lined the upper walkways, and wooden benches were bolted to the concrete floor, along with healthy distractions such as tabletop football and table tennis. A social space for the inmates during the day, but now empty and quiet. Lock down ended an hour ago, and by now inmates would be sleeping or masturbating. Even so, part of our job was to invade their privacy every hour by peering into their cells. The bosses claimed it ensured prisoner safety, but it always felt like an intrusion.

My soles slapped concrete as I made my way toward the ground floor cells on the right. At the far wall, facing the gate, were doors to the bathrooms, a television room, and a chapel, while a library and computer room were on the upper floor, giving the block a T shape when viewed from above. The canteen was elsewhere in the prison complex and shared with inmates from blocks A, B and D, but there was a snack machine available for food outside mealtimes, assuming the inmates had funds. There were no pay phones; our inmates could not be trusted to access the outside world without strict supervision.

Movement in my peripheral vision. A shadow rushing silently down the metal staircase. I rotated to face whoever was out of their cell but saw no one. When I turned away, it reappeared, a black mass sprinting towards me, but when I steeled my nerves to stare it down, only Laney and I occupied the space. Was I spooked by the accident and change in routine? Although I had not personally herded inmates into their cells, I had to trust my colleagues did their jobs properly, but trust was something I found difficult after years of constant betrayal. Sighing, rubbing my temples, standing there like a bloody fool and staring at the empty staircase, helped no one, least of all myself. Sometimes, my mind played tricks on me. What it feared might happen if I relaxed, it had never deigned to reveal. I envied people whose brains worked for rather than against them.

Forcing myself to move, I headed to cell twenty-four, the one closest to the gate on the ground floor. As I looked through the viewing window, pimples rose across my flesh and tiny hairs vibrated. There was no thermometer to check whether it was colder here, but it felt as though icy air was seeping from the cell. A shadow obscured the ceiling and stretched tentacles of gloom towards the cots where sleeping inmates lay.

'Everything okay?' Laney asked, her footsteps padding towards me.

How long had I been standing there?

I pulled back and smiled at my colleague. 'Have a quick peek, would you? Does it look normal?'

Her features scrunched together as she inspected the cell, creating gullies that ended at the hub of her nose. 'Fast asleep.'

'Check the ceiling,' I urged, feeling a little ridiculous.

'What me looking for?'

'Is it too dark?'

'No.' She withdrew from the window and placed a cool palm on my forehead.

'I'm not sick,' I said.

'Yuh feel okay,' she confirmed. 'Maybe it stress after the crash?'

'It was weird, and I'm angry I didn't note down the Audi's number plate. Maybe you're right.'

'You think the man cause the accident?'

Up close, Laney smelled of cocoa butter and vanilla, and her presence was reassuring. When I checked again, the cell looked normal. Visual disturbances often accompanied my migraines, but those tended to be kaleidoscopic fractured lights.

'It looks fine now, sorry.' I slid the panel closed.

Laney nodded, pinching her lips between her teeth. Did our age difference make her feel responsible for my well-being? She looked out for me like I was a chick she had recently hatched.

'Honestly, I'm fine,' I said. 'Let's finish this check.'

I reached the adjacent cell as her footsteps faded. Both cots held sleeping women and no tricks of light interrupted my view.

Not everyone on the ground floor was asleep, but they were all calm, and I had no need to enter a cell. Each had its own toilet, so only medical emergencies or continual screaming required the guards on the night shift to open a reinforced-steel door and deal with an inmate. Night terrors were the most frequent problem. Many of the women had terrible dreams.

Laney had already reached the last of her upper cells as I climbed the metal staircase towards mine.

Betty Wilson's cell was the first I inspected. Wilson was a nasty piece of work. She and Masterton pretty much ran the block, and when they fought each other for control, everyone, guards included, shuddered with fear. Dread filled me as I imagined what tensions the day shifts had faced while the two matriarchs bristled at Powell's arrival. Wilson was reading by torchlight. She glanced up from her book when she heard the scrape of metal and waved at me. My smile felt like rictus, and I was glad to move on. Her nickname was the Angel of Death. A cliché, but one she embraced. As a nurse, she killed twenty patients before the authorities figured out what was happening. She was on the run when they caught her and didn't express an ounce of guilt for the lives she had destroyed. She had been at Witchwood for ten years and, as a poisoner, her offers to work in the kitchen were always declined, but her celebrity lived on, and journalists contacted her for interviews at least once a year. Steph kept a book on Betty Wilson in her bedside cabinet. A year ago, she asked me to get it signed, but assured me she was joking when my jaw dropped in horror.

In contrast, most of our inmates seemed ordinary unless triggered, exhibiting all the complicated and flawed aspects of humanity: sometimes vain, often generous and kind, but also liars and manipulators when it served their interests. Strong, vulnerable, sad, joyous, angry or frustrated, there was no aspect of womanhood absent at Witchwood Prison. Like the non-murderers housed in other wings, our women looked forward to visits from family members, especially those with children on the outside, and found a myriad of ways to fill the rest of their time.

The upper-floor cells were single occupancy where we warehoused prisoners who couldn't be trusted to mix with others without supervision. The ten cells separating Wilson and Powell revealed only blanket-shrouded bodies of sleepers. By the time I reached C48, Laney was already waiting at the gate. Her brown eyes followed me to the final viewing window as if she was as curious as I was about our newest resident.

Powell sat cross-legged on top of her blankets, staring at the wall opposite where fifty or more photographs decorated the concrete blocks. She appeared catatonic, but I assumed she was meditating. What I couldn't understand was the girl's appearance. She looked like an adolescent even though she had turned eighteen. Her pale face, upturned nose and delicate ears reminded me of fairy folk, and her body was painfully thin with no curves to suggest maturity. While it was unusual to see such a fragile-looking creature in this place, that wasn't what rattled my brain. It was her hair. When I saw her on the news, her pretty face was surrounded by long white hair; now patches of raw scalp glowed pink between thistle-like tufts. Her corkscrew curls had been hacked away. Did she do it to herself, or had her first day at Witchwood been so stressful her hair had fallen out? Surely, Reynolds would have mentioned it if she knew. Had Smith not included it in her report, or had it happened this evening?

During Queen Victoria's reign, it had been customary to sheer the scalps of female patients and sell their hair to wigmakers, but not now. My mind flicked to Clark and Humphreys. It seemed extreme, even for them. After sliding the viewing window closed, I hurried to the gate.

'She asleep?' Laney asked.

'Meditating, I think. Did someone chop off her hair?'

'Not that me know.'

'It looks terrible,' I said as we exited the block and stood outside the gates.

Things kicked off in the early hours.

Laney and I were due to begin our second round of checks when the screaming started.

'All-hands-on-deck,' I called on the radio while Laney unlocked the gate.

'Where's it coming from?' I asked.

'Upper floor,' Laney replied.

We raced up the steps and followed the sounds of anguish to cell thirty-seven, Betty Wilson's room. She was in the corner, hands flailing through empty air as if trying to bat wasps from her face. Her mouth was wide, and her scream continuous, like a high-pitched foghorn. If she kept going, she would damage her vocal cords.

Evans and Williams shouted from the gate.

Laney answered. 'Wilson have a meltdown. Contact the doctor.'

Hands outstretched to display empty palms, a technique animal handlers used with dangerous beasts, I approached the woman whose nightmare made her oblivious to my presence. Still, it was good to take precautions.

'Wilson, it's Miss Jones. You're having a nightmare.'

The murderer's face was glossy with tears. Her arms still waved manically, but at least the noise stopped. She shook her head emphatically. 'It's her. She sent them.'

'No one here, Wilson. Nothing attacking you. Just a bad dream.' Laney's soft voice put me at ease. My breathing slowed, and my muscles relaxed.

Dr Richard Preston bustled into the cell, carrying a small bag filled with restraints and tranquillisers. We made room for him to approach the distressed prisoner.

The doctor squatted beside Wilson, keeping his bag safely out of her reach. 'Betty, can you tell me what's wrong?'

Wilson stared at him, confused, perhaps not recognising her name after years of being Wilson, but his voice appeared to calm her. Maybe it took her back to a simpler time, when her father read her a bedtime story, or the family doctor would offer sweets after a check-up. Laney and I stayed alert, ready to intervene if the scene turned nasty. It was impossible to tell how any inmate might respond, but Betty Wilson was particularly dangerous.

'She sent demons to taunt me.' Wilson's voice sounded broken, cracked, weak from screaming.

'Who sent demons?' the doctor asked.

'The new girl. The witch.'

The doctor glanced over his shoulder for confirmation.

'She mean Melissa Powell. She join us today,' Laney said.

'Powell?' the doctor asked, facing Wilson again.

The inmate nodded.

'Betty, why do you think Powell sent demons to taunt you?'

Wilson shook her head and lifted her arms.

Laney stepped forward and placed her hand on Doctor Preston's shoulder. 'Can you give her something to help her sleep?'

Wilson recoiled. 'No! No! I have to keep them away.'

The doctor nodded and withdrew to retrieve a syringe.

'Help me, Miss Dawson,' Wilson begged. She made a pitiful figure, cowering in the corner, almost unrecognisable from the usual font of spite.

Laney and I would need to take an arm each if Wilson attacked the doctor.

'Let's get you back into bed,' Laney said.

'Make her stop,' Wilson begged. 'Please. Make her stop.'

'We will,' I assured her. 'Miss Dawson and I are going to help you back to bed now, okay?'

Wilson nodded, too exhausted to fight. We held her arms as she stumbled onto her cot, then gently lowered her. While Wilson's eyes focused on Laney's face, the doctor injected her with a tranquilliser. The frightened woman's eyes fluttered before closing. We waited with the doctor for a minute before leaving the cell and locking the door behind us.

While Laney spoke to the doctor, I marched down the corridor to C48. Through the viewing window, Powell looked the same, ramrod straight, facing the wall of photos. No, my treacherous mind suggested, Powell was staring through her wall and the ten others between her cell and Betty Wilson's. Did I glimpse a satisfied smile on Powell's lips?

Laney joined me. 'Powell asleep?'

'No.' I unlocked Powell's cell, and Laney followed me inside. 'Good evening, Powell. This is Miss Dawson, and I'm Miss Jones. We need to ask you a question.'

Powell's lips curled upwards at the edges until a cruel grin stretched her pale cheeks. The smile didn't reach those wide, unblinking, turquoise eyes. 'Good evening, Miss Dawson, Miss Jo-ones.'

'What happened between you and Wilson today?'

'Wilson?'

'Another inmate, an older woman. She was screaming a few minutes ago,' I said, studying Powell's face. Her features remained calm, so I tried a different approach. 'Why did you cut your hair?'

'I didn't. A guard shaved it.'

'A guard from *this* prison?'

'She said I had lice, but that was a lie.'

'Them wonderful photos,' Laney said. 'You take them?'

'People send them to me. I got a new one today. Would you like to see?'

Melissa Powell lifted a photograph from her lap and tilted it towards the door. My eyes widened as I expelled a squeak.

'You gonna stick it on the wall?' Laney asked.

Legs trembling, I backed away. Laney Dawson bid Powell good night and followed, locking the door. She held my arm to manoeuvre me along the landing.

'What?' Laney asked.

Lights created a halo around my vision, and a sharp pain ripped through my skull. Incapable of forming words, I couldn't tell Laney the photo showed the exact spot where I stood to check the abandoned car for damage earlier this evening; probably taken an hour or two before I arrived, when it was still daylight. Mist softened the shadowy edge of Witchwood Forest on the right, but the fast-flowing river was perfectly clear. What did it mean? It made no sense, and I could not form words to answer Laney's question. Shaking my head, I hurried down the metal staircase to meet the other guards waiting at the gates.

'Jones, you look like you've seen a ghost,' Sarah Reynolds

said, staring at me. 'Jones and Dawson with me for a debriefing, Evans and Williams take over gate duty, and Humphreys and Clark, break room. Got it?'

'Yes, Ma'am,' the others replied. I was still too shaken to speak.

Laney and I followed Sarah Reynolds to her office. The supervising officer poured three coffees from her old-fashioned percolator. Her pupils grew wide as she sipped.

Reynolds grabbed a stack of paper, tapped it against her leather-topped desk, then leaned across the neatened pile. 'What happened up there? You look like you're in shock.'

Laney nudged my arm. Heart racing, still struggling to breathe, I bowed my head, incapable of looking either woman in the eye.

'Dawson, what happened?' Reynolds asked.

'Powell show us a photo. The edge of a wood and river.'

'And you recognised this place, Jones?'

It took a moment to tamp down the scream that filled my mind. When it was quiet enough to process her question, I nodded.

'Finish your coffee, gather your thoughts. What about Wilson?'

'The doctor give her a tranquilliser,' Laney said.

'And you asked Powell about Wilson?'

'Wilson say Powell send demons to her cell.'

Reynolds laughed.

Caffeine would not calm my racing heart. After taking a deep breath, I spoke. 'The RTA on my way in. The photo. It was the view from the abandoned car.'

Laney gasped.

'And there's something else. Something even weirder...' I had not put the pieces together until that moment, but they spilled from me now, clearing my head and making the pain subside. 'Powell said a guard cut her hair, and a man was walking away from the abandoned car, holding a plastic bag which brushed against my arm. A strand of long hair – white like Powell's – stuck to my sleeve. It can't be a coincidence.'

Sarah Reynolds studied my face. Something she glimpsed in my expression made her frown, but she did not probe deeper. She sipped her coffee, then licked her lips before saying more.

'Relax here for ten minutes, then start your paperwork. When you're back at the gate, Dawson will do the first visual inspection, all of them if you don't feel up to it, Jones. Are we good?'

'Yes, Ma'am,' I said. 'I know it doesn't make sense.'

Reynolds patted my shoulder, then left with the stack of papers tucked under her arm.

Laney squeezed my hand. 'Yuh okay?'

'I'll be fine.'

During the short walk to the guards' office, insistent voices surrounded me, desperate to communicate, giving me an intense feeling that, if I could only untangle the sounds, everything would make sense. Laney showed no sign of hearing anything strange. Logic assured me the noises did not belong to the spectral remains of long-dead lunatics; they originated from inside my head, but logic could not explain why Powell had the photograph.

Most guards hated doing paperwork, but my mind entered a peaceful zen-like state every time I emptied my pigeonhole. The tranquillity of tunnel vision descended and cleansed me of worry as I checked rotas and memos, bringing order to chaos. Did Reynold's ritual of tapping paper against her desk come from the same place?

There were notes from the morning shift, detailing Powell's arrival and processing, but they did not mention her haircut. The names of the guards who handled her care were Patterson and Ives.

'Laney, do you know Patterson or Ives? Would either of them have cut Powell's hair?'

Her groan suggested she believed it was a tale spun to garner sympathy. Even if Laney was right, I could not ignore the day's weird coincidences. When I searched for less bizarre answers, which did not involve an inmate's hair being retrieved from an abandoned car, a migraine chipped at my vision like heat cracking tarmac. There was nothing in the shift reports about headlice or shorn hair.

Laney tutted and called me paranoid. Was I joining disparate dots to create a wild conspiracy with no rational foundation? I pigeonholed the conversation for Steph who was bound to be intrigued.

Pen in hand, I thought about what to include in my report. How many of the night's events should I commit to hard copy? Even as I added a bare skeleton of the information, it all seemed implausible. Such ramblings would not help my case if I faced a disciplinary hearing, and they used these notes as evidence against me.

When we arrived for our final shift at the gate, Laney checked every cell, and reported that all the inmates were asleep. An hour later, I checked the cells on the left, including Lily Masterton's. Luxurious waves of auburn surrounded her peaceful face – glamorous even in sleep. Unlike me, I doubted Masterton woke on a drool-drenched pillow.

It was five o'clock when we handed over to the morning shift and headed to Reynold's office for debriefing. Finally, we were set free, and I drove home to prepare breakfast for Steph. Her shift started earlier and ended later than mine, so I always made sure food awaited her return. It was the least I could do for the person who tolerated so much from me – the night terrors, the constant need for reassurance, my refusal to discuss my childhood.

I slowed as I passed the accident site. The Nissan had been removed, and only a few tyre tracks remained. Accident site. Had it been an accident? I sensed human design at work, serving a purpose I could not hope to understand.

At least my adventures would amuse and intrigue my partner. For the first time since joining Witchwood Prison, I was eager to share my experiences with her.

CHAPTER TWO

WHEN I heard Steph's jeep pull up outside, I rushed to the door like an excited puppy, kissing her flushed cheek as she entered. Her skin glowed, and the earthy smell of fresh sweat gave my mind a sense of peace and wellbeing. She collapsed on the sofa and let me untie her shoes, revealing feet swollen from hours of standing.

When I started to massage them, she pulled away. 'It tickles.'

The dark circles beneath her eyes made her look as tired as I felt. I'd already taken my full allowance of pills, trying to stave off a migraine, but I refused to retreat to bed until she had eaten, knowing she would not have touched food during her shift.

I brought her a mug of tea and a pasta bake. After thanking me, she wolfed them both down. She often teased me, claiming I'd taken on the role of mother in our relationship, but Steph was everything to me. Without her, I would be empty, an automaton.

Revived by the food, she smiled and stroked my cheek. 'How was your day?'

'Weird,' I admitted.

'Did you meet Melissa Powell?'

'Honestly, it's really mixed up and confusing. Are you sure you don't want to sleep first? Have a good night's rest before you call the white coats to take me away.'

'I'm intrigued.' Her face was animated, her pupils wide.

'I've got something to show you.' I retrieved the hair from my pocket.

'Is it Melissa Powell's?'

'I don't know for sure.'

'What do you mean?'

'On the way to work, I found an abandoned car. A bloody giant loomed out of the mist. He was holding a carrier bag; the plastic rustled as he brushed past me, and afterwards, I found this strand on my jacket sleeve. What if he ran the car off the road to grab the bag – the hair? Do you remember how Powell looked, staring out of the prison bus?' Of course, I knew she would. 'Well, when I saw her in the prison cell, her head was shorn. A guard must have done it, right? It looks just like Melissa's. What if the guard smuggled a bag of it out the prison, but the person she planned to sell it to stole it instead?'

'It's a shame there's no root, or I could ask someone to do a DNA test,' Steph said.

While I hadn't considered testing the hair, I was pleased to hear we couldn't. Until we learned the truth, it would remain a coincidence and an intricate conspiracy – like Schrödinger's cat.

'Can I have it?' she asked.

'Of course. What are you going to do with it?'

She responded with a charming smile, plucked the spiral of hair from my fingers and carried it to the kitchen. Steph returned without her trophy, having squirrelled it somewhere for later, and was all affection, dragging me to bed and nestling between my thighs, showing me how much she loved me.

☽⛥☾

'Good evening, everyone. A guard from the morning-shift is missing,' Reynolds said. 'Foul play cannot be ruled out. I want you to keep your eyes and ears open and be careful getting home. Drive in convoys if you can. I'll update you when I have more news. Right then, let's lock C down for the night.'

'Miss Reynolds,' I said. 'Were there any more issues with Wilson?'

'Wilson is in Psych, so we won't see her this shift. Get to it and stay vigilant. Call me if you notice anything strange, anything at all.'

The prisoners seemed subdued during lock down. Even Masterton. Carrying a rock in my chest, I checked the chapel, computer room, and bathrooms. *Report anything strange. Christ, everything feels strange.* Reynolds had not specified which guard was missing, but I was certain it was Patterson, and Powell was responsible. She had to be – Powell had the photo.

When the inmates were all safely locked in their cells, Laney and I peered through Powell's viewing window. One thing remained the same – she was sat on her bed, straight-backed and staring at the wall of photos.

The call from Sarah Reynolds came while Laney and I were in the staff room eating microwaved rice and peas. As we entered her office, two male detectives stood up.

Reynolds poured five cups of delicious coffee before making the introductions. 'This is Detective Smith and Detective Michaels. Detectives, this is Wanda Jones who found the abandoned car yesterday evening, and Laney Dawson.'

'Hello Ms Jones,' Detective Michaels said. 'Could you take us through the events of yesterday?' He looked so young it would not have surprised me to hear he didn't shave yet.

I can handle this. 'I was driving to work along the Newtown Road and pulled up behind a parked black Audi. I spotted taillights pointing upwards and passed a man, the Audi driver, who was walking away from the abandoned vehicle. I tried to speak to him, but he drove away. I'm kicking myself for not noting down the registration.'

'Can you describe the man?'

I recalled the giant in a wizards and witches movie. What was his name? Hagrid. Yeah, but it might be better if I didn't describe him as Hagrid after a killing spree. 'Really tall, maybe six seven, white. He looked unkempt with dark, wavy hair and a beard. He was carrying a plastic bag.'

'Could you see what was in the bag?'

I chewed the inside of my cheeks. 'It was hair.'

'Hair?'

'Yes, long blonde hair. Lots of it.' I fought the urge to wriggle, knowing it would make me look guilty. 'A bit of it was stuck to my sleeve after he pushed past me.'

'Do you still have it?'

My head shook before I considered the ramifications of my lie. They did not need to know I had given it to Steph.

'And this man drove away in the Audi. Did you see anyone else?'

'No, and when I reached the other car, it was empty. Joyriders maybe.'

'Did you touch anything?'

'No.'

'Do you know Moira Patterson?'

Connections had already formed in my mind between Powell's hair and Patterson's absence, and Detective Michaels' otherwise contextless question confirmed my suspicions. A guard had cut Powell's hair, somehow smuggled it out of the prison, and veered off the road. The abandoned Nissan must belong to Patterson; what other reason could there be for asking whether I knew her? 'She's a guard who works the morning shift. Is she the one who's gone missing?'

'Have you ever spoken to Patterson?'

'The silver Nissan. Was it her car?'

'Please answer the question. How well do you know Moira Patterson?'

'I don't know her at all, but she was at Powell's intake yesterday morning. Did she cut Powell's hair and smuggle it out in a carrier bag?'

'Do guards remove inmates' hair from the prison?' Detective Smith asked.

'Absolutely not. We have an incinerator for all biological waste.' Reynolds' calm and assertive reply made me realise how flustered I felt.

'Melissa Powell is infamous,' Detective Smith said. 'Perhaps Patterson wanted to sell the hair.'

'How she get it past security?' Laney asked.

'We'll need to investigate,' Reynolds said. 'I'll speak to the warden, and we'll pass any relevant findings to the police.'

Detective Michaels wrote in his notebook before looking directly at me again. 'We're told Powell showed you a photograph yesterday.'

'Yes.' I shifted my posture, unable to get comfortable. The tension was palpable. Trying not to fidget, I focused my attention away from my body and towards the police officers. 'A view from the abandoned car.'

'Do you think Powell arranged Patterson's disappearance?' Detective Smith asked.

Reynolds frowned. 'I don't see how she could. It's a maximum-security prison block. She hasn't had visitors or access to a phone.'

'Still, we will need to interview Miss Powell. Do you have a room we can use?'

'Of course, but the night shift has a skeleton crew. It would be more convenient if you could return in the daytime,' Reynolds said.

'Time is not on our side if your guard has been kidnapped,' Detective Smith urged.

'I'll need to discuss it with the warden. Do you have any more questions for my guards?'

'Not at the moment.'

'Jones and Dawson, you are free to go. Thank you for your time,' Reynolds said.

We left the room and marched silently through the corridor. My body felt distant, disconnected. No voices, but something moved behind the wire-reinforced glass windows of dark and empty offices. I didn't tell Laney; we didn't speak at all until the staffroom door closed behind us.

'Sorry,' Laney said. 'Me thought you was paranoid.'

'I did sound a bit out there.'

'You was right though. You think Patterson plan to sell the hair?' Laney's wide eyes reminded me of a wise owl. Except owls weren't wise, were they? Their huge eyes dominated their skulls, allowing them to see everything while removing the ability to understand what they saw. Laney might not see conspiracy, but she was more intelligent than any owl.

'Maybe.'

'How she get the bag past security?'

'Bribed someone?'

Despite the vapours which moved above the old radiator as it blasted out heat, I felt cold.

'Shit! You think Powell had her kidnapped or killed?'

'I hope not. How the hell are we supposed to deal with a prisoner who can make us disappear?'

'Yuh scared?' Laney asked.

'Aren't you?'

'Terrified. Me know Patterson. Wouldna think she capable of doing nothing like this. Me canna wrap me head around it.'

'Tell me about it,' I replied.

)☽⛤☾(

The moment I stepped through the gate into C block, my hair bristled, and my skin itched. Static electricity charged the air. Laney expected me to check the ground floor cells and avoid the upper floor, but my feet carried me to the staircase. My colleague's stare followed in my wake, but she respected me enough not to argue.

I ascended slowly. Excess energy buffeted me on the landing as if it had mass. I headed towards Wilson's cell, number thirty-seven. Although it was empty, I wanted to inspect it.

Wilson's personal items were scattered around the two by three metre cell, and her mattress had been dragged or thrown across the room. The tap was running – impossible without constant pressure on the faucet – and water flowed from the basin. The light blinked on and off although the main switch for the cell lights had been turned off hours before. I took a step back and inhaled deeply, doubting the reality of what I had seen. Would the room be tidy again when I checked a second time, the chaos clearing like those shadowy tendrils of yesterday?

Trembling, I approached the window again, not sure whether I wanted to confirm or disprove what I had seen. My childhood had been full of adults denying reality as I perceived it, not only my parents but also their friends, neighbours, even my teachers. As a result, I second guessed everything, but it was exhausting. I wished more than anything to believe my own eyes. Water splashed under my boot. I bent to touch it, swirling my fingertips through the warm liquid to be sure it was real.

I lifted the radio to my lips. 'All-hands-on-deck.'

Reynolds' voice crackled. 'What's happened, Jones?'

'It's Betty Wilson's cell. Can you come down here and look, Ma'am?'

'I'm on my way. All guards, meet at the gate. Jones, return to the gate and wait for me, understood, over.'

'Okay, Jones out,' I whispered.

As I stumbled along the landing, I glimpsed dense and shifting shadows outside Powell's cell. I prayed my imagination created the undulating shapes which ended in spindly, twig-like limbs and razor claws. My white knuckles gripped the banister as I picked my way downstairs. Laney opened the gate as I approached. She did not ask what was wrong but wrapped her arms around me until my cheek pressed into her ample bosom. I felt like a child, waking from a nightmare to their mother's comforting presence. Not that I had ever experienced such comfort, but I had read about it in books. By the time the others arrived, I could form words again.

'Jones?' Sarah Reynolds asked.

'Cell thirty-seven has been torn apart. Was it checked earlier?' I asked.

The other guards shook their heads.

'Show me,' Reynolds said. 'Dawson and Evans come with us. The rest of you wait here.'

Laney led the way, and I followed. Evans walked beside me, ready to catch me if I fainted on the stairs. I must have looked ill. The cell door was open, and Laney and the supervising officer were already inside when Evans and I reached it. Laney tugged at the button on the faucet to stop the water, but her hands kept slipping.

'I'll call maintenance,' Reynolds said then used her radio to contact the night manager, telling them it was urgent. 'Get this stuff out of here,' she told Evans. 'Williams, we need you in cell thirty-seven, out,' she said to her radio.

'Get Williams to help. Dawson, Jones and I will be with Powell.'

'Where should we store it all?' Evans asked.

'Outside the gate. And clean up this water before it leaks into the cell below.'

'Yes Ma'am.'

Laney and I followed Reynolds along the corridor. Williams passed us as she hurried to join Evans in the cell.

Reynolds scratched her eyebrow. 'What's going on here?'

'Do you think we should contact the warden at Powell's last place of residence? Find out whether weird things happened there too,' Laney asked.

The shift manager shook her head. 'I'll speak to them, but I can't see how it could be Powell. I've checked the reports. Powell hasn't had access to a phone or received post since she arrived.'

Actions spoke louder than words, and the fact that the three of us were marching towards cell forty-eight suggested Reynolds made the same connections that I had but could not justify her suspicions. Combined with her compulsive eyebrow scratching and paper tapping, it made me feel less alone, less strange.

I doubted she was conscious of these habits, but they probably helped calm her, allowing her to maintain the equilibrium she was famous for. I started noticing my tiny rituals a couple of years ago, after Steph pointed them out. What had once calmed me, now added to my anxiety, making me wonder who else noticed and thought it weird. I knew nothing of my shift manager's childhood and would never ask but suspected we were the same. If only I could learn to project strength the way she did, my life would be easier. There was hope for me yet.

The shadows outside Powell's door had dispersed. Either I imagined them, or they were for my eyes only.

We glanced over the railings as the gate opened to admit the maintenance manager and his assistant. Laney followed Reynolds. After a moment's hesitation, I hurried after them, pinching the back of my hand in case I was dreaming, hoping I would wake up beside Steph and laugh at my nightmare.

'Does she sleep sitting up?' Reynolds asked.

I glanced through the viewing window. 'I've never seen her anywhere else.'

'I'm going in,' Reynolds said.

Laney unlocked the door. Reynolds stepped inside, and Laney followed. I hovered on the landing.

'Powell, are you awake?' Reynolds asked.

The inmate's smile made me shiver.

'Powell, I'm Miss Reynolds, but you may call me Ma'am if you prefer. How are you? Can't you sleep?'

'I heard noises, Miss Reynolds, Miss Dawson, Miss Jo-ones.' When Powell stared at Reynolds, she reminded me of a schoolkid listening intently to a teacher rather than a hardened criminal. I almost felt sorry for her.

'What sort of noises?' Reynolds asked.

'Like someone was moving things around in a cell and water dripping.'

'Did it wake you?' Reynolds played the role of concerned guardian.

Unable to guess what my manager was thinking, I shuffled my feet, feeling inexplicably guilty. Apart from me, everyone in the room seemed perfectly calm and incredibly polite as if they were engaged in a civilized conversation at a tea party on a well-groomed lawn. Only the distant grunts of workers reassured me that I had not tumbled down Alice's rabbit hole.

'I don't sleep deeply, and the detectives gave me coffee.'

'I hear you've been eating meals in your cell. Do the other inmates frighten you?'

Powell's eyes fell to her lap as if she forgot her next line and had to check the script. 'Some of them are mean, and I have everything I need here.'

'You told the guards you received a new photo yesterday...'

Powell nodded.

'But you haven't had any post since you joined us.'

Another silent nod.

'So, it's an old photo...'

'No.' Powell's petulant frown made her appear even more childlike.

'Who gave it to you?' The concerned guardian retreated, and Reynold's voice grew sharp enough to slice through bullshit.

Powell stiffened and turned away. 'That's all I'm saying.'

'I don't think so, Powell. If you don't tell me who gave you the photograph, I will have all your pictures removed from your cell by morning.'

We waited for a response, but none came. I glimpsed the edge of a sneer on Powell's profile. Was she calling my manager's bluff?

'I'll be back in an hour,' Reynolds told the prisoner. 'If you still refuse to answer, you will lose all your photos and post privileges for a week.'

Reynolds marched from the room, her jaw clenched and eyes dark. Laney locked the door. We strode along the landing in single file to the dismantled cell. All but the mattress was removed during our brief time with Melissa Powell, and the water had been turned off. The maintenance worker mopped the floor, and the mattress leaned against the wall.

'Thank you,' Reynolds said to the man. 'Do you know why it was leaking?'

'Spring mechanism corroded. We switched off the water an' we're fitting a replacement. The boss 'as gone to source one.'

Evans and Williams returned. 'Only the mattress left, Ma'am.'

'Be careful on the stairs,' Reynolds told them, squashing herself against a wall to let them pass. 'We'll check the cell below.'

There was no water in cell thirteen, and Hodges had not stirred from her sleep.

'What a day!' Reynolds exclaimed as we headed to the gate. 'If this carries on much longer, I'll end up with no hair like

Powell.'

If it was a joke, it fell flat.

When it was our turn to sort paperwork, we rushed to clear it then spent the second hour checking online for information about Melissa Powell. Dust danced under the fluorescent strip lights, which hung from the high ceiling on heavy chains. I rubbed my upper arms to get warm while trying to ignore the whispering shadows in the corners; they only wanted to tell me my name, something I already knew. *If you must bother me, at least say something interesting*, I thought.

Laney discovered a fan site, and we read it together. The idea of this strange, almost pitiful woman having such avid fans left a nasty taste in my mouth. Lily Masterton received love letters, acknowledging this allowed the bitter sting of poison to become a more generalised sense of despair.

A History of The Highgate Priestess in a Nutshell.

Words from the Coven. Collected from diaries, newspaper reports, and interview transcripts.

Melissa Powell began her life as an innocent, like all of us, ripped from the dark blanket of a human womb. Born of a twenty-five-year-old mother, Hortense Powell, and unnamed father; Melissa was nursed, bathed, and protected by the Temple's acolytes while her brain and body developed. Sadly, we could not find photos of her as an infant, whose aquamarine eyes must have startled anyone who met her.

She grew into a strange teen; told she was special by those followers (since deceased) who adopted and raised her. The seventh child of a seventh child, and yet there was no word of support or condemnation issued from siblings, aunts, or uncles during her trial.

Photos followed this introduction – four sharp-faced women and two untidy, dark-eyed men glared from the screen. They hardly seemed like loving guardians, but I was not the best person to judge. My mother wore floral dresses and a smile and was still a bitch.

Temple leaders raised the young Melissa Powell, isolating her from the contamination of other children. Diary entries reveal that they tucked her into her bed each night, promising her great power, but no one kissed nor embraced her, except to hold her still when they brushed tangles out of her wild blonde curls. She never heard the word love escape their lips.

Is that why Melissa Powell didn't shed a tear when she was on the stand? Records of police interviews describe Melissa shaking her head when asked what she saw on that fateful night. She'd been discovered – the sole survivor – covered in the blood of her guardians and others who had joined them.
Perhaps frustrated that Powell failed to provide answers, the police drew their own conclusions, repeated in the newspapers and later in court. They claimed she had murdered almost forty people.

Her lawyers pleaded her innocence – she couldn't remember what happened after the chanting started. Promised them that she, a weak and helpless child, had sat at the centre of the dank ecclesiastical vault, surrounded by voices, and left her body behind. When she re-joined with her flesh, it was already over, and her only memories of those hours were being distantly aware that the chanting stopped, replaced by screaming, silence and later the soft buzz of flies feeding and breeding until someone carried her upstairs and placed her in an ambulance.

One doctor argued that the accused was in shock, but that doctor was ignored in favour of their preferred narrative that Melissa Powell, The Highgate Priestess, was a mass murderer.

CHAPTER THREE

I WOKE suddenly, convinced someone had whispered my name. 'Did you say something?' I asked Steph's back.

Her purr-like snore assured me she was sleeping. The house was silent except for her soft breaths. Just a dream. I let my heavy lids close and rolled over.

'Wanda.' Breath tickled my ear and ruffled my hair.

I sat up, heart racing. Nausea made my stomach churn and acid rise in my throat. Daylight nudged between the curtains, allowing me to confirm the room was empty.

'Wanda.' The soft voice came from the doorway, not my lover.

The air felt icy, but it was fear that made my body tremble.

'Who's there?' I croaked as bile coated my tongue.

'What's wrong?' a sleepy voice asked.

'Sorry, I didn't mean to wake you.'

'Bad dream?' She resumed snoring before I could reply.

I cuddled into Steph's back, listening to bird song and the clicks and whooshes of the water boiler while my eyelids grew heavy.

A nightmare sent me into the darkness of Witchwood where dense canopies of leaves blocked moon and sun. I followed a voice that whispered my name, my steps guided by a ball of eldritch energy above my head. Shadows, from beyond the puddle of its green light, extended claws of darkness towards me.

As I reached the high fence which surrounded the outer

perimeter of Witchwood Prison, wire unknitted itself and swept aside like a curtain, allowing me to pass through. Two-thousand-watt floodlights illuminated crab grass, rabbit holes and mole hills. I stepped carefully, not wanting to fall into another and even more bizarre world.

'Wanda...' No longer a single whisper, but three female voices all calling my name.

I paused at the six-metre-tall brick wall topped with razor wire, separating the prison grounds from No Man's Land. Bricks rearranged themselves to reveal a secret doorway. It swung open when I touched a crystal doorknob and revealed the prison garden, tended by prisoners during the day to supply fresh fruit and vegetables to the kitchens. One bush with small, dark berries did not belong there. Cultivating belladonna wasn't permitted.

My dream had transposed the front and back of the prison complex; instead of concrete cell blocks, I faced a black door, gleaming like a beetle's carapace, between narrow barred windows and Victorian red bricks. The door opened as I approached, and beyond this portal, hundreds of inmates wandered freely. Not one of them noticed me.

'Wanda...' A cacophony from dozens of throats.

Drawn to another door, I drew back its heavy bolts, opened it, and entered a cellar. The room was enormous and only partly illuminated by flickering candles, its high ceiling and far walls invisible, hidden behind dense shadow. Thirty or more people sat in concentric circles around a girl in a white nightgown with flowing blonde curls. Her face was slack, and her eyes rolled back, exposing white orbs between pale lashes.

'Melissa?' I asked.

'Wanda...' My name was on the tongue of almost every person in the room; only the girl in the centre remained silent.

The candlelight wavered, and shadows stroked each head in the room.

Oblivious to any threat, the congregation chanted my name, even as ebony demons dropped from the darkness, but I saw their sharp teeth, wicked claws, and mischievous cavorting, and feared for every soul who had brought me here. One devilish creature caught my eye and winked before they all piled onto the folded limbs and bowed heads of every person bar Melissa and me and tore them to shreds. Human screaming met inhuman laughter as my mind fled the horror, and I awoke in my bed, panting.

My eyes bulged, and I could not draw breath. My fingers scratched my throat, tearing at the noose around my neck. I stared in horror at handfuls of blonde hair before discarding them, but the pressure on my windpipe tightened. I sat up, coughing feebly, scraping hair from my throat until, at last, the pressure eased, and I bent over, touching my forehead to my trembling thighs as I wheezed, every cell of my body straining in concert to fill my lungs with air.

On my right, Steph was sleeping. How could she sleep while I struggled and coughed beside her? I spent my nights, like my days, in a state of hyperawareness, constantly alert to the slightest sound of distress. Nothing could have kept me asleep while she choked and coughed until her throat was raw. Her obliviousness mirrored that of the victims in my dream. Exhaustion or not, it felt like betrayal.

I assured myself there had been no real threat to my life, only a nightmare clinging to my semi-conscious mind. It was the only answer that made sense. The rhythmic rise and fall of Steph's narrow shoulders calmed me; my heartbeat slowed, and my breathing became easier.

I remembered every vivid detail, but when I searched the duvet for hair, I could not find a single strand. The dream's symbolism was blatant: from the belladonna in the vegetable garden to the dying congregation in the cellar – Melissa Powell was poisoning the prison.

My shaking hands fumbled with my mobile phone. It took me three attempts to type my password. It was one o'clock in the afternoon; a mere three hours after I fell asleep. I stumbled out of bed and grabbed my dressing gown, wrapping it around me. Cold. Too cold. Our heating was on a thermostat, and sunlight streamed between the curtains, but the bedroom was like a freezer.

Not wanting to wake Steph, I headed downstairs and collected our post from the doormat. While I waited for the kettle to boil, I flicked through the letters: an electricity bill and flyers from various would-be MPs begging for our votes in the upcoming elections.

After coffee, I headed to the bathroom, glimpsing involuntarily at the reflection I usually ignored. My neck was striped with purple, white, and crimson. A single strand of blonde hair clung to an angry welt.

'What the fuck? I'm going mad.' I peeled away the offending strand, confirmed it was identical to Melissa's, then dropped it into the toilet bowl and drowned it with urine.

Steph would not wake for hours, but I did not dare return to our bed. Instead, I drove to the edge of Witchwood, hoping to dispel the nightmare by confronting it. I stood at the ridge and gazed at the river. The bank was steep, but I believed I could climb down safely. The bubbling and grinding noises of rushing water grew louder as I descended, and when I reached the water's edge, it was almost deafening. I followed the river to the forest and strolled between trees, picking up broken twigs to throw into the racing current, watching as they were whisked out of sight. The trills and whistle of a bullfinch competed with the warble of blackbirds, the deep xylophonic notes of a cuckoo, and the calls of other birds I could not identify from the tangled melody.

The memory of my dream prevented me from wandering deeper into the woods. I stayed near the edge, keeping the dancing sparkle of sunlight on water within sight, and following it downstream. The fresh aroma of pine needles cleansed my head.

I grasped one end of a twig that was caught between the roots of a gnarled oak which emerged from the eroded bank to drink from the river, wiggled until it was free and watched it float away, twisting and turning between meandering banks, knowing it would not meet the towering perimeter fence nor enter the grounds of Witchwood Prison; *it* would never feel the stranglehold of an inmate's fingers, squeezing and squeezing until *it* snapped under the pressure.

I retraced my steps and sat behind my steering wheel. Surrounded by steel, I purged my fear with tears, sobbing until lights flashed across my vision, and my brain recoiled from the rusted blade of a migraine. Scratching my oesophagus, I forced down my meds without water. Eyes squeezed shut and head in hands, I staggered onto the rear seat and curled into a tight ball to battle the pain. Unable to see or think, the only thing I could do was wait until the worst of it passed.

Hours later I drove home, covered in vomit. I sat in the shower, scrubbing bile from my hair. Steph would wake soon, but I had not yet decided whether I would share my dream with her. Her inevitable ghoulish delight might reopen my still raw wounds.

)O(

The third evening after Melissa Powell joined Witchwood Prison, I drove to work reluctantly, half-tempted to call in sick. I only grabbed a few hours of sleep and was swallowing migraine tablets as if they were sweets. At least I had a rest day to look forward to, assuming I survived the coming shift. I envied Laney, who would escape after tonight.

Laney was already in her usual spot when I entered the staff room.

'Yuh pale even for you,' she said.

I carried my mug to the sofa. 'Hilarious.'

'Don't let them in yuh head.' She was mothering me again. When I didn't reply, she continued. 'Headache?'

A few years ago, I admitted I suffered from headaches, having waited until my boss knew I could do my job before requesting permission to bring medication to work. My irritable mood almost provoked me to snap at Laney and demand she stop using my medical history as ammunition. Instead, I changed the subject. 'Have they found Patterson yet?'

'Me no think so.'

The other guards filtered in, poured hot drinks, and relaxed.

Clark looked smug, cradling her mug while trying to attract our attention.

'What?' Laney asked.

'Masterton's entire wardrobe wor slashed this morning. She wor taken to solitary in a jumpsuit.'

'Sound!' Humphreys held her belly and laughed until tears rolled down her cheeks. 'Who did it?'

'It could only have been Masterton 'erself, but she blamed Powell,' Clark said moments before Reynolds entered.

'Good evening, everyone. We're two down this evening: Wilson's still in Psych and Masterton's in solitary. Lee and Powell are confined to their cells.'

'Any news on Patterson?' I asked.

'None yet,' Reynolds said. 'Okay, let's start work.'

Laney and I weren't due at the gate until later, so after lockdown, we headed to the office to process our paperwork, chatting as we worked.

Humphreys had reacted strangely, and I was eager to find out why. 'What was up with Humphreys earlier?'

'Before yuh time. Masterton play a cruel trick on she.'

'How long ago?'

'Seven, eight years. How much yuh know of Masterton's history?'

'She's a serial killer. My other half watched a documentary where they compared her to the Moors Murderers.'

'Me can tell yuh if yuh want. Take yuh mind off Powell.'

'I'm listening.'

'Yuh know Lily Masterton kill at least fourteen people, and that unique...' Laney made air apostrophes. 'Blend of glamour and sadism get she millions of views and likes on social media. Not as blatant as some psychos. Yuh hear about that arsehole in Canada, film himself torturing cats and killing a man?'

'Luka someone or other?'

'Yea. Well, Masterton have a couple of things that keep viewers in the yard.' In case I did not follow, Laney jiggled her breasts, making me laugh. 'Without posting no video evidence of the crimes. Worst thing me see, mind me didn't watch all the videos, is a vile homage to Myra Hindley. She film herself masturbating with a child's toy, squirming around on the moors while five-year-old Paul Thompson be suffocating a few feet below.'

I shuddered.

'When she arrive at Witchwood, she spend weeks planning and executing cruel pranks on guards and inmates. Most disturbing is when she collect menstrual blood and pour it over Humphreys' head.'

'Our Humphreys?'

'Yea. Humphreys off for three months – stress and anxiety. Take she a year before she stop panicking every time an inmate approach.'

'Shit!'

'So, me know what me talk about. Celebrity craziness, it pass in time. Hang on til we get through this difficult period – excuse the pun.'

'Masterton is still a huge pain in the arse,' I said, although I knew what Laney meant. This thing with Powell was new and strange, but eventually it would become part of our routine.

'True, but us learn how to deal with she. This weird mystique around Powell will dissolve when you realise it all bullshit,' Laney said.

'Thank you, Laney.'

'Irie. How thing with Steph?'

'Oh, you know.'

'Me not, that why me ask. You be stressed all the time.'

'We don't have much time together, shifts and all. When we're both home, we're mainly sleeping.'

'Me feel you. Luckily, me no need much sleep. Yuh two okay though?'

'I think we are. It's just…'

She waited for me to continue. I scribbled some notes while I decided how to phrase everything, to make her understand without hours of background knowledge.

'She sometimes seems more interested in the women we work with than me.' There, I admitted it, relieving some of the burden. The worry had been growing inside me for a long time, and it lightened the load to have shared it with someone I trusted.

'She a weird one for sure.'

'One of many reasons I want to quit.'

'Make sense. What yuh want to do?'

'Our plan is for me to work with animals once Steph qualifies. We need the money, but each day, it's harder to motivate myself. I don't know how I'll cope without you here to soften the blow.'

'Yuh be fine without me. Stay away from Powell, and remember what me tell you, and me be back before yuh know it. Why yuh no book a holiday with Steph? Enjoy each other.'

'A lovely thought. I'll see when she can get some time off.'

)⊕(

'I didn't ask Reynolds whether she wants me to speak to Powell,' I said when we arrived at the gate.

'She woulda tell you if she did. How many times? Stay away from cell forty-eight.' Laney headed right and started with the upper corridor, leaving me no excuse to check Powell's or Wilson's cells.

'Anything weird in forty-eight?' I asked when we reconvened at the gate.

'Just Powell staring at an empty wall, but Wilson cell back to normal,' Laney said.

The first hour was uneventful, but it did not lull me into a false sense of security.

The alarm in Lee's cell wailed at two o'clock in the morning. Our boots clanged against metal treads as Laney and I raced towards cell twenty-eight. Blood dripped from Lee's fists.

'She ripping out my heart,' Chow Lee screamed. '*Nǔ wū*, she dragging me down. Why she pulling me to Hell? ...No, stay away; you not taking me back.'

Lee rushed out before we could stop her and leaped down the stairs, falling to her knees at the locked gate preventing her escape. Laney put an arm around Lee's shoulders while I told Reynolds we needed a doctor, then we led the prisoner to her cell.

After we bundled Lee into her cot, loosened her fists and removed balls of black hair, we cleaned the puncture wounds on her palms. The radio crackled; the doctor was unavailable. Laney and I stayed in the cell; afraid Lee would hurt herself if we left.

'Down, down, into cellar,' Lee wailed. 'I not going back.'

'What cellar?' I asked, trying to keep my voice steady.

'A nightmare,' Laney said.

'No, cellar real. Candles. Demons, they pulling out hair, teeth, heart,'

'Yuh no lose yuh hair or teeth. Yuh heart still pump in yuh chest. A bad dream, not real,' Laney said.

'The cellar; can you describe it?' I urged.

Laney glared at me.

'It's important. Tell me.'

'I sinking through floor, concrete scratching my skin, to big cave. Demon… panther with eyes of fire. More of them. More demons dropping from ceiling, pulling at clothes. They tugging out hair and teeth. Panther punching my chest. Claws squeezing my heart and ripping it out.' Lee's fingers massaged her scalp. Despite the hair we removed from her fists, I saw no bald patches. 'My hair,' she claimed. 'The demons...'

Laney stood up and nodded at me to leave, but Lee grabbed her wrist.

'It not my fault. Lily wanting to teach lesson. I ripping up letters. Lily making me.'

'Us be right back,' Laney said, shaking her arm free.

'No!' Lee screamed. 'Stay!'

We slipped through the door and locked it before Lee wrestled her way out of bed.

'Masterton...' I said.

Laney shook her head.

'That's why her clothes...'

'Stop,' Laney growled, making me pull away from her in

shock. 'Yuh sound as crazy as Lee and Wilson.'

My eyes burned, and I chewed my lip, refusing to show how deeply her words wounded me. My mother had hurt me the same way every time she shut me down, calling me crazed.

Reynolds arrived at the gate. 'Is she safe?'

'Me think so, but us…' Laney glared at me again. 'Feed she psychosis.'

'Did you speak to Juvie?' I asked Reynolds, meaning Vinnie Green, Powell's previous residence.

'I haven't heard anything yet, but I wouldn't worry. Stuff like this happens when a new high-profile joins us.'

'See.' Laney smiled. 'Exactly what me tell you.'

Maybe, I could have countered all their arguments with a simple question: how many other prisoners could make a guard disappear or plague inmates and guards with nightmares involving cellars and demons? But they expected me to ignore what was inexplicable and dismiss every bizarre event as hallucination or coincidence. I acted my part and held my tongue, pretending to believe them. A voice in my head suggested Reynolds might be pretending too. Afraid, like I was, of sounding insane.

'Do you want us to visit Powell?' I asked. 'Lee said there was an incident with letters earlier.'

'Actually, I have a job for you,' Reynolds said. 'I need you to repair the letters. Keep aside anything which pertains to prison security, and we'll return the others to the inmate.'

'Of course,' I said, before Laney could protest.

'I'll stick them in your pigeonhole.'

'Yes, Ma'am. Should we check Powell's cell?' I persisted.

'I'll come with you. Although, I suspect we've given her more than enough attention already.'

Reynolds sat on one side of Powell and Laney on the other. I stood in front of the previously photo-filled wall. Reynolds had made good on her threat. The scraps of sticky tape made me visualise a modern art installation, maybe by Tracey Emin, depicting a decaying cell held together by Sellotape which would force the middle-class audience to ponder deeply on the state of our penal system and the way inmates were left to rot. I briefly feared the wall would disintegrate if the tape was removed before dismissing the idea as crazy.

The atmosphere was calm. Laney Dawson and Melissa Powell smiled. Reynolds' forehead wrinkled in a deep frown.

'Good evening, Miss Jo-ones,' Powell said.

'Good evening, Powell,' I replied. 'What can you tell us about Lee?'

'Lee?' Powell asked.

'The Chinese woman who follows Masterton around claims you dragged her to a cellar.'

'The cellar.' Powell nodded.

'Tell me about the cellar,' I said.

Did Powell read something into my eager tone? I noticed a sly smile reshape her lips. 'I told Lee karma would punish her.'

At last, the truth was within reach. 'Where is the cellar?'

'In her mind, of course,' Powell said, as if explaining something to a child.

I scowled and rubbed my ear. If I could trap her in her lies, trick her into admitting a connection to at least one strange event, the other pieces might fall into place. 'What of the photo? And Patterson?'

Powell shrugged. 'I didn't take the photo. Your mind is playing tricks, seeing what you want to see.'

All the glamour and mystery she had embodied dropped away, and I saw she was the same as everyone else, a manipulator who resorted to gaslighting when cornered. Reynolds nodded, encouraging me to continue.

Powell was lying. If I could study the picture again, I was sure I could prove I was right. 'Where's the photo now?'

'The detectives wanted it. May I have my photos back please, Miss Reynolds?'

Even with all her hair hacked off, the young woman was beautiful, and those turquoise eyes were hypnotic. I looked away to clear my head.

Reynolds took it as a sign to take over the interrogation. 'I still want to know who gave you the photo.'

'A grey-haired guard from the morning shift. Maybe she felt guilty for punching me.'

There were no bruises on Powell's face, but why assume she had been punched there when a stomach would work equally well? It was little wonder a guard assaulted her, even I wanted to slap her. My eyes moistened as I imagined her cowering under the bulk of an angry guard. Despite my anger, I felt a sudden urge to protect her, and this empathy cleansed me of my rage. Was Powell inside my mind, changing the way I saw her, or was this emotional seesaw real? She was tiny and fragile. No, she was a cold-bloodied mass murderer who had arranged a guard's disappearance and tortured the other inmates. Pity and anger blinked on and off like vertiginous hazard warning lights. I leaned against the wall, trying to recover my balance.

Reynolds frowned. 'If your story checks out.'

'And my letters?' Melissa asked.

Reynolds offered me a sympathetic frown. 'They're being restored. You'll have them soon.'

'Thank you, Miss Reynolds, Miss Jo-ones, Miss Dawson.'

'One thing though, Powell,' Reynolds said as she stood up. 'You will no longer threaten to punish inmates. If you have a problem with another prisoner, you will address the issue with a guard. Do you understand?'

'Yes, Miss Reynolds.'

Sarah Reynolds left the cell, and Laney wasn't facing the inmate; only I caught Melissa Powell's wink.

)O(

There were newsletters, time sheets, and next month's rotas to check before we could start Powell's jigsaw puzzle.

'I don't think I can do this much longer.' Before vocalising this thought, I hadn't considered quitting. How would I support Steph or pay rent?

'The paperwork?' Laney's brow furrowed.

'Any of it. I'm ready to hand in my notice.'

'Why? Yuh a good guard, and management respect you. Yuh could be warden in five years, governor in fifteen. And me miss you.'

'I dreamed of Powell last night.'

'Understandable.'

'Is it?'

'Course.' Laney squeezed my hand.

Her kindness made me want to weep. 'I saw her in a cellar, like the one Lee described.'

Laney pulled back, physically severing any connection between her and the taint of what she believed was paranoia. My chaotic thoughts refused to settle even while I focused my available attention on the paperwork, all the while, holding onto the vain hope that Laney would press me for details on my dream. Of course, she did not mention my dream or the cellar and never would. She had accused me of feeding into Lee's psychosis, and perhaps she feared feeding into mine, but I was right before. Why did she doubt me on this?

'You're lucky, Laney. You'll escape this crap for a couple of weeks.'

'Me canna wait.'

At least it was my rest day tomorrow; a chance to clear my head and rid myself of this unhealthy obsession with Melissa Powell.

When the other paperwork had been completed, I emptied the contents of a transparent plastic bag onto the table. 'Where do we start?'

'Put them in piles of same paper. Make it easier,' Laney said.

'Makes sense. We'll need more bags or envelopes. This will take a while.'

Making a semicircle of my arms, I dragged a pile of scraps towards me. Breath tickled my ear as something leaned over my shoulder. Laney bowed her head and shuffled pieces of paper. I scanned the room. We were alone. No one, except the ghosts of long-dead patients, breathed down my neck.

'You must be excited to see your folks,' I said, trying to distract my morbid thoughts.

Laney was happy to discuss her holiday plans while we matched up the pieces. Her ten-hour flight left at seven the following morning. It was a short taxi ride from Kingston airport to where her parents, siblings, aunts, and uncles would spend the following ten days together. 'Me love Jamaica. When the grandkids grown, me go there and spend me old age in the sunshine.'

It sounded like heaven to me. I stared at the chaos beneath my fingertips. Some of them were easy to separate, and those which felt and looked the same we would leave until last. I grabbed a pile of ivory parchment with a business logo at the top and started arranging the edges.

Laney completed the first letter. After flattening the creases with the outer edges of her hands, she covered it with strips of tape.

'I'm going to read it,' I said.

She shrugged and slid it across the table with a resigned sigh.

Messrs Gray and Andrews LLP.
Old Bailey
London

28 May 2016
Dear Miss Powell,

As per your instructions, the property in Highgate, London has been let to The Friends of MP, at a consideration of £1 per annum. Please, do not hesitate to contact us if we can be of further service.
Sincerely yours,

Bartholomew Gray LLP

'The date is almost four years ago. It has to be the murder

house, right?'

'What you think they do there?' she asked.

'Carrying on her great work.'

Laney tilted her head, then laughed. 'Mass murder?'

'Or summoning demons.'

Her smile dropped. 'What the hell yuh talking about, Wanda?'

'Ignore me.'

'No, tell me.'

'I've been dreaming of the night it happened. She's in a cellar, and these black ink-like creatures drip down from the ceiling and kill everyone. If I'm right, it's probably the place Lee saw.'

'Yuh serious?'

'Do you think it's crazy?'

Laney shook her head, but I took her expression to mean yes.

My skin prickled. 'Then how do you explain what happened to Wilson's cell?'

'Me can't.'

'Shit! It's almost time to quit. I'll finish this one. We'd better bag the rest.' I put two final pieces in place, fixed it with tape and read the handwritten letter out loud.

High Priestess,

We are your servants throughout your days.
The package is safe, and we enclose two photographs as requested. The waterfall is in the Scottish Highlands, the beach in North Wales. We hope they are suitable for your purposes and wish you glorious travels.

Yours eternally,

The Friends of MP.

'Package, do you think they mean Patterson?' I asked.

'No address or date,' Laney said. 'Could mean anything.'

'And Powell hasn't received post since she arrived. I wonder what it was...'

'Best no overthink it, Wanda.'

)⊕(

I described my dream to Steph while she sipped coffee, emphasising the overlaps with Chow Lee's claim. Steph begged me to smuggle one of Powell's letters out of the prison and looked disappointed when I assured her it wasn't possible.

My dreams returned me to the vast catacomb and Melissa Powell whose dress glowed white at the centre of the chamber. My unconscious mind knew I must face the Highgate Priestess. I weaved past men, women and a few children, all chanting, all calling out my name, until the noise thrummed in my head.

Pitch black. Flesh tight. The noise changed: no longer my name repeated on a loop, but a celebratory melody promising bodies and souls to the Dark Lords who governed all hearts. When the song ended, the screaming began. If only I could have helped them, saved the wounded and dying, but my body refused to move. My gaze dropped, focusing on the cradle of my lap; instead of my muscular thighs, I saw only the spindly legs of a malnourished child shrouded by Melissa's white gown; heard only tearing flesh and sinew, and the thuds of limbs, torsos, and heads as they hit the floor. My hair moved, ruffled by the frantic air. Melissa's flesh, which I had unwittingly inhabited, ignored my instructions when I told it to stand up, and not one finger or toe moved. Even those turquoise eyes, the pupils of which were tucked tightly behind bone, couldn't be persuaded to shift. The fight evaporated and, with sullen resignation, my mind became one with Melissa's.

The stench of coppery blood and fetid intestines burnt her nostrils. Her stomach boiled but could not expel the bile produced by her sickened liver. All barriers between us melted, and I felt what she felt, knew what she knew, because I was Melissa. I

49

realised, even if my guardians were right, and I was a conduit between two worlds, I could not control the murderous rage of the demons whose leathery wings flapped heavily above the now silent congregation.

Blissful silence, even though I knew it meant they were all dead.

My guardians? I was a conduit. No, not me, Melissa Powell, but her thoughts felt like mine while I occupied her tiny body.

CHAPTER FOUR

BY the time I woke, Steph was ready to leave. Our nights off work rarely aligned, and once again, I would be spending the evening alone.

'Take it easy, okay.' She kissed my cheek, making me long for those early years of our relationship when every kiss was deep and passionate. Was it exhaustion that kept us as sedate as a long-married couple? 'Got anything planned?'

'I thought I might drown my sorrows.'

She frowned, perhaps wondering whether I was joking. 'I love you,' she said, before heading out.

While I sipped my coffee, I thought about Patterson. Was she chained up in the house Powell leased to *The Friends of MP*?

I mentioned that idea to Steph last night, but she had dismissed it. 'You haven't a shred of evidence, Wanda. The man with the bag might have been Patterson's accomplice. She probably sold the hair to a wealthy collector with morbid sensibilities.'

She was right, of course. There was no evidence except the photo which the police had confiscated, and the strand of hair I flushed down the toilet.

If I had been convinced of *The Friend*'s involvement and known that they still used the Highgate house as the base for their nefarious dealings, sheer exhaustion would have prevented me from grabbing my car keys and driving to London on a whim, enraging Steph in the process. But already, her conviction that things were not as I imagined, was weakening my resolve.

If I ignored the tingle in my spine and let the matter drop, this would become yet another example of me allowing Steph's logic to override my intuition, further eroding my individuality, my sense of self. Eventually, every independent thought might dry up as my brain decided it was simpler to allow others to dictate what was real. It would make life easier, and I would avoid ridicule from colleagues who considered me paranoid or over-sensitive, but I did not want to give up on the mystery, not yet.

With ten hours of darkness to fill, I could grab a powerful torch, drive to the edge of the forest, and conduct a thorough investigation of the crash site. It wasn't that I expected to find anything, but I was too buzzed to stay home, knew I would drive myself crazy if I did not leave the house.

Under the grey twilight sky, I parked on a gravel verge. Failing light cast the grass in shades of insipid green, and the forest's edge resembled the wall of an ancient city, solid black below clusters of towers and peaked roofs. The single light that flickered beyond the treeline resembled a will-o'-the-wisp but was probably someone moving around with a torch. After retrieving my tyre iron from the boot, I grabbed a heavy flashlight and strode towards the forest.

It was dangerous, I knew that, but I couldn't turn around and drive away. Before entering Witchwood, I flashed my torch twice. Two flashes replied. Whoever it was, they stood some distance ahead and slightly to my left. With my torch beam trained on the ground, I watched the shadows between the trees for more flashes.

Eyes blazed and undergrowth rustled as a fox sprinted into bushes. An owl hooted and another screeched. Twigs snapped underfoot, and moths dive-bombed my torch like kamikaze pilots, their lacy wings brushing my cheeks. Long shadows descended from high branches, only to vanish when I faced them.

Eyes narrow, I searched for traces of torchlight, but the darkness seemed impenetrable. Three times, I allowed complete blackness to swallow me in its gigantic throat while I flashed my torch. A faint pinprick of light returned the signal. Groaning, I stalked between variegated trunks, trying to narrow the distance.

Music wafted between the trees. The hairs across my body stood on end; my tongue tasted like metal, and my conscious mind screamed, desperately trying to dissuade me from bulldozing my way into a trap; Patterson had wandered the same route and never been seen again. Somewhere in this forest, wolves, goblins, or witches planned to snare me as well, but I had not felt this alive since childhood.

Voices joined the soundscape, a chorus of low and high notes, all vowels. A light appeared ahead, its unbroken beam swaying in time with the strange music. Close now, almost there, but who would I meet? How many of Powell's friends were waiting to greet me, and what did they want?

Everything warned me I was not welcome. Humans did not belong in this forest at night. The otherworldly music added to my sense of unease until it built into a crescendo of fear. My feet stopped abruptly, but momentum pumped my arms and torso onward. If I had not wrapped myself around a tree trunk, shredding my palms and cheek, I would have somersaulted head over heels. My heart raced in my throat and my knees shook while my mind rolled over and over. Although I clung to the tree, my consciousness kept moving, deeper into the woods, surging between trees, pushing me closer to the dancing light and a portal to the land of elves and fairies from which I could never return.

'Go home,' I whispered, but I had lost all sense of direction, and when I tried to turn away from the light and flee, my body refused.

My consciousness returned, pulsing with promises of safety ahead. Believing myself bewitched, I marched towards my doom in a trance. With each step, my mind reached for other explanations – I was asleep in my bed, and this was a dream like the others. Accept it and know peace.

My toe caught on a root, and I fell face-first, elbow bouncing off my tyre iron as I hit the ground. The pain was enough to convince me I was awake, in the middle of the woods, and in mortal danger. I scrambled upright, retrieved my weapon, and continued. Why? Because my desire for knowledge overwhelmed all caution; I needed to understand this mystery, could not leave until I discovered Powell's secret. No one could hurt me. I was strong and armed. Fear argued that Patterson was strong too, but I told it to shut up.

Screams reverberated around the trees, blood-curdling, chilling expressions of terror. Flickering lights massed on my right. I retreated and hid behind the wide trunk of an oak. The spectral procession did not prove the existence of ghosts. If I was not dreaming, and the hot throbbing pain in my arm assured me I was awake, it was the projection of misfiring neurons replaying something stored in the depths of my subconscious, some childhood terror or the scene from a film or book consumed when my mind was too young and malleable to process or understand the difference between fact and fiction, dreams and consciousness, history and the present day.

Five men in wide-brimmed hats and knee-length breeches bent to their task, heaving ropes, and behind them, to my horror, I saw their captives: three women and two adolescent girls. If I thought, for one moment, what I witnessed was real, I would have tried to rescue them, attempted to rewrite the history of this forest. Instead, I gazed impotently at the scene.

The prisoners wore sackcloth, their hair shorn like Melissa Powell's, and around their necks, they wore the tools of their demise. What I saw made me tremble so violently my knees would have buckled were it not for the tree's support, yet I could not avert my eyes. Their shoulders bent under the weight of the nooses, fear and resignation leeching the vestiges of their strength. Why were these poor women accused of witchcraft? Had they refused to marry or dared to heal the diseases plaguing their neighbours? They were the unfortunates in whose memory the forest was named, and I was relieved when they vanished from my sight.

My eyes scoured the ground, afraid to look up and see those broken and humiliated women dangling from an ancient tree.

Only when I entered a small clearing did my gaze rise again. The circle of trees bounced discordant music back to the epicentre of the glade where I stood, completely disorientated, squeezing my head between my hands to protect my eardrums. The source of this cacophony was an old ghetto blaster, the style of which I recognised from films set in the 1980s. Too loud. It filled my head and stopped new thoughts from forming.

A torch swung at the end of a rope like a pendulum, its moving spotlight illuminating the stereo and a large metal chest beneath. The combined weight of flashlight and rope was too great for the supple branch, bending the limb until its fingertip tapped against the stereo as if trying to silence the music. Apart from these weird props, I appeared to be alone in the clearing. Although, whoever led me here could be nearby, watching from the shadows. I staggered the final steps, pressed a button, and the noise ceased. When the whine of tinnitus faded, I listened for footsteps or voices, but heard nothing.

A knot held the torch in place with a yellow ribbon woven through it. A key dangled from the ribbon and a note that said *open me*. I put down my flashlight and makeshift weapon, removed the stereo, loosened the knot, and grabbed both torch and key. There was a keyhole in the metal lid, so I slid the key inside, turned it until it clicked, hoisted it open, gasped, fumbled with my phone, and called the police.

When I got through to Detective Smith, I told him I needed an ambulance. 'It's the missing guard, Patterson. She's unconscious. They gagged and bound her and put her in a metal box. There are bruises on her face, but she's alive. Can you find us from the phone signal?'

Detective Smith asked whether I was in danger. Phone pressed to my ear, I used the beams of both torches to check if people were hiding between the trees but saw no one. Once I was certain I was alone, I tore the gag from Patterson's mouth.

'I think we're alone. How long before you arrive?'

'Soon. Keep the line open.'

Patterson's pulse was strong and steady although she didn't

wake. Drugged? Bruises covered her cheeks, and her lips were split, but the blood was dry. Her head had been roughly shaved, an act of revenge or a demonstration of power.

'She won't wake up.'

'We'll be with you soon. The paramedics are following.'

I sat beside the box. Fifteen minutes later, I glimpsed dozens of lights moving in our direction.

'We're here,' I shouted, pointing the torch at a tree trunk to light their way.

Detective Smith handed me a flask of hot cocoa and guided me to the far edge of the clearing to give the paramedics space to work.

'You're either stupid or brave,' Detective Smith said, as I sipped the drink.

'Can't I be both?' I asked.

The detective grinned. 'How did you find this place?'

'Someone led me here.'

'Who?'

'I only saw their torchlight.'

'How do you know it's Patterson? I thought you never met her.'

'I just know. It has to be her.'

'The experts will deal with your friend. I'm sending you home.' He locked his arm around mine, and I leaned against him as we picked our route between trees. Our progress felt excruciatingly slow, but he silenced my apologies.

'I reckon I could sleep for days.' Even the threat of more nightmares would not keep me awake much longer.

'We will need to ask you a few questions before you can go to bed.'

'If you need me alert, you should have brought coffee, not cocoa. Can you ask me on the way?'

'Sure. An officer will drive your car; you can ride with us. We might not get through all the questions on the journey, but at least we'll make a start. Why do you think they wanted you to find Moira Patterson?'

A discotheque of blue lights ahead, but I had no energy for dancing.

'I don't know. What did Powell tell you when you interviewed her?'

'We're not allowed to share that information. You understand.'

'Have you spoken to anyone at Vinnie Green? Laney and I suspect Powell caused trouble there too. And she owns a house in London but leases it to *The Friends of MP*. We have a letter from them. I guess MP is short for Melissa Powell. They must have kidnapped Patterson. I'm sure the tall man with the bag of hair was one of them.'

'We're looking into it,' Detective Smith conceded.

'Are we in danger?'

'The prison guards?'

'Yes, and me particularly?' I asked.

'You followed a strange light into the woods where you suspected your colleague was kidnapped, and now you wonder whether you're in danger?'

We reached the police car. Detective Smith passed me to Michaels and opened the back door before climbing into the driver's seat. Detective Michaels helped me into the car. Tension drained from my body, and I slumped in the seat, my spine merging with the back-support.

'You have a point, but it isn't as straight forward or stupid as it sounds. I didn't follow the light of my own free will. Something compelled me.' Was I trying to convince him or myself?

Detective Michaels sat beside me. 'You think something supernatural is going on? I'm afraid it isn't my area of expertise, Ms Jones. Maybe you should contact a priest.'

Detective Smith chuckled.

'I'm being serious.'

'So am I. Let's look at this logically. You've found yourself at the centre of something your mind finds difficult to explain, and you've allowed your imagination to take the reins. We all crave excitement and adventure. Whatever compelled you to go into those woods was part of you, not the external influence of another.'

I shrugged. 'Maybe you're right.'

'You work with dangerous women, Ms Jones. You know the effect they can have on people. I bet you receive fan mail for the more famous ones. I've often wondered whether acts of horrific violence speak to an ancient part of our minds, and that's why evil people such as Hindley, West, Bell and Masterton are attractive to otherwise sane people.'

'Hybristophilia.' I thought of Steph.

'Exactly. It's the dark side of the action hero; a primitive part of us admires those who use extreme violence.'

'What do you think Powell wants?' I asked.

'We're trying to figure that out,' Michaels admitted. 'But for now, ignore the child inside you who wants an adventure. I don't want to find you in a metal box or worse.'

The car pulled into my street.

'Have you got everything? I need sleep.'

Michaels paused before he nodded. 'Phone me when you wake up. Here's my direct number.'

With his card in my fist, I staggered towards my front door. The police waited until I was inside, then drove away. Leaving his card on the kitchen table, I downed a glass of water before heading upstairs. Steph was not due back for three hours. If I set my alarm, I could grab forty winks before making her breakfast.

Melissa Powell's face filled the darkness behind my closed eyes, making it impossible to sleep. I sat up, rubbing my ear, raking my hair, massaging my scalp to ease the burning tingle there. I glanced at Steph's bedside table, scrambled out of bed, and searched the drawer and the pile of books stacked in the cubby hole below. What I wanted wasn't there. A sense of urgency pushed me down the stairs. It was in the bookcase, the spine broken and unreadable; yellow-edged pages fanned open as if each one had been studied hundreds of times. *The Highgate Priestess, an insider's tale* by Onyx Black. After I brewed a pot of coffee, I wrapped myself in a warm jacket, and took the book into the garden.

My alarm sounded, telling me it was time to make dinner. The first chapter had detailed Ms Black's experience of talking to spirits and scrying before she entered the house in Highgate. After putting the book back where I found it, I turned on the stove.

My amygdala recoiled at the prospect of sharing my adventure in the woods. While I had saved a colleague and deserved to feel proud, a voice in my head told me Steph would not approve, might even interpret it as an act of obsession and diagnose me as pathological. Although, as I listened to the warning, I doubted its veracity. If either of us was obsessed with murderers and true crime, it was her not me. But when she asked about the detective's card, I claimed the police came to our house.

'Why did they come to the house?'

'For more information about the tall man.'

'What did you tell them?'

'Won't you eat? You must be hungry.'

'Wanda, what aren't you telling me?' She couldn't have known I was lying to her, but her eyes glared darkly, watching me as I gnawed my bottom lip and rubbed my ear.

Instead of answering, I dug into my bowl of chili, knowing I owed her an explanation, but afraid she might ridicule whatever answer I provided and undermine my intuition with her logic.

CHAPTER FIVE

WHEN I arrived at the prison, I headed directly to Reynolds' office. No time like the present. 'Ma'am, I've told the police we have Powell's letters.'

'You've what?' Her cheeks flashed purple.

'I found Patterson last night, and the detectives drove me home. It slipped out. Sorry.'

'Is Patterson...'

'She's alive. I found her in a metal box.'

'Well, you know how to bury the headline. Look, we'll talk again after lockdown. Not a word to the other guards until we've spoken. What time are the police due to arrive?'

'I don't know, Ma'am. Maybe they won't.'

Reynolds frowned. 'I suppose I'd better let the warden know.'

I retreated to the staff room where my temporary partner, Greer, was sipping coffee. She was a young guard with career ambitions who was normally stationed on B block where they kept non-violent convicts: thieves and sex workers mostly. The temporary transfer would help her climb the organisational ladder.

'Anything I should know?' she asked.

'Never enter a cell alone.'

'What's Melissa Powell like?'

My skin prickled. 'Don't worry. She's mine.'

Greer's pout made my stomach churn. Another bloody fan.

The arrival of other guards and Reynolds distracted Greer.

'Masterton and Powell are in the Hole. Wilson is in Psych. Here's to a peaceful shift,' Reynolds said without glancing in my direction.

'They're droppin' like flies,' Williams said, nudging Clark.

The inmates were twitchy and directing them to their cells was like herding cats, but there was no threat of violence behind their glazed expressions. Most seemed confused and a few fearful, but not dangerously so. Greer and I evacuated a few stragglers from the bathroom before returning to the gate.

'Jones with me; Williams and Rose, you're on the gate; Humphreys and Clark, tackle your paperwork, and Greer, tidy the staffroom.'

I followed Reynolds. It felt like she was leading me to my execution. When we reached her office, I took a seat while she poured herself a coffee.

'Talk to me. How and where did you find Patterson?'

Reynolds remained standing, forcing me to look up. While I knew this was a powerplay straight out of a management textbook, it still made me feel small.

'In Witchwood Forest in a metal box.'

Reynolds put a hand on the back of her chair. 'How was she?'

'Alive but unconscious.'

'Why did you decide to go behind my back? It's up to me to decide whether the letters are important.'

I did not feel guilty but allowing her to play the blame game would not hurt me and might help her feel in control. 'I'm sorry. I was exhausted. My brain wasn't functioning properly.'

'So, you broke protocol and invited them to look?'

Heat spread across my cheeks. 'It's relevant to their investigation.' Did I sound defensive?

'That is not your decision to make.' Was she calling me a grunt, implying some decisions were above my pay grade? 'Humphreys and Clark will finish piecing the letters back together if the police don't confiscate them as evidence.'

'But?'

'You're lucky I don't suspend you. Chain of command exists

for a reason.'

I imagined Steph's justified rage when she discovered I had lied and channelled that guilt, hoping it would make me appear suitably ashamed. 'Yes, Ma'am.'

'I'm giving you the benefit of the doubt, but you will minimise your contact with Powell when she returns to C block. Clark will take over as her handler.' Reynolds ground her teeth between words, angrier than I had seen her before.

'Yes, Ma'am.'

It felt like a punishment – a fuck you, but part of me was relieved.

)⊕(

Steph peered at me over her mug. 'A friend of yours was transferred to ICU today.'

'Who?'

'Moira Patterson.'

Of course. If Steph did not already know I had lied to her, she was bound to find out, and then there would be no point trying to justify myself.

'Has she regained consciousness?'

'Not yet. She was drugged and savagely beaten.'

'Melissa Powell's responsible. Patterson's the guard who cut her hair.'

'Powell didn't drug and beat her.'

'No, but her friends did. The ones who leased the house in London,' I said.

She glared at me while placing her mug on the table. 'Do you have proof?'

'The letters. I'm sure the police will find all the proof they need when they repair Powell's letters.'

'The ones Lily Masterton tore up?'

'And Chow Lee, the inmate Powell dragged to the cellar. The cellar in my dreams!'

'Darling...' Steph's voice sounded sweet but threatened poison.

62

'Yes?'

'You know I love you, and I find all these Melissa Powell theories fascinating...'

Please stop talking before you say something hurtful. What I needed was a mosquito net to protect me from her doubt and repel the sting of her words. All those years she had begged me for information about the prisoners, but now she was throwing my confidences back in my face, weaponizing them. It felt like I was a kid again.

'But you must realise how implausible it all sounds.'

'Who else would have done that to Patterson?'

'Wanda...'

'No. Don't patronise me.'

'I'm not, baby, but...'

'Please don't.' Pressure built behind my eyes before tears rolled down my cheeks, depositing bitter salt on my tongue.

Steph held me, but she did not take back her words. They joined my self-doubt and made me question my sanity. I knew it was all Powell's doing, didn't I? Even if I didn't know how, I knew who. Steph wanted to take my certainty and crush it, leaving me with nothing to assuage my confusion. Didn't she understand how fragile I was behind my mask?

Steph went to bed at eight, but I knew I could not sleep. I went for a run, hoping to slough off some of my tension. There were few times in my life when I felt free, but even as a child I escaped my family, teachers and peers, temporarily at least, while running, stretching my legs, feeling the power of each muscle in my thighs and calves, bouncing off the ground, and breaking every chain restraining me. My love of running was probably why my PE teacher took me under her wing. I struggled with team sports, having never learned how to behave in a group dynamic or achieve a shared goal, but on the track, I was unbeatable. Now, I used it to clear my mind, expelling stress and sweat through my pores, cleansing myself.

I sprinted past neighbours' homes. Identikit houses for identical families – father, mother, two children, and a dog or cat. Father at work, mother taking care of kids, although some had jobs, part-time because the housework, cooking, children, and pets were her primary responsibilities. I passed such mothers, wheeling pushchairs occupied by babies and toddlers, or pushing scooters or bicycles as they returned from dropping off children at the local primary school. Most seemed peaceful, happy even, in their own little bubbles as they ignored my friendly waves. I envied their serenity but resented their parochialism.

The housing estate had enough trees to absorb the pollution caused by commuting fathers, leaving or returning in their ubiquitous people carriers. It probably seemed like heaven to most of my neighbours.

A dog leapt over a low wall. It ran at my heels until distracted by a startled cat. I veered right along a lane which followed the edge of a field where horses grazed. One day, I might open a veterinary surgery here. There were plenty of animals to keep me in business. Fantasies of other lives, outside the prison, played in my mind before I outraced them, focusing only on my movements, the healthy warmth of my limbs, and the luxurious absence of all other thoughts. Liberty.

When I returned at half-nine, a police car was pulling up to my house. Two police officers stepped out: one was a woman in her thirties with short ash-blonde hair. Her uniform belonged to a low-ranking constable while her grey-moustached colleague wore a navy suit with threadbare cuffs.

The man introduced himself as Detective Inspector Lewis when he shook my sweaty hand. 'And this is W.P.C Samantha Marrs.'

Marrs rolled her eyes.

'Come in. Can I get you anything?' I asked.

'Please don't bother yourself. We're fine,' D.I. Lewis said.

Marrs' thin smile suggested she was used to men answering for her.

The detective inspector did not wait for us to get comfortable before asking his first question. 'You've been speaking to Detectives Michaels and Smith. I understand you discovered

Moira Patterson in the woods and work as a guard at Witchwood Prison where Melissa Powell is currently residing at Her Majesty's Pleasure; is that correct?'

D.I. Lewis sat on a sofa and Marrs took the armchair.

'Yes.' I lowered myself onto the couch opposite the D.I. and glanced at the stairs, not wishing to disturb Steph.

'I'm afraid the detectives were involved in a fatal collision this morning,' he said.

The room spun around me. I felt my face drain of colour while my stomach clenched.

'Excuse me.' I ran to the bathroom and vomited. When I sat down again, my hands would not stop shaking. 'Were letters found in the car?'

'Letters?'

'Melissa Powell's from the prison. They hoped they'd shed light on who kidnapped the guard.'

'What were you doing in the woods, Miss Jones?'

'I gave the detectives a full statement. Were the letters recovered?'

'Let me ask the questions, Miss Jones. Tell me what happened in the woods. Why were you there? You found the abandoned car as well, didn't you?'

'What are you implying?'

'Only that your name crops up a lot in this ongoing investigation.'

'Am I a suspect? Do I need to call my lawyer?' I asked.

'No, this is an informal interview, Miss Jones.'

'For which your secretary is taking notes.' I glared at Marrs, but she kept scribbling in her notebook. 'I think I'd like to record it on my phone if you don't object.'

'Of course, go ahead,' D.I. Lewis said.

He waited while I fiddled with my phone, looking for the right app.

'Why were you in the woods the evening before last, Miss Jones?'

Why did he keep repeating my name? It was obvious his questions were directed at me, not his colleague. Did he think I was stupid? 'I saw a light and went to investigate.'

'You didn't think it might be someone taking their dog for a walk?'

'It could have been, but as you said earlier, it was close to where I found Patterson's car.'

He asked me to describe the box and everything else I had seen in the clearing, what I did when I discovered Patterson, how I spent the forty minutes between making the emergency call and the detectives' arrival, and my relationship with Patterson. It felt like an interrogation, and my exhausted brain kept getting muddled. I wasn't sure whether to grab a whiskey bottle or call a lawyer.

'The letters. What do you know of them?' D.I. Lewis asked.

'Only two had been reconstructed. The rest were in pieces.'

'Powell tore up the letters?'

'No, two other prisoners,' I said.

'Why?'

'A powerplay. Masterton wanted to remain the dominant force on the block.'

'Masterton?'

'Lily Masterton.'

'The serial killer?' The detective raised a bushy eyebrow.

'Yes.'

'Who else?'

'Chow Lee.'

Lewis glanced at Marrs. Her pen hovered above the notepad. She nodded when she caught his gaze.

He switched his full attention to me again. 'Did you read the letters?'

'One was from a group who call themselves *The Friends of MP*, another from a solicitor mentioning a property in Highgate. That's why the detectives came to the prison. Did they suffer, or was it quick?'

'Their deaths would have been instant.'

'They seemed like good men.' I did not add the qualifier, *for cops,* or suggest D.I. Lewis embodied the worst aspects of the force. 'Is that everything, Detective Inspector?'

'Do you recall the name of her solicitor?'

'No, sorry… Look, I'm exhausted, and I really need some sleep.'

'Of course. Thank you for your help. I'll leave my card in case you find yourself at the centre of anything else.'

I grimaced.

'Good morning, Miss Jones.'

'Goodbye,' I said.

'Sleep well.' Marrs offered an empathetic smile.

I locked the door behind them and squeezed my temples. *Dead?*

Should I wake Steph and tell her everything? Surely, she would forgive my lie when I relayed the detective's grisly deaths.

When I reached the bottom of the stairs, I discovered Steph glaring down at me. 'Why did you lie?'

Fuck! How much did she hear? 'I thought you'd worry.'

Steph descended without breaking eye contact. 'What other lies have you told?'

'None.'

'I'm not sure I believe you, Wanda. I mean, how can I?'

'I'm sorry,' I said.

'Are you in danger?'

'I don't think so.'

'Tell me everything.' Her tone allowed no room for negotiation.

It took me until midday to tell her everything. At least she got a couple of hours' rest before the police arrived. We agreed, the next time our days off synchronised, to take the train to London and knock on the door of the house where Melissa Powell murdered thirty-six people.

CHAPTER SIX

THERE WAS A new inmate on C block – a wrinkled bag of flesh with thistledown hair called Bryant. She did not lift her head when I opened the viewing window, either deaf or preoccupied. I watched as she wove a long piece of thread around and between her fingers. I might never know why she had been sent to a maximum-security wing, but it was hard to believe someone so old and frail had killed anyone. I often wrestled with the idea that my charges must be locked away to protect society. Masterton, Wilson, and Powell were dangerous women, but the rest?

Women who killed were abhorrent to the judges who sentenced them. Whether it was despair or sadism which drove them to violence was a moot point. In the eyes of those wigged-authorities, women were supposed to be soft, gentle creatures, carers, and mothers; to be female and a murderer was a crime against nature as well as society. To maintain their vision of reality and sleep soundly, they embraced this lie like a frayed teddy bear. Yet Steph and Laney called *me* delusional. I understood women better than those judges. Young, for instance, a quiet woman who would not look out of place at a church fete, was here because her son died from severe neglect. She had been an addict when she arrived. Now she was clean, she spent most of her hours reading. Some might wonder how any mother could have been oblivious to their child's suffering, but my mother ignored mine. Young was no longer considered a threat to society, and the parole board was due to hear her case next month. I hoped she wouldn't breed again. *Breed!* How much misogyny had I internalised? Such thoughts were beneath me, the sort of things my mother might say. Young deserved a second chance, even if some people might petition for sterilisation to be a condition of her release.

Hodges, in contrast, had not taken drugs to escape from reality, she had faced it head on. After thirty years of abuse, she slit her drunk husband's throat. Hodges' solution was easier to grasp than Young's. I understood anger too well; impotent rage was my constant companion which I tried to sweat out while pumping iron or on long-distance runs. Pent-up fury had a tendency to explode – a hole punched in a wall, plates smashed, insults yelled, or the burning tip of a cigarette pressed into a daughter's arm. Such things happened regularly during my childhood.

Guards like Humphreys might tug an inmate's limb until a bone snapped or kick a pitiful ball of human flesh while the prisoner begged for mercy, and far too many of our inmates "slipped" in the shower or down staircases. Then there were the more subtle humiliations, like a shaved head, or a letter from a loved one left undelivered, or a week in solitary, or visitation rights cancelled at the last minute. All of them happened in Witchwood Prison. People paid scant attention to where they stepped on the narrow line dividing civilised intellectual from rabid animal, kindness from cruelty. The difference between women in prison and those on the outside was often the freedom to walk away. Melissa Powell made me feel trapped. If I stayed, I might kill the Highgate Priestess.

Wilson was back in cell thirty-seven. A blanket covered her head, but I watched the subtle movement of her outline as she breathed. Melissa Powell had also returned. Reynolds must have accepted Powell's version of events or verified them, because the inmate faced a wall of photos.

I met Greer at the gate. 'All calm on the eastern front.'

Exhausted, I nodded off on the sofa while waiting for Steph to come home and woke to the smell of tomato soup.

I sat up and rubbed my ear, feeling guilty. 'I'm sorry. I didn't cook.'

'It's okay. I can see you are tired.'

'Do you forgive me?' I asked.

'For lying? Yes, but don't do it again. You've got two rest days coming up, haven't you?'

'I'm working tonight, but then I have two days off.'

'Me too. We can go to London.'

Now, I was wide awake. 'Really?'

'If you still want to.'

'It could be dangerous,' I said.

'I love dangerous. It's why I love you.'

I fell asleep with Steph beside me, her spine curled into a loose comma.

A scratching sound from above brought full consciousness. It sounded like nails or claws dragging against wood. What the hell was it? I put on my dressing gown, grabbed a torch, and set up the ladder. The torch was heavy enough to use as a weapon if a rat charged at me.

'What's wrong?' Steph's sleepy voice floated from the bedroom.

'There was a noise. I'm checking the loft. Go back to sleep. It's late or early, or something.'

More scratching and shuffling overhead.

'Did you hear that?' I asked.

'It's probably birds on the roof. Come back to bed.'

'In a minute.'

I climbed the ladder, switched on the torch, and opened the hatch. I stuck my head and shoulders through the gap and swept the space with light. Nothing. The attic was empty apart from a grey plastic bag that glinted, reflecting the torch beam back at me. 'Steph, did you put a bag in the attic?'

'What?'

'There's a grey plastic bag. I'm going to…'

'No wait,' Steph said. 'It's your birthday present. Don't you dare peek.'

'My birthday isn't for three months.'

'All the more reason not to spoil the surprise.'

'Then you're probably right. It's birds.' After alighting, I folded the ladder, leaving the torch beside it in the shallow cupboard before returning to bed and wrapping my arms around Steph, kissing her neck and shoulders. 'Sorry I disturbed you.'

Some hours later, my phone woke me. When I answered, the line was dead. It was eleven am. More movement above, beyond the ceiling. I resisted the urge to check the loft space again. Instead, I grabbed my dressing gown and padded to the kitchen to make coffee.

My thoughts clambered over one another, smearing self-doubt. My boss was angry; I had lied to my partner, become obsessed with an inmate, and might have been responsible for the deaths of two detectives. Would Steph be hurt or killed next? Why had we agreed to visit the murder house together? She called me dangerous, and perhaps she was right. Imagining monsters in our attic wasn't normal. I should catch up on sleep during my days off, not make a cross-country trip to visit a homicidal cult. I turned the coffee machine off. Caffeine would only make me more anxious.

)☉(

Partnered with Greer again. She followed my instructions and checked the downstairs cells while I took the upper landing, dismissing anything that might disturb my equilibrium, telling myself that the disorder in Wilson's and Masterton's cells was normal mess, not signs of demonic attack, and the shadows outside Powell's door were cast by a cloud crossing the moon.

A woman's sobs echoed from below; a mother, missing her children, or a daughter who recently received news of her parent's poor health, or someone feeling trapped and alone in their concrete cell. Life outside the prison walls did not stop when a family member was locked away, warehoused, stored to protect all those good citizens yet to be punished for their transgressions.

As quietly as my boots allowed, I crept along the landing, peering through each window, watching women sleep while noting every shadow. Each opportunity, however ephemeral, to delay my arrival felt like a win. For twenty minutes, I managed to resist the force which drew me inexorably towards the final cell, knowing that something terrible yet inevitable awaited me. Did I seek a confrontation to purge myself of repressed stress? Such thoughts entered my mind as I meandered towards destiny, but I brushed them away, unable to define my purpose even as I slid open the viewing window of cell forty-eight and saw the prisoner in her usual position. My hands were slick with sweat as I unlocked the cell like a thief in the night, sneaking around another's home. Ignoring protocol, I entered without backup, cleansed of anger and resentment, filled with a hunger for knowledge, needing to understand what made this inmate so enigmatic.

The prisoner was not startled when I stepped inside and shut the door. Powell sat cross-legged as usual on the prison mattress, facing her wall of photographs and postcards: a hundred vivid landscapes, some famous – the Pyramid of Khufu and the Taj Mahal in hues of saffron, others unknown, anonymous verdant forest scenes, wooden cottages in hickory and gingerbread shades, empty beaches, iridescent waterfalls, and a steep riverbank, which looked like the edge of Witchwood where I found Patterson's abandoned car, but could not be the picture the police confiscated.

I stood between her sagging mattress and the photo-studded wall. Powell did not react to my intrusion. Her line-free face was a blank slate. Her wide, turquoise eyes remained unfocused, as if deep in reverie, and beyond her mesmerising gaze, tufts of blonde hair glowed like a halo. My desire to understand drew me towards the cot. Keys rattled on my belt as I sat beside her. The underarms of my shirt dampened, and my heart quickened. I stared at Infamy's profile, studying her soft mouth and slight underbite, the elfin ear which rose to a delicate point amidst the pale stubble of her roughly shaved head; the pronounced domes of her eyes shone beneath pale-lilac eyelids, which never fluttered. How long would she have remained that way if I had not disturbed her? Melissa Powell turned her head when I touched her shoulder, and for a moment, my reflection floated in tropical waters.

When I stood up, the clanging of keys sounded like church bells.

The prisoner extended a pale hand and gripped my wrist. 'Stay.'

I sank back to the mattress, unnaturally calm.

'Which is your favourite?' She pointed towards her wall of worlds.

My eyes settled on a photograph of a waterfall plunging between silver birch trees to a pool the colour of Powell's eyes. A curtain of clear water reflected light in a myriad of rainbows. 'That one.'

'Bring it to me.'

I followed her instruction without entertaining the idea of refusal and placed the photo in her open palms. Cupped in her hands, the scene came alive. The water moved and cool spray bounced from the glossy paper onto my face. I smelled flowers and ozone and heard the whisper-roar of water.

Powell passed the animated image to me. I held it securely between forefinger and thumb, watching entranced as fish leapt and birds settled on tree branches. The logical part of my brain flexed its muscles and assured me this was a hallucination, but Powell's breath against my cheek was the gentle spring breeze which completed the scene.

The dull pain of a hand hitting me squarely between my shoulder blades propelled me forwards, and I was in the sunlit glade, paddling in cool water while the humid air thrummed with life.

Fuck, I thought as I splashed to the pool's edge to drag myself onto dry land. At first, I assumed I was dreaming, but when I pinched my arm and felt the sharp pain, the solidity of the scene did not flicker.

Trying to untangle the problem of my relocation, I considered recent events one by one: I had been in Melissa Powell's cell, sitting on the cot beside her. We looked at the photos on the wall, and she told me to choose my favourite. My eyes settled on the image of a waterfall, the same one which hissed and spluttered beside me now. Trees stretched towards a blue sky where a white sun blazed, even though it was night. The pale earth beneath my fingers felt soft and warm, and crumbled when I rubbed it. Birds squawked and insects hummed. My skin prickled as the water evaporated. Everything seemed real. Only the impossibility of my sudden arrival gave me reason for doubt.

Where the hell am I? Where's Powell?

What has she done to me?

Think! Think!

Powell had hit my back. The spot between my shoulder blades was still warm, tingling.

Powell's cell. Then here. Pushed from one reality to another. Impossible. People didn't fall into photographs, and this water was real; it was wet and cool. This was no photo.

So, how did I get here?

This was crazy. A hallucination. Imagination or drugs. Was the pain between my shoulders from a jab, not a slap? If my body and my keys were still in the cell…

Naked apart from my underwear – no uniform, no keys. Powell was going to escape. I had to warn someone. Every moment counted.

Wings fluttered above as three birds took flight, chirping angrily. I leaned against a tree until my legs stopped shaking.

The pool nestled in a bowl-shaped valley. The ground surrounding it rose steeply, like an amphitheatre with trees crowding the stalls. To my left, a narrow brook burbled gently between grassy banks. To my right, the waterfall churned the surface like a whisk. Behind the waterfall was a rock-face too steep to climb. No footpaths between the trees. No trace of humanity to guide me home. Alone, but at least my mind had not conjured monsters to plague the hallucination. The only monster was in the cell with my keys unless she had already escaped.

I knelt at the pool's edge, scooping cool water in cupped hands, splashing it on my cheeks. Nothing changed. The water evaporated, but the scene did not.

Maybe there was a cave behind the cascading water, a hidden escape route? Unable to reach it from the bank, I waded through the pool until the water reached my chest. Waves pushed me away, but I shoved back, determined to breach the veil and see what was hidden. Two forces, muscles and water, equally balanced. While I could hold my ground, I could not pass. A deep breath filled my lungs before I dived beneath the surface. Behind the violent churning was a calm spot where water had carved a bowl into the rockface. Water pounded my spine as I ploughed through. There was a narrow cleft behind the waterfall, and beyond it, I glimpsed the prison cell and Powell on her bunk, chin resting on her chest. I squeezed forward, sucking down air as my skin tore against the rock. Almost there. Almost back. Melissa Powell had not escaped.

It was like cellophane, the barrier between the cave and Powell's cell. It stretched, but even when I raked it with my nails, it did not break. Half-blinded with tears, I waited and watched, but Powell did not move, even when Greer crept into view. The stupid guard turned her back on the most dangerous woman in Witchwood prison and gazed in wonder at the photographs. Her fingertip came closer and closer. Her nail, yellow and brown, filled my view. I moved back, afraid of being squashed like an ant. The finger withdrew, and a blue eye filled the cell. I waved, hoping she could see me, before realising that was insane. Her eye grew smaller. Lines wrinkled the bridge of her nose as she frowned. Greer turned to the prisoner, who still had not moved. Her hand rose and slapped Powell's face, making the prisoner's cheek bloom red. My face flushed as I was pulled from the cave, fast like the pinging of elastic, and saw the cell on its side. One cheek burned, the other was pressed against a blanket. Before I could speak, the guard marched out, and I was alone.

My skin felt too tight. I lifted an arm and rubbed a pale, tiny hand and delicate wrist. The arm had none of the muscle mass I had spent years building.

No. No. No!

The photograph was back on the wall.

Every hair on my body bristled. My earlobe burned hotter than my cheek. Rubbing the silky flesh to calm myself didn't help; the realisation that the lobule was too small to be mine only increased my panic. A terrifying thought filled my mind. It couldn't be true, but what was the alternative? Somehow, Powell had pushed my consciousness into a photograph and walked away with my body. The mass-murdering witch had left the cell, wearing my face.

How?

Did it matter how? I was trapped in Powell's body, in Powell's cell.

I stood up, feeling thin and fragile – insubstantial. Did she ever eat, or did she simply absorb the energy of the universe? I paced between the tiny, barred window and the heavy door, pausing occasionally to stare at a reflection that wasn't mine. Was the face in the mirror a symptom of psychosis? Even stressed and sleep deprived, I couldn't believe I was hallucinating. If I were, I would feel the leather belt around my waist, the keys attached to it, my uniform, and silky hair rather than prickly stubble when I rubbed my scalp. If I shouted for help, the guards would come running, but they would never believe my story; no sane person could. They would bundle me off to Psych or throw me in the hole while Melissa Powell escaped, wearing my body, to kill again. She could kill someone I knew, maybe Steph.

Shit. Shit!

No! Not Steph! What can I do? Wake up. Wake up. It isn't real. It's real. I'm fucked.

No. Calm down. It's stress. A bad dream. I'm mad. Insane. I'm sane. It's real.

It can't be real.

Think! Stay calm. The guards won't listen if I'm agitated.
They won't listen, anyway.
They might if I'm calm.
A deep breath didn't help; even the air made me dizzy.
How can I be calm?

My head was still spinning. My pulse raced and my blood pressure soared. My mouth tasted of metal, and my hammering heart bruised itself against my ribcage, trying to break free. The spinning head, the metallic mouth, the hammering heart – I wore them, but they were not mine. If Powell's body went into cardiac arrest while I was trapped inside, would she die, or would I?

I rested my head on a pillow, which smelled of damp and bleach. My eyes shuttered, and I concentrated on my breathing. I must have fallen asleep because, when I opened my eyes again, dust motes danced in the silver light which crept through the window. The echoing clatter of cell doors being unlocked, then the clanking of boots on the metal stairs, told me the night shift had left, and it was time for the morning crew to wake the kitchen workers. In an hour, they would come for her – for me.

Two guards I didn't recognise entered the cell.

'What's wrong, Powell?' one asked. She was slender, Lebanese or Syrian and had intense, beautiful, almost orange eyes.

The other guard was slightly taller. Her hair was braided and tied at the back, exposing a high forehead and beautiful face.

'I'm not Powell,' I said, chewing my lip. 'Is Sarah Reynolds still here? I need to talk to her.'

'She doing it again,' the second guard said. Her accent reminded me of Laney's; perhaps she too descended from the Windrush generation.

I sat up and tried to smile, but Powell's muscle structure was unfamiliar, and I suspected my face did not appear as friendly or safe as I hoped.

'Do I know your names?' I hated the way my voice sounded, but I wanted to gain their trust, so that they might let me speak to Reynolds or phone home. What if Powell was there with Steph? Did she know where I lived? Probably. She seemed to know everything.

'I'm Miss Zane,' the first guard said. 'We've spoken many times.'

The Jamaican guard put a cool palm against my forehead. 'No temperature. Me is Miss Bennette.'

They seemed kind, and I needed to confide in someone. 'I'm going to sound crazy, but I promise I'm not. I know this is Melissa Powell's body, but my name is Wanda Jones. I work the night shift. My supervising officer is Sarah Reynolds, and my partner is Laney Dawson, but she's visiting her family in Jamaica. Last night, I was with Elaine Greer. Powell did something to me, and I think she escaped the prison with my body.'

My tale did not provoke laughter, at least, but the guards seemed unsurprised. Had Powell pretended to be other people before? Miss Zane and Miss Bennette allowed me to speak uninterrupted, but it was obvious from their expressions they did not believe a word.

'Will you be staying in your cell again today?' Miss Zane asked.

'One of our most dangerous prisoners is loose. You have to believe me.'

'Powell... settle down. You is safe here. No one escaped,' Miss Bennette assured me.

My hand darted out like a cobra and grasped Bennette's wrist.

'All hands in cell forty-eight.' Miss Zane used her radio.

I let go. 'I'm sorry. I didn't mean to frighten you. If Sarah Reynolds is still here, would you ask her to visit me, please?'

'Cancel that call,' Miss Zane said.

'Us going to leave now, Powell,' Miss Bennette said.

While desperately hoping the message would be passed to my supervising officer, or at least noted in the day's records, I was certain my words would be forgotten.

After the guards left, I scanned the collage of landscapes. If Powell knew how to jump into these pictures, she could travel anywhere.

I clambered onto the desk and pressed my face against the

barred window, examining the vegetable garden below, the pink clouds above, and the grey wall of D block. For three years, I had felt trapped in the prison, feeling sorry for myself, unable to see a significant difference between the inmates' circumstances and mine. How wrong I had been? A prisoner couldn't drive home after eight hours to lie down beside their partner. The only solution to my predicament was if I could get someone to believe my story, and inmates were notorious liars, or so we all thought. I might die in this cell, and no one would know what Melissa Powell had done.

The guards returned with a breakfast tray and told me to get off the desk.

'Miss Reynolds?' I asked.

'I will leave her a message for when she returns.'

It was more than I expected. 'Can I make a phone call?'

'You don't have phone privileges, Powell. Do you want to write a letter?' Zane asked.

I nodded.

'I'll bring paper and a pen after breakfast.'

I kept my head down all morning and stayed in the cell, determined to write a letter to Steph, hoping it would be sent. It was the most important thing I would ever write, the only thing able to free me from this nightmare. *Dear Steph*, was the easiest part; I wrote it beneath what I hoped would be my temporary address. The next section was far more challenging. It must sound lucid and compelling, convince her both of my true identity and that something magical, something impossible had happened to me. In our many post-work conversations, we had discussed Powell's manipulative behaviour and how she knew things she should not; relaying the private details of Steph's life or mine would not be enough. It must be written in a style which Steph would instantly recognise as mine. I glared at the white page, willing the right words to materialise, but language eluded me.

One sentence, an urgent prayer, filled my mind. *I hope you are safe.*

The door opened. Cursing the intruders for breaking my train of thought, I rotated in the chair and saw Tyson and Stevens in the doorway. They invited me to play poker.

'Not right now. Can't you see I'm busy?'

Chastised, they fled, and I was abandoned to my fractured thoughts, without the calm concentration I spent the past hour cultivating. My pen danced across the page, but only nonsense appeared: *Have you seen me since Thursday? I mean my body without me inside it.* I screwed up the sheet and wrote the greeting and first sentence again.

'Melissa, alright are ye?'

Irene Hodges entered the cell, dragging the stench of cooking oil with her. Another inmate, desperate for my company, dragging my attention from my task. It seemed Powell had made a few friends on the block. It would do me no good to tell the women I was not Melissa, or that I craved solitude.

'I have a headache,' I said. A lie. For the first time in ages, I sensed no threat of a migraine.

Instead of accepting this excuse like the others, Hodges planted herself on the mattress. The smell of grease was overwhelming. 'Has Masterton been botherin' you again?'

'No. I didn't sleep well.'

'Amos needs thee in't library. Didn't forget, did thee?' Hodges asked, placing a rough palm on my forehead.

I recoiled.

'Sorry,' the older woman said. 'I thought a cool touch might 'elp. Shall I walk wi' thee t' library?'

'I really don't feel up to it,' I grumbled.

'They don't care bout no headaches. Unless I'm pukin' us guts up, I'm always in't kitchen at five, headache or no.'

I forgot inmates were not entitled to sick days. Three years on night shifts had purged it from my memory. 'Okay, give me a minute. I need to... you know... and privacy would be nice.'

Irene Hodges smiled. 'Gotcha. See thee later.'

I used the toilet, washed my hands and face, checked Melissa's meagre choice of clothing, and threw on an ugly dress.

'I thought you weren't coming,' Amos said as I arrived at the library.

'Sorry,' I offered.

'I won't tell the screws if you don't,' Amos said. 'Trolley's over there.'

The trolley was full of books. Most looked tattered and well used, but a few appeared new.

'Bring them over here,' Amos said.

I stacked the shelves after Amos separated those books she would deliver to inmates. The work wasn't terrible, and we were too busy for conversation. Time passed quickly, and when my shift finished, I skulked back to my cell, ignoring the waves and calls from Melissa's friends below.

The perfect letter still eluded me; version after version was screwed into a tight ball and discarded as useless. Impossible to draft something so far beyond my linguistic capability; I was no poet; language didn't submit to my will. Each time I described entering Powell's cell and sitting beside her only to find myself thrust into another place and time, it sounded like the ravings of a lunatic.

In the end, I decided the experience was too complex to express. It would be easier to tell Steph what happened rather than show her. A deep breath helped me focus, and I wrote the following in careful script: *Somehow, Melissa Powell switched bodies with me.* It was short and to the point, and at least it sounded sane. Implausible but sane.

I remembered the tightly coiled strand of hair, and the way Steph had removed it from my fingers with the reverence reserved for holy relics. If Powell met my girlfriend and told her about the body swap, would Steph be horrified and rush to save me? I feared her reaction would be more nuanced. She might be thrilled to meet the priestess or play along with what she imagined was erotic role play. When I pictured the two of them making love in our bed, jealousy froze my veins, making my emotions brittle.

Rather than weep over the pile of paper, I curled up on the cot, nursing my dark thoughts. Unable to purge myself of misery, I ground my teeth against the tear-soaked pillow, knowing I must find another way to reach my partner. The letter would never be adequate for my purpose, but with luck it might interest her enough to apply for a visitor's permit and speak to me in person. The words filled my head, and I rushed back to the desk to transfer them to the page.

What if Powell was not allowed visitors? She might be considered too great a security risk. I added a plan B, then read the letter back to myself.

Dear Steph,

I hope you are safe. Somehow, Melissa Powell switched bodies with me, and I need your help to convince the guards. Can you come and talk to me as soon as possible? D.I. Lewis's card is in the kitchen drawer. The one full of out-of-date warranties. Please phone him and try to make him understand what has happened. You could be in danger. I don't know whether Powell will come to our house or head for London, but please stay safe.

Love always,

Wanda.

It was not perfect, but I hoped it would be enough.

Someone from the afternoon shift took my letter. It would be read before it was sent, all letters were. If sending it endangered anyone's safety, they wouldn't, but maybe someone would be intrigued enough to speak to the detective. It was a meagre hope, but the only one I had until Laney returned.

Each time my anxiety spiked, I wanted to punch a wall or scream. I forced myself to stay quiet, for fear of being sent to solitary or worse. When I grabbed the pillow and shook it, two photos floated out of the pillowcase. I wept when I saw the modern semi that Steph and I shared. Did it mean Powell visited me while guards thought she was meditating? Was it Powell who whispered in my ear and made noises in my attic? Was her plan to drive me crazy? If so, she had succeeded.

A four-storey townhouse dominated the second photo. If I had to guess, I would say it was the murder house. When both images had been fixed to the wall, secured there by the edges of Powell's other photographs, I stared at my starter-home and the Renault parked outside while hitting myself between my shoulder blades. Nothing. Refusing to accept defeat, I tried harder, slamming a puny fist against my spine, eyes streaming with frustrated tears, but I did not move from the mattress.

After forcing down grey mince and peas from a plastic tray, I decided to exercise. It seemed vital that I strengthen this waifish body, but I couldn't manage a single press up. After a few star-jumps which made my calves ache, I thumbed through a library book. It had been checked out before by Lee. The subject was astral projection. Had Lee used it to protect herself against the *me wu*? Although I did not understand Chinese, I was sure *me wu* meant witch. If I did not wake in my own bed tomorrow, I would speak to Chow Lee. After her experience in the cellar, maybe she would believe me.

)⊕(

I hung around the recreation area as it neared lockdown, eager to catch sight of Reynolds. Other inmates tried to distract me with card games. I lost them all, unable to concentrate on the hands I was dealt.

At last, I spotted my colleagues approaching the gate. My best chance was to explain my plight directly to Reynolds, but she wasn't there. Did Steph call when I didn't return home? Were the police hunting for me in the woods, expecting to find me dead or alive in a metal box? Or had Powell met Steph, pretending to be me? Were they heading to the murder house together? Were they already there? Was Steph still alive?

Williams strode towards our table and told us to go to our cells. She sounded like the furious mother of unruly teens. The other inmates dispersed as ordered, but I sprinted across the atrium and clung to the bars.

'It's me, Wanda Jones.'

Something slammed into my shoulders, and I hit the floor. My arms jarred as they were pulled behind me, and one wrist snapped like the twig it resembled. Tears flooded my vision as pain ripped through my body – a rag doll tugged to its feet by Clark and yanked towards the stairs.

'My wrist is broken,' I sobbed.

'The doctor will see you after lock down,' Clark growled.

)☾⊕☽(

Hours passed, and no doctor or guard came to check I was okay. My wrist throbbed, white hot, but it was my emotional torment that carved through my chest. I pressed the emergency alarm. Eventually, the cell door swung inward, and Patton, Best and Reynolds entered the cell.

I held my arm towards them feebly. 'I think it's broken, Ma'am.'

Patton gripped my wrist between her finger and thumb. Daggers of pain, like broken glass, shot from the pressure points to my fingers and elbow. I screamed.

'We need the doctor at cell forty-eight,' Reynolds told the radio. 'Broken wrist.'

She sank onto the mattress beside me, sending new shock waves of pain through my nerve-endings. I sucked air through my teeth.

'Powell, Powell, Powell,' she said. 'What are we going to do with you?'

'I know it seems insane,' I said. 'But I'm not who you think I am. I'm Wanda Jones. You're my supervising officer. You love good coffee and brew it in a percolator. You drive a four-year-old Mercedes, an automatic, so you don't have to concentrate as hard and can relax on the way home, listening to seventies' rock.

'I found Patterson in the woods and waited for the ambulance and police. I messed up and told the detectives we had Powell's letters. You gave me a reprimand, the first one I've had. Maybe one of Powell's friends found out… not from me, because Detective Inspector Lewis and Officer Marrs came to my house and told me Smith and Michaels crashed their car on the way back to the station and died. I didn't like D.I. Lewis, too old school, all W.P.C this and Miss Jones that, like he was stuck in the 1960s.

'Last night I was on duty, working with Greer because Dawson's on holiday in Jamaica. Powell brought a photo to life, sent me into it, and walked away with my body. She escaped, Ma'am. She could be anywhere.' My wide and pleading eyes tried to hold her gaze, but Reynolds kept glancing towards the other guards.

'How do you know so much, Powell?' she asked.

'I've met Laney Dawson's son and grandkids. My favourite music is the blues. My partner is Stephanie Walker, a student doctor. Someone needs to check she's okay. Powell might go there; she has a photo of my house on her wall, right there.' I pointed. 'What can I say to make you believe me?'

All three guards frowned. Their narrowed eyes bored through my desperate turquoise stare. When the doctor arrived, Reynolds and the guards pressed their backs against the walls to make room.

He probed my wrist and asked me to wiggle my fingers. 'I can't be sure without an X-ray, but I'd say it's sprained. I'll bind it and give you something for the pain.'

Reynolds moved towards the door.

'Don't go,' I shrieked. 'Check the Highgate house. She's probably there. Ask the police to check. Please, Ma'am, I'm begging you. Don't leave me like this, without hope.'

My supervising officer left me alone with the doctor, Patton and Best.

'Stay still,' the doctor said.

Teeth ground against each other as I forced myself to stop wriggling and let him do his job. After he left, Best and Patton stared at me.

'She uses the photos,' I said, exhausted. 'Sue, before you joined Witchwood, you were a social worker; you keep cats, and Anna, you started here after school on a management training programme and still live with your parents. Sue, you drive a...'

Everything went dark.

)◈(

Amid a puddle of drool, and with my good hand tucked inside the pillowcase and my bound wrist resting against the cool wall, I pulled my nightmare-addled brain into consciousness. If only I knew how to send myself into the photographs, I could warn Steph, or at least check she was okay. As I tried to sit up, I accidentally put pressure on my sprained wrist and could not hold back the scream that tore through my windpipe.

Zane and Bennette arrived first. Zane hovered in the open doorway. Bennette edged around the first guard and approached the bed, palms displayed; a zookeeper trying to calm a psychotic tiger.

Two more guards arrived, and Zane stepped further into the cell to give them space. Then another two. It was a swarm. They morphed into bluebottles circling a ripe corpse. I shuffled back on the mattress until my spine pressed against the wall.

'Powell, why did you scream?' Zane asked.

'I'm not Powell,' I whispered. 'I'm not Powell.'

A doctor entered the cell, carrying his battered leather bag.

)◈(

My head felt full of fog. I tried to roll over, but I was chained to a metal framed bed. The ceiling was pure white, and a striped curtain separated me from the rest of the room. Weeping and the incomprehensible mutterings of other women filled the ward, seeping through my skin until my eyes became waterfalls.

'Where am I?' I asked.

86

A shadow shifted in my peripheral vision, and I craned my neck to study it. It reminded me of the thing I had glimpsed outside Powell's cell on the night Wilson was taunted by demons. The shadow stretched its claws, and its darkness striped the sheet shrouding my body; then it grew until it reached the ceiling. Hints of crimson moved within the darkness.

'Are you real or a hallucination?' I asked.

It shrank again, seeping into the floor or hiding under the bed. The slap of shoe leather approached. Metal rings clinked as the curtain was drawn back to reveal a woman wearing a peppermint mask and gown, her dark eyes narrow beneath unkempt brows.

She pointed a syringe at me as if brandishing a weapon. 'It's an anti-psychotic.'

Although my muscles tensed, the needle sank smoothly into my skin.

'Finally, I meet the legend who sent two raving inmates to my ward.' The eyebrows rose, and the head tilted, as if I was a challenging puzzle she could solve with the correct application of theory and logic.

'Am I in Psych?' I asked.

'What do you remember?'

'How far back do you want me to go? My parents didn't love me, or Melissa Powell stole my body to escape the prison.'

The doctor's ears shifted as if she was smiling beneath her mask. 'What happened last night? I see you sprained your wrist.'

'Someone jumped on my back.'

The head nodded.

'I'm a guard on the night shift. My name is Wanda Jones. I've been working at Witchwood Prison for almost six years, three of which have been on C block. Sarah Reynolds is my line manager. Laney Dawson, Alma Humphreys, Angela Evans, Pat Williams, Sue Patton, Anna Best, Amy Clark, Elaine Greer and Theresa Rose are my colleagues. I found Moira Patterson in the woods last week. My partner is called Stephanie Walker; she's a student doctor. I believe Melissa Powell has taken my body to London, to the Highgate house, where thirty-six people died. She uses magic and has a wall full of photos, hundreds of landscapes. She pushed me into a photo of a waterfall and stole my body. No one wants to believe a mass murderer escaped Witchwood Prison, but it's true. Powell also had a photo of my house; she used it to move around in my attic, waking me with strange noises, messing up my sleep patterns, making me exhausted and vulnerable. The cellar, the one she dragged inmate Chow Lee into – you remember Lee; she was sent here from C block – well, the cellar she described is identical to the one I dreamed. I think it's under the house in Highgate. I don't know the exact address, but her solicitor will. It's a lot to accept, and it's easier to believe I'm delusional or lying, but I promise you it's all true, and if you can arrange a meeting with Stephanie Walker, I think I can prove it. She works in the ICU.'

The doctor dropped the used syringe into a dish and squeezed my hand. Her sad eyes, troubled by more than empathy, reminded me of the saying – physician heal thyself. How many terrible things had she witnessed? How many patients arrived, wounded in such severe beatings that they hovered between life and death? Were they still raving, even while she nursed them back to health, knowing when they were well enough, sane enough, they would be returned to the arena to face more lions? How many strange stories had she heard? Did she dismiss them all as psychosis?

The pressure around my fingers eased, and the woman slipped away. It was the last soliloquy I would allow myself while I was in Psych. The hospital bed would only be provided until my wrist healed. If I continued to convince them of my insanity, I would end up in a padded cell. Abandoned. Alone with the ghosts of Victorian lunatics. No phone calls, no visits, and no access to Laney Dawson when she returned.

I needed to prove I could be calm and well behaved, like I had at friends' birthday parties when my mother would drop me at the front door. 'Remember, you're a lady. I don't want you spoiling your pretty dress.'

Parents of other children pointed to my good example, extolling my virtue: 'Look at how well behaved your friend is while you're racing around the garden, knocking over tables, and making a mess. Maybe I should swap you.' I would press the toes of my polished shoes together, never feeling worthy of the compliment, but wishing a kind woman would claim me as her own, if only for a weekend. A mother who could smile at juice-stained clothing was the greatest treasure I could imagine. My mother taught me, from an early age, how to pretend to be something I was not, act as if I wanted to stand quietly on the side-lines rather than play. Convincing a doctor of my sanity should have been simple, and I expected my time in the psych ward would be brief.

Stupid to dwell on my childhood. Even innocuous memories could be the catalyst which dragged me back to a time of powerlessness and terror. Compared to such deep-seated trauma, my current predicament was a stroll through a sunlit park. As my eyelids grew heavy and I felt my consciousness drift away, I prayed I would not remember my dreams.

School bag stuffed with my most treasured possessions, I set out on a great adventure. I imagined the relief of my parents when they discovered my absence, and realised I was no longer their problem, although they would be angry if they knew I stole coins from the whiskey bottle beside Father's chair, unless they considered it a small price to pay for their freedom.

I marched to the park, intending to spend a night in a concrete tunnel which connected two play areas, and ran beneath a grass mound. It was already occupied by children much older and larger than me. Abandoning the tunnel, I pushed past flowers and headed for the trees. Mud caked my shoes; a crime my mother would not forgive, and another reason I could not return home even when darkness descended, and strange noises disturbed my sleep. The big kids had probably left the tunnel by now, but it was dark, and I was not sure I would find my way back. Tomorrow, I would catch a bus and travel somewhere – anywhere – where no one knew me, and I would be free to play and get dirty.

'Birds,' I told Edward, my teddy bear, when something made the leaves rustle above our heads.

'Climb up and check,' he insisted.

I sat him against the trunk and tested the ladder to check it was secure. Branches tore my dress as I climbed towards a black square. I entered an attic. Nothing was visible in the darkness, except the sliver of light I crawled towards. Dust filled my nostrils, and my giant sneeze made the light rise and dance in the air. I grasped plastic, opened the carrier bag, and discovered a shiny blue-green egg in a nest of pale ringlets.

Time jumped; I stood in a queue at a bus stop. A man asked my name, but I ignored him. I paid three coins to the driver and sat down, waiting for the bus to take me to a happier future. Tongues clicked and blood roared in my ears as I waited for the bus to move. Eventually, a woman in a black jacket with bright silver buttons climbed on and made her way down the aisle. She leaned across the empty seat beside mine. I wanted to tell her to sit down and let the bus leave, but the words were stuck in my throat.

'Where's your mummy?' she asked.

I sat at a table; pieces of paper arranged in a circle before me.

Laney turned her mug upside down and placed it at the centre. 'Ask when you get your body back.'

The mug jerked between the scraps, and I picked up each one it settled on, but the message made no sense: Melissa, house, travels, appeal, cellar, monster. 'I don't think it understood the question.'

Laney shrugged, retrieved her mug, and put it against her lips. 'Reynolds make the best coffee.'

Chow Lee sat cross-legged on the table. She had been strapped into a straitjacket, her arms forming an X. Bending forward at the waist until her shoulders were tucked between her knees, she pecked strips from the circle. When she straightened her back, her cheeks were swollen from the ball of paper which filled her mouth. I watched in horror as she chewed. Ink-black drool escaped the corners of her mouth and ran down her chin, making her look like a ventriloquist's dummy.

'Stop,' I said. 'We need to put the letters back together. I have to find out what she's doing.'

My eyes followed the lump's progress when Lee swallowed, wondering how she could breathe. After it vanished behind her collar bone, she widened her mouth to laugh, revealing blackened teeth and tongue. From behind me, I heard Steph's voice. She said I was crazy. Although I knew she couldn't really be here in the prison, I tried to turn around and assure her I was perfectly sane, but I was strapped to the chair. When I strained against the cuffs, a sharp, hot pain sliced my wrist, shocking me awake.

A tall figure with six arms grinned at me from the foot of my bed. Two exaggerated appendages extended vertically from its head, like a hare's ears or the horns of an oryx. It was not a monstrous shadow. How could I have thought so, even for a moment? It was Steph who watched me, and when she noticed I was awake, a warm smile made a crescent of her mouth.

She sat on my mattress and stroked my fingers. 'I got your letter.'

'Thank God. Did Powell visit you?'

'No. Why would she?'

'But you believe me?'

'Of course, my love. I knew something was wrong when you didn't come home.'

'Steph, I'm glad you're here.'

'At first, the warden refused to let me see you, so I spoke to the detective. He must have put in a good word for me, because the prison phoned and said I could visit. How are they treating you?'

'Five-star service. They even throw in a syringe of controlled drugs for their loyal customers.'

'I can't stay long, but I'm on your side, Wanda. I'll break you out of here, whatever it takes.'

My dressing had been removed, and the doctor was inspecting my wrist when I woke.

'How long did I sleep? Has Steph left?'

Eyebrows pointed towards the bridge of the doctor's nose, suggesting a frown. 'There's no one here called Steph. Do you mean Beth?'

The drugs she gave me made it hard to separate my dreams from reality; both seemed equally vivid. I had felt Steph's thumb against the back of my fingers, but I doubted the doctor would lie when her job was to strengthen my sense of reality, not gaslight me. The most insignificant detail might hold the key to distinguishing fact from fiction, so it was vital I paid attention to everything, including the colour palette of my perception. Green and white were the dominant hues in this room, while the terrifying black and red shadow, which visited me whenever I was alone, could not be real.

A few hours later, Chow Lee was brought back to Psych. Guards strapped her to the bed beside mine. A curtain obscured my view, but I heard her struggle, and the straining creak of metal when she pulled against her restraints. I waited until I was sure we were alone before speaking.

'Chow Lee?'

'Fuck off!' Lee did not use the continuous 'fucking', the tense she arbitrarily applied to most of her verbs.

She had probably been told to fuck off so often the phrase was carved into her vocabulary, immutable. I received her message, loud and clear.

'Come with me,' said the woman in the black jacket.

'Fuck off!' I'd heard teenagers use that phrase, and I repeated it now. The woman might seem kind, like the angels I wanted to go home with after birthday parties as if I was a gift bag or party favour, but I feared her plan was to reunite me with my parents, and I could not allow that, not when stolen coins weighed down my bag, and my shoes were muddy. She recoiled and frowned, teaching me the power of words.

She tried to grab my hand, but I kicked and punched, desperate to remain free of her grasp. Once she got hold of me, there would be no escape; I knew how strong adults' hands were. Long after bruises faded, I recalled my mother's vice like grip, or the punches, which made me double up in pain. If I told this woman all my troubles, if she knew how bad they were, she might help me escape, but Mother made me promise never to share family business and assured me things would be far worse if I ever broke my promise.

I lied instead. 'I'm sorry. I didn't mean to say those words. Mum's waiting for me, and she'll worry if I'm late. I paid my fare, didn't I? Look, I have my ticket.' I dug into my pocket for the precious piece of paper and brandished it before her like a golden ticket.

Doubt flickered across her face, and her eyes flicked to the front of the bus. I waited, certain she would accept my explanation and clamber off the bus to hassle some other poor kid. The engine would roar into life, and I would be on my way – free at last.

'What's your name?'

Her question caught me by surprise, and I made the mistake of telling her the truth. 'Wanda Jones.'

The moment I saw her satisfied smile, I knew I had been reported missing.

'Your mum *is* worried.'

She took my hand and pulled me along the aisle. Passengers stared as we passed, some angry, others sympathetic. The woman with shiny buttons sat beside me on the back seat of a police car. Instead of Mother, who I vividly remembered standing at our front door, flinty eyes glaring as I dragged out those final steps still hoping for reprieve, the black and red shadow filled our doorway; his welcome-home smile revealed a mouth full of fangs.

'Doctor Armitage, we need you on C block.' I recognised Reynold's voice as it crackled over the airway.

'On my way,' the doctor replied.

'I wonder who it is,' I said.

To my delight, Lee replied. 'Not Lily, please.'

'Is that why you're here? Did Masterton do something to you?'

The squeal of metal as she strained against her restraints.

'Lee, it's Jones. Powell took me to the cellar too.'

'The cellar…' Her voice sounded dreamlike, as if she only vaguely recalled something from her distant past. 'He's here, the demon, watching you.'

'Demon. What does he look like?' I asked.

'Black, red, long, long ears.'

My chest burned, my head spun, and blood pounded my eardrums. Lee saw it too – the shadow, which could not be real. The nightmare, which crowded around my bed, had also dragged Chow Lee to Powell's cellar. My head shook until my entire body trembled, and metal rattled against metal, and teeth chattered against teeth, and that thing still stood at my doorway where my mother should have been; its huge mouth and sharp fangs, waiting, waiting until we were alone, so it could gobble me up.

A long time ago, I adopted a kitten. It must have wandered away from its mother and got lost – succeeded where I had failed. I cradled it in the palm of my hand and dripped milk into the tiny triangle of its mouth, used a towel from the laundry cupboard to make its bed in my wardrobe. If Mother found it, I knew the kitten would be taken from me. She could not abide any joy in my life, as if happiness was a sin or the path to sin. She took no pleasure in the misery she caused, but her ambivalence to my suffering did not soften the blow of her cruelty. So, I did everything I could to keep my secret, ensuring my room was always tidy, and collecting clothes, fresh from the ironing board, to put them away. Mother never thanked me or questioned my helpfulness, acting as if my behaviour was above suspicion, which only made the shock of returning from school and discovering both my kitten and the towel were missing harder to bear. Unable to ask what happened without admitting my deceit, I stayed silent, and she never told me, although I spotted the towel on the washing line and knew it was her.

It was not Masterton who was bundled into Psych by guards. It was poker-playing Tyson. I did not know her well, not even who she killed or why. She was pleasant and easy-going without being overly friendly, and I could not imagine her doing anything worthy of a trip to the psych ward or solitary.

Once Tyson had been restrained and the guards left, Doctor

Armitage brought a chair to my bedside and sat there, holding a clipboard and a biro. 'How are you feeling? Do you know your name?'

'Melissa Powell,' I said.

She leaned back and smiled. 'Good, good. We'll have you back on C block in no time.'

'What happened to Tyson?' I asked.

'Don't worry, Powell. Your friend will be fine. She got some unwelcome news and needs a few days of rest to recover. Soon, you'll both be where you belong.'

)⊕(

A couple of days later, Doctor Armitage seemed professionally brisk as she unfastened my restraints. 'Detectives are waiting for you in an interview room. When they've finished, you'll be transferred to C block.'

Two guards waited by her desk. Head bowed, determined not to present any challenge to their authority, I joined them, hoping the sour smell came from the overweight guard on my right, rather than my armpits. It was funny how physical fitness was a prerequisite for new recruits, but guards who had been at Witchwood for years allowed their bodies to grow soft. Was Melissa taking care of my flesh? If she wasn't, the muscle mass I had built would quickly turn to fat.

D.I. Lewis and Officer Marrs sat on one side of the table while I was handcuffed to a hoop on the other. My bandaged wrist rested on my lap; the pain now muted to a dull ache. I was thankful they had not put a metal bracelet around it.

'What day is it?' I asked.

Marrs stared at a notepad, chewing the end of her pen. D.I. Lewis answered my question. 'Monday.'

Three days lost.

'Tell us where Wanda Jones is,' the detective demanded.

Bubbles of hysteria burst from my throat as I leaned forward, beating my chest.

'This isn't a game, Powell. Jones left her car here on Friday morning. She made a call to your solicitor's office in London, so we know you're involved. Where is she?'

I wanted to say, I'm right in front of you. Instead, I said, 'At the Highgate house,' hoping at least to interrupt Powell's plan and extract my body from the demon-infested cellar. 'Melissa Powell stole my body. *She* left *my* car behind. There's a photo of *my* house in *her* cell, in her pillowcase. I think she visited me there.'

D.I. Lewis whispered something to Marrs, then spoke loud enough for everyone to hear. 'Escort Powell back to her cell. We have what we need.'

After the detectives left, I was unchained from the table and given to the guards at C block.

CHAPTER SEVEN

ONE corner of cell forty-eight was too dark, but the guards did not notice. Confined to a tiny room again; how many times had the same thing happened throughout my childhood? At least no one was likely to walk in unannounced while I knelt on the floor and stared at the shadow.

'I know you're there.'

The darkness stretched, becoming impossibly tall yet almost humanoid. Details imposed themselves on the blackness – a pair of burning eyes which stared down at me from the ceiling. The metre-wide torso, with peaks of muscle and bone, was covered in stripes of bright red, the same colour as its eyes, which moved across its leathery skin. Instead of four limbs, the creature had eight, six arms and two powerful-looking legs, longer than its other limbs, so long that its pelvis blocked the cell window. I craned my neck to study its face, trying to find kindness there.

'What's your name?' My trembling whisper made the long ears twitch.

A single word was projected into my mind. *Harrokabis*.

'Why did you stay? Why didn't you leave with Melissa Powell?'

No reply.

'Can we be friends? I need a friend, Harrokabis, now more than ever.'

Silence.

'When you're ready to speak to me, I'll listen.'

As I staggered to the wall of photos, the knees of my feeble legs rotated left and right, sending lightning bolts of pain up my thighs. To ease the agony, I resorted to shuffling, sliding first one foot then the other across the concrete floor. I touched a photo, half-expecting to be sucked inside and spat out elsewhere, hoping for an urban destination, somewhere with phones and a bus route, but the cell remained solid around me.

After everything I had seen, I still doubted its reality, doubted everything I perceived. My mind could not be trusted. Throughout my life, people had questioned my reality, my memories, and my emotional responses. Steph did so sympathetically, suggesting I responded the way I did because of past trauma. My parents did it to justify or deny their actions, but the result was the same. Whenever there was any doubt, I assumed I was wrong, and Steph's memory and perception were more reliable than mine. Repeatedly, I discarded my truth in favour of hers. Now I was alone, with no one to steer me to safer shores, I was unable to trust the broken machinery inside my skull.

Was I here? Was Harrokabis real? How could I trust my perceptions when faced with such strange magic? Lee said she saw the shadow-demon unless I imagined that conversation too.

Everything was so tangled; I could not unpick it. Talking to a shadow, hearing its voice, waiting to be swallowed by a photograph, it was all insane. Psychotic. Everyone thought I was Melissa Powell. Was Wanda Jones only a dream I once had?

Years ago, a watchful PE teacher noticed bruises across my lower back. She called me aside, and I figured it was finally time to tell someone the truth. She believed me enough to take me to the headmaster, who called my parents. He accepted their version of events: a clumsy child who had tumbled from the top of a climbing frame and hobbled home, too ashamed to admit what had happened. Father focused on the same patch of skin to punish me for my taletelling, causing more pain while leaving no new evidence. What did it matter if the monster in my room was real? I'd lived with monsters all my life.

As I stared at Harrokabis, the alien nature of the enormous

being became more obvious, from the leathery, canine triangle of its blunt nose to those tree-trunk legs, jointed in three places, bent like concertinas. Cruel fangs glistened in a mouth that never completely closed, and long, bat-like ears rotated to catch sounds. The constantly moving crimson stripes that decorated its torso reminded me of something. When I was seven or eight, my favourite toy was a slinky, which I wore like a gauntlet. I often sat at the top of the stairs to release the metal spring and watch it descend. The veins of red light which shifted through the monster's body reminded me of that toy.

I fought against my desire to recoil when its six biceps twitched and taloned paws flexed. It was naked, but no genitals were visible between its strange legs, which made me wonder whether its species reproduced. I marvelled that I could form such base thoughts while faced with a supernatural, possibly immortal, entity. This creature of nightmares might be my only ally until Laney returned. It had stayed when Powell left, and I needed to find out why.

'Harrokabis.' The corners of its wide mouth lifted when I said its name. 'Why are you here? Did Melissa abandon you?'

Its ears drooped, and it lowered its gaze.

A wave of profound loneliness broke against me.

'She called me cruel.'

My stomach vibrated with the bass of its voice. Strange pronunciation and gravelly sibilance made it difficult to understand. For some reason, the deep timbre when it spoke aloud made me assign an arbitrary gender. It was then that I stopped thinking of the beast as an it and instead perceived it as male.

'You only wanted to protect her. That's all you ever wanted, isn't it?'

Crimson eyes lifted, burning through me, pinning me in place. He craved companionship, someone who could see past the horror of his outer shell. I'd witnessed the same look in the rheumy eyes of abandoned dogs.

I wasn't afraid that such a creature might exist. If it was real, it could be tamed, reasoned with, or fought. What terrified me most was that it wasn't real, that my mind had conjured it, because if my mind could convince me there was a monster in my room, it meant I could not trust my senses. How could I know that the floor was real or the walls? How might I believe in the existence of anything – including myself?

I reached up and touched a paw, stroking the coarse fur on his wrist. It felt warm, corporeal, comforting. 'I won't abandon you,' I said, not sure whether it was a lie, but knowing it was what he needed to hear.

My priority was Steph's safety. Did the demon know where my girlfriend was? Would he know whether Powell meant to harm her? Melissa Powell knew where I lived, had a photograph of my house, but I forced myself not to ask, not yet. I did not want the monster to believe my interest was purely selfish, sensing that he needed a deeper connection with me. First, I needed to earn his trust.

His chin brushed the back of my hand. I released his wrist and touched his cheek, tracing the slender blades of his teeth.

'How did you meet her?' I asked.

'She stepped into my world as a child, her eyes glistening, reflecting the light, unaware of her power, a timid rabbit cowering before a predator.'

Harrokabis took me there with the strength of his will. The land seemed familiar, like a place visited in dreams; a vast tundra of volcanic rock veined with lava, mirroring the colours of his pelt. His home.

'She studied me through those enormous pupils ringed with an ocean. Eventually, she spoke.'

'Where am I?' I asked, but my voice was wrong – tiny like an eleven-year-old girl's.

Unlike the waterfall in the photograph, the projection was incomplete; it was visual and auditory, but not multi-sensory. I did not feel any heat from the ground despite the steam that rose around me. It looked as though Harrokabis stood ten metres away, but I felt his cheek, his mouth, his fur between the fingers of my left hand, and my right wrist throbbed under an itchy dressing.

'The borderland. There are worlds within worlds connected by invisible membranes. The borderland separates them from each other. A place where creatures from different worlds can meet if they free their minds.'

'You live here, in this borderland?' Melissa asked.

'We are its guardians, my siblings and I; it has been our prison for millennia.'

I glimpsed movement in the distance, huddled hordes like storm clouds staining the horizon.

Young Melissa took a tentative step, carrying me towards our terrifying host. Closing my eyes didn't help, the scene was inside my head, a shared memory, a dream. I hit my sprained wrist against my hipbone, gritting my teeth against the scalding pain. It was enough to remind me of who and where I was.

'How did Melissa reach the borderland?' I asked.

Harrokabis' legs folded beneath him like the telescopic arm of a cherry picker until his snout drew level with Melissa's face. He became perfectly still, apart from those perpetually active ears. Alert, listening. They had drooped earlier when he recalled something painful. Did they react to his emotions, revealing them like a cat's tail?

'Melissa stumbled upon my land without training or psychic preparation. I was drawn to her; I had never encountered grief more powerful than hers. She asked if I was an angel. I told her no. Then she asked if I was a demon, as if such things are binary.'

'You don't have to crouch,' I said. 'I'm not afraid.'

Harrokabis straightened his legs and towered above me, his knotted thighs level with my eyes. I held my breath to stifle the scream which curdled in my chest.

'Melissa snatched anxious breaths and wrung her hands. "Sister Geraldine and Brother Charles sent me here. They gave me pills to dull the pain in my stomach, and sour tea, which made me want to vomit. The edges of the world softened, the shadows breathed, then I arrived." Tears glistened on her cheeks. "I was in the cellar, sat on a cold, hard floor, blood staining my underwear. Is my body here or there? Do you know?" Wanting to reassure her, I said, "Only your astral body is here. Your physical body stays wherever you left it."'

'Unless someone steals it.' Anger blazed through my eyes – Melissa's eyes.

The scene collapsed, imploding until all that remained was a dark circle which sucked me into its mouth then spat me out. My spine hit the cell door, bruising my shoulders, and jarring my wrist.

Tears spilled from my eyes. 'Why did she do it? Why me? I'm a good person.'

'If she chose someone else, would it be better? Who would you sacrifice? It had to be a guard, someone who could leave the prison. Melissa has work to do in London, and the two of you... well, you're compatible.'

'You mean I was vulnerable.' Nursing my wrist, I clambered onto the bed and sat with my back against the wall. The chill eased the muscles in my shoulders. My obsession with Melissa Powell, imagining her webs of influence, had made me vulnerable, and now I was caught. Laney warned me, but I did not stop.

'You sound defeated. Imagine what it was like for a child. Melissa hated the Highgate House and everyone in it. They told her she was special but locked her away. She was a slave that they dressed in king's garments. I knew I could help her. Despite what your courts ruled, Melissa is a gentle soul.'

'Gentle?' I did not disguise the venom in my voice. 'Compared to your kind, perhaps, but gentle humans do not go around killing and torturing each other.'

Harrokabis glared at me. Instinct made me recoil, and my body curled into itself protectively, knees hiding my chest; chin obscuring my throat. My damaged wrist pressed against the mattress, making me yelp.

'Your wrist is hurt. Let me help.' The pads of his strange hand felt like velvet. Long fingers ending in crescent-moon talons sharp like scimitars extended from paws as big as my head. Gently, he cradled my forearm, knitting my ligaments together with his magic touch.

My muscles tingled as nerve endings snaked into place, and the swelling eased. Harrokabis unwrapped my bandage to reveal pale unblemished skin. There was no bruising, and when I flexed my fingers, I felt no pain. Incredible. *Impossible*, my mind assured me. *It was never sprained, only bruised, and now it's healed. The rest is pure imagination.*

'It has been damaged before,' Harrokabis said.

'My father…'

The monster bowed his noble head. 'An accident?'

'No… maybe… I doubt he planned to do lasting damage,' I said.

'What happened?'

'The usual.' I shrugged. 'I can't remember what I did to make him angry.'

'Families are supposed to protect each other.' Harrokabis cocked his head, looking more canine than ever.

'That's a lie we tell ourselves. People don't magically shed their flaws when they become parents.'

'Melissa could not remember her parents. Perhaps, in your case, remembering is worse. I asked whether anyone looked after her. She told me Brother Dennis read to her and gave her chocolate.'

I shuddered. 'Did Brother Dennis hurt Melissa?'

The creature's eyes darkened. 'Deeply. I did not understand such things then, or I would have warned her. He was all she had apart from me. When I promised her my friendship, her smile was a beacon. "I would like that very much, Harrokabis," she said before vanishing. It was a month before I saw her again.'

'A month?' I said, mentally running through everything Harrokabis had told me. 'She could only reach you when she was menstruating.' I recalled my first period. No one had told me what to expect. I feared I would die when I woke one morning in a puddle of blood, clutching my burning belly. Mother's eyes as she bundled my sheets revealed disappointment rather than sympathy. "Eve's shame," she called it.

Harrokabis nodded. 'I loved her. She shared her secrets,

all of them, including the shameful ones she told no one else. Brother Dennis hurt her at night, she did not tell me how, but the way she crossed her legs and pinched her lips when she revealed this made me suspect he believed himself her lover, and I felt a surge of hot jealousy in my chest.

'Two years after our first meeting, she asked for my help, and I was eager to oblige. "Tell me what you want, and I shall do all I can to help you." Her gratitude was the colour of sunset skies – yellow, orange, and pink. She wanted to leave, and the solution seemed simple. I already hated her gaolers, especially Dennis and his night-time visits. I called a meeting and discussed it with my siblings. A group of us descended from the ceiling and entered a dank chamber with grimy brick walls. Melissa sat, legs crossed, in the middle of the flagstone floor. Thirty-six others chanted around her.'

Back in the cellar with my spirit squeezed into the thirteen-year-old girl at the centre, candles flickered, and the shadows became corporeal. Breath warmed my neck, and fur tickled my arms.

'The stench of destruction filled my wide nostrils. Blood spray made my fur glisten in the candlelight. I crouched beside my beloved, urging her to wake and leave the cellar, but her eyes were empty. She could not move, and I feared lifting her in case I damaged her delicate bones. My siblings returned to the borderland. I stayed after the carnage was complete, but she did not wake. I finally left when men descended the stone steps and filled the cellar, believing she would be cared for, removed from this Hell. Melissa did not kill anyone, but they locked her up. My choices had been flawed. Instead of setting her free, I condemned her to imprisonment, but she never blamed me.'

Bodies torn apart, piled high. 'It was terrible,' I whispered.

'What else could I have done?' Harrokabis asked.

'Anything. Anything but that.'

The monster faded, becoming a shadow, a smudge of darkness in the corner. I'd judged him harshly, but I could not apologise. Those people, however cruel they had been to Melissa, had been ripped to shreds. No one deserved to die like that. Covers pulled over my face, I fell into a fitful sleep, reliving the horror until the guards woke me the following morning.

It was important to be a good inmate; my survival in the short term depended on this. Guards were human, with all the associated flaws and pettiness; Laney Dawson would not return for many days, and my relationship with Powell's demon was fragile. Joining the others was the best way to ensure my safety while I tried to figure out an escape plan. Dressed in a shapeless, floral-print dress, and an ugly cardigan, I left the cell. The noise on the landing was intense. My knuckles tightened around the guardrail.

Prisoners were herded into a single line, waiting to be led to the cafeteria for breakfast. I joined the queue. A guard escorted me to the dining hall, which was even noisier than the cell block. Four women, including Hodges, busied themselves behind the counter, preparing food. Two more leaned over the trays of meagre offerings with ladles and grim faces. All six wore hairnets and plastic aprons.

The woman who served me seemed disinterested and bored, offering everyone the same rough greeting. 'What-cha-want?'

I sat alone with a tray of scrambled egg, toast, and a warm beverage which resembled dirty bath water. The table was constructed from the same durable plastic as the desk in my cell. Its surface and the floor were spotless. At least one hundred inmates crowded around tables in the cavernous room. The windows were large, but out of reach, and fluorescent strip lights blinked and flickered. I felt constantly observed, but when I lifted my head, eyes flitted away, settling elsewhere, returning the moment I looked down again. Inmates whispered behind hands. I overheard a few words – Wilson, Masterton, Psych, and body-swap. I managed a few mouthfuls of lukewarm powdered egg before giving up and striding to the door.

'You need to put your tray on the rack,' a guard said, sending me back to the table.

Cackles followed in my wake. 'She's used to table service.'

'Room service.'

A guard returned me to C block where a dozen women queued for their turn in the dining hall, their stomachs rumbling. I marched back to my cell, offering friendly smiles to the guards I passed.

'Are you still here, Harrokabis? I'm sorry I judged you. Perhaps there wasn't anything else you could have done. How did Melissa react?'

Shadows congealed and solidified into a form that still shocked me. 'She did not visit me again for some time. After returning to the borderlands, I expected her to forget the friend who saved her. When she finally returned, I was ecstatic to see her. She wept in my arms, telling me she was sorry; she had missed me terribly, but it took time and planning to find her way back. She never witnessed the carnage but heard about it second-hand from police and lawyers. When she asked, I assured her I killed no one, only stayed by her side and protected her. She believed me, then said a group had been in contact, asking her to sign a lease, and in return, they gave her the tea she needed to reach me.

'She described Vinnie Green. "It isn't bad. They treat me okay, and I've learned to read and write." I had hoped she'd find a lovely family who worshipped their clever, adopted child. "Don't look sad. I'm okay, Harrokabis. My life is better now. I have friends my own age, but sometimes I am lonely. Can you come and keep me company?" She looked expectant. Her eyes were clear, and her expression exuded a strength and determination I had not seen before. She had grown up. "Are you inviting me to stay in your world?" She slipped her hand into mine. "Yes, I am." She pulled me into a tiny room, much nicer than this cell, with curtains and warm lighting. I lay on her narrow bed, curled against her spine. We were safe, and her steady breaths calmed me. I resolved to protect my beloved for all of time. I whispered this promise into her hair as she fell asleep. Some of the happiest times of my long existence were those years with Melissa.

'I taught her how to access worlds through photographs and postcards. We travelled together, and I shared her joy when she felt fresh air on her face, moved silently between trees, or swam in cool pools. Nothing could hold her spirit captive. She learned how to send others to these distant lands. Teenage girls paid Melissa for the experience; those who mentioned their adventures were bundled off to a psychiatrist, but most kept quiet and returned regularly; some used photos of their homes so they could visit their families.'

My rage boiled, imagining Melissa as the puppeteer of all those girls. I grabbed the photo of my house and shoved it under the beast's nostrils.

He pulled back, wrinkled his nose, licked thin lips.

'Send me there, or at least check on Steph for me. She could be dead.'

'Why would she be dead?' he asked.

'Melissa… she had this photo… she knows where I live, where Steph lives. She could be there now.'

'Mel wouldn't hurt anyone.'

'Please… I can't stand not knowing whether she's okay.' I stared at my facsimile home, desperate to go there, but trapped in the cell. 'How do I do it?'

'It takes practice.'

'Please, Harrokabis.'

The creature vanished. I felt relieved and grateful.

Harrokabis reappeared a few seconds later. 'The house is empty.'

'She's probably at work.'

He did not look convinced. 'Someone has emptied the wardrobes.'

'Steph and I planned to visit the Highgate house. What if she went with Melissa?' My mind reeled. I paced the room, glaring at Harrokabis until he faded into shadow and disappeared.

'Steph is fine.' His voice was crisp and emotionless.

His body flickered. I wrapped my arms around him afraid he might leave forever. 'Wait. Don't go. I need you.'

'You do?' He cocked his head and peered at me. Half-hidden behind lashes, his eyes communicated desperate longing.

'I can't do this without you.'

His twitching nose reminded me of a timid rabbit. I pressed my head against his chest, wrapped in his long arms.

'Where's Steph?'

'In Highgate. She has not been harmed. They are treating her like an honoured guest. She was chatting and eating breakfast when I saw her.'

The honoured guest part worried me; it made me think I was not privy to a vital piece of the puzzle. Something was going on, but I needed more information to figure out what. Were they fattening her up for slaughter? 'Are you sure they won't hurt her?'

'I sensed no threat.'

'Steph thinks Melissa is me. She's probably having fun.'

'I'm sure she is. Do you want to hear more of my story?'

Without waiting for my answer, Harrokabis continued his tale. 'We had lived happily together at Vinnie Green, and did not expect Witchwood to be different, but from the moment I arrived, hidden inside Melissa's skull, I was shocked by the malevolence of those paid to take care of her. Of course, she had told me how adults treated her at the house in Highgate, but it was infuriating to see such cruelty first-hand. Only three of the women here were kind to Melissa: Miss Ives, Miss Dawson and you. I know you fear her, but you and Melissa are the same. It's why I stayed, and watched, and waited for you to call me.'

My stomach twisted. Melissa and me the same? We had one thing in common; my parents' views on religion were as extreme as Powell's caregivers. Apart from that, I was nothing like the mass murdering bitch!

While it was easy to believe another neglected and abused child had been dragged through the legislative system and punished further, normally they were convicted of killing their abusers. Melissa's body count was thirty-six. They hadn't all abused her, had they? Harrokabis claimed Melissa killed no one, but each time she winked or smiled at me, even when she said my name, elongating it as she always did, I had sensed I was in the presence of powerful evil.

Miss Zane opened the door and poked her head into the cell. 'Have you forgotten your shift at the library, Powell?'

'My wrist,' I said.

'Just avoid lifting anything with that hand. You can't miss work, or you'll lose your privileges.'

After she left, I turned to Harrokabis. 'I'll be back as soon as I can.' I bandaged my wrist and washed my face.

The calendar on the library wall said it was Wednesday 12th October. Laney should return in seven days, but would I be able to convince her of my identity? Harrokabis remained my best chance of escape.

Amos was ordering new books for the library. Most would be transferred from other prisons, but there was a small budget to buy approved books requested by inmates. While she typed, I cleaned the shelves. The mindless work gave me time to process Harrokabis' story, allowing me to admit that there were parallels between mine and Melissa's childhoods.

We broke for lunch. I forced down some limp salad leaves but left the inedible looking chicken. Afterwards, Miss Ives took me outside. It took us half an hour to walk the inner perimeter. Beyond the tall fence lay a grass boundary 200 metres wide, surrounded by another unscalable fence then the dense and varied trees of Witchwood. Clouds parted mid-way through our walk, and the sun warmed my face, filling me with energy. No one was on the running track, but twelve inmates played football, and another twenty used the basketball court, none of whom I recognised from C block. Guards were in attendance, but the prisoners sounded relaxed and seemed to enjoy their leisure time. No one was working in the vegetable garden, so Miss Ives gave me a quick tour, pointing out different vegetables, telling me they were planted and tended by inmates and used in the kitchen. Of course, the belladonna I'd glimpsed in my dream did not grow there in reality.

We headed inside, while Miss Ives explained such outings could only happen twice a week. The thought might have crushed me were it not for my eagerness to hear Harrokabis' story. Inmates greeted me as I passed, but my purpose created a wall between myself and them.

'I'm back.'

He appeared on my mattress; his arms crammed together, and the curve of his lower back resting against the wall. I sat beside him, legs straight and ankles dangling over the edge of the bed.

'You smell of outside,' he said.

'I walked around the garden. It was nice.'

He smiled and patted my arm.

'What happened when you arrived at Witchwood? Why did Patterson cut Melissa's hair?'

'A welcoming party of press vans lined the street. When the prison bus slowed to turn onto the driveway, journalists rushed towards us, tapping on the barred windows. Our police escort pulled over, but the bus continued through the first gates, where guards boarded to search the vehicle. No smiles from the men, but a dog sniffed Melissa's hand, whining submissively when I greeted it from behind her eyes.

'We skirted the car park and red-brick mansion and stopped beside an ugly concrete annexe. The chains on Melissa's seat were released, and a guard helped her to her feet and guided us off the bus, through a tunnel and two sets of doors. Paperwork was signed and custody transferred. Two new guards arrived, greeting us with frowns. One introduced herself as Miss Patterson and took us to a shower room. "I'm going to remove your clothes so you can get clean," she said. "If you try anything stupid, there will be severe consequences. Do you understand?" We were stripped and led to a shower rose. Guards watched as water pounded Melissa's head and shoulders. A machine blasted moisture from our skin, then a masked nurse sprayed us with powder, making our nostrils burn. Patterson told us to sit and pulled out electric clippers. "It's too tangled to brush, but it'll grow back. You probably have lice, anyway." I watched as Melissa's long hair fell to the floor.

'Patterson ordered us to dress, shoving us between the shoulders. It was an act of aggression, not a gentle push to guide us towards our destination. She gathered bundles of Melissa's hair and shoved them into a plastic bag. "I said get dressed, inmate." Melissa restrained me, begging me to stay calm, otherwise I would have ripped through the old hag.

'Patterson approached another woman in uniform. "Get her to C block while I dispose of this." We both know she kept the hair. A trophy!'

'Inexcusable.'

'We made her pay.'

I saw the metal box again. 'I know. I found her.'

'We were escorted into a chamber with a high ceiling where the skylights were at least ten metres above our heads.'

I knew the cell block like the back of my hand but did not interrupt. As I absorbed the details, I saw it through the demon's eyes, unfamiliar and fascinating. Metal staircases rose on either side of the foyer, leading to a balcony festooned with netting to catch anyone who jumped, fell, or was pushed. The upper walkway formed a square crescent, and steel doors punctuated the walls.

'Like exclamation points,' Harrokabis said.

Women milled around the central area, dressed in street clothes.

'Like the ones worn by the teens at Vinnie Green. Frowning faces turned towards us as we entered. There were whispers, then one voice shouted out her name. "Melissa Powell, the Highgate Priestess." The guard gripped Melissa's arm, and we were guided towards the staircase and up to the mezzanine.

'"Mass-murdering bitch!" was shouted from below. I bristled, but Melissa told me to ignore it. We were led to our cell at the end of the landing above the gate. The number forty-eight had been stencilled on the metal door. Two boxes were stacked on the small desk, containing Melissa's possessions – clothes, letters, and our precious photographs.

'The guard removed the handcuffs. "Don't worry, Powell. They're excitable when new people arrive. There's a panic button here by the door, but it's only for emergencies. Use it if you're being attacked or have a medical problem." Then she left, shutting the metal door behind her.

'We pulled our photos from the smaller box, carefully, because tape made them stick to each other. We were still busy at this task when a woman barged into our cell. We met our visitor toe-to-toe. The red-haired woman was almost a foot taller than Melissa.'

'Lily Masterton,' I said.

'"So, you're the priestess." Her emerald glare bored into Melissa's face. "I expected someone more impressive, to be honest." The woman barged past us and grabbed a handful of photographs from the box. "What are these?"'

'"They're ours," we said. "Put them back."'

'The woman laughed. "You're new, but you'll learn. Everything here is mine, understand? Don't think you're better than the other plebs." We asked our aggressor's name, and she sneered as if we should already know. "I'm the boss. You can call me Master."'

'Melissa laughed. Photos dripped from the woman's fist, creased by the pressure of her fingers. She thrust her arms forward, shoving Melissa who stumbled and fell. We gritted our teeth and made to stand up.

'"Stay down, bitch," the woman warned. Two guards hurried into the cell. *We're safe. Everything is okay*, Melissa reassured me. "Masterton, out," the older guard shouted.

'Masterton pursed her lips and launched a ball of spit before marching out of the room, head held high. The guards edged sideways, distancing themselves from the inmate, before helping Melissa to her feet. A guard asked if Melissa was hurt and told us our door would be locked and our dinner brought to our cell. It sounded more like punishment than protection, and I was already plotting revenge. However, the idea of solitude appealed to Melissa, and no walls or doors could hamper my movements. The lock ground into place after the guards left.

'I could have killed them all, but my gentle and wise beloved shook her shorn head.'

'She did not want you to hurt Masterton?' I asked.

'Would you?' Harrokabis replied.

'I would have wanted to crack the bitch's skull.'

'My plan was more subtle. When I returned from my reconnaissance, I found Melissa wandering between tall pines, bird song echoing off tree trunks, while the tap, tap, tap of a woodpecker kept rhythm. Melissa filled her lungs with fresh, cool air as I lolloped by her side and briefed her on my discoveries. "The woman who pushed us is Lily Masterton. She's a serial killer who targeted men, women, and children. She was convicted of fourteen murders, but her body count was double. The guards are nervous around her, and she uses inmates as her personal army, including a Chinese woman called Chow Lee, who's in here for torturing and killing her pimp. Another inmate is making threats – an ex-nurse called Betty Wilson. She's planning to send us to the medical wing. If she offers you anything to eat or drink, refuse it. I will deal with her first. Patterson bribed a guard to help her smuggle out a bag of your hair. *The Friends* will need to intercept and retrieve the package, or someone might use it for spell work."'

'Who did Patterson bribe?' I asked.

'Does it matter?'

It was not my number one priority, but the corruption bothered me, even if I was not able to tackle it. 'I suppose not. What happened next?'

'We left Scotland, switched photos, and entered the Highgate house to scribble instructions on their notepad. By the time we finished watching children play in the park, a reply had been added. *Problem dealt with*, and a new photograph, ink still shiny, waited on the table; the one that troubled you.'

Time behaved strangely. It felt like years had passed since I found the car, not days. From the moment Melissa Powell arrived at Witchwood, I sensed something was wrong, but even in my most paranoid moments, I never imagined astral travel and a demon lay at the heart of the mystery.

'Melissa asked me to bring the photo to the prison. I held it between my claws, careful not to smudge the ink or tear a hole.'

'Melissa claimed a guard gave her the photo.'

'The guard was not innocent. Your righteous anger will be appeased when I reach that part of my story.'

'Still…'

Harrokabis' mouth twisted into a sympathetic half-smile. 'Melissa's bedroom had been preserved exactly as she left it, almost bare. She rubbed her index finger across the windowsill, not a speck of dust. People played tennis in the park, sweating as they sprinted across the courts, grunting as they swung rackets at balls. The tallest mausoleums of the west cemetery stood proud above the treeline to our right, and, to our left, beside the school she was never allowed to attend, cars crawled along a busy main road. In the distance, spires of other places of worship stabbed the heavens.

'After dinner, which she ate in our cell, Melissa spent a couple of hours beside the river near Witchwood Forest, listening to music from the sixties on Patterson's car radio until the police switched it off. Betty Wilson was in her cell. Unlike Lily, who looked deceptively innocent, Wilson's evil was reflected in the disdainful crease of her mouth and the deep crevices across her brow. I hated the awful grating sound of her teeth grinding in her sleep, so I pinched her nose, and she woke, flailing.'

'Wait,' I said. 'Tell me more about Patterson's accident. How did it happen? Where did she go? I met a man who was carrying a bag of hair, but where was the guard?'

'They didn't tell us how they did it. Could he have moved her first and come back for the hair?'

I considered this. 'It's possible, but he was a big man. He could have carried both.'

'Maybe they wanted you to see the hair but not the body? I'm sorry I can't fill in all the gaps for you.' He stroked my tufty head. 'Shall I continue?'

My eyelids kept sliding down. The smell of him was a heavy blanket that lulled me towards sleep, but I nodded, hoping the solution to my problem might lie in the next part of his tale.

'Wilson tried to push me away, crawling from her mattress to the corner of the room. I released her nose and tugged playfully at the strands of grey growing like moss from her sweaty crown. Guards sprinted upstairs, making the metal treads vibrate. Later, Melissa told me the sound reminded her of Brother Anthony's kettle drums.

'You entered our cell and towered between Melissa and the wall of photographs. Your legs made a narrow triangle, and your boots were planted firmly on the concrete floor in the stance of someone who is used to fighting. I noted everything: your short brown hair and warm eyes, five-feet-nine-inches tall, and it was obvious you worked out; inmates who used the gym at Vinnie never achieved the hard contours of your body.

'I studied Dawson next; braids twisted into a neat bun on top of her head; taller and wider than you, but her body language seemed gentle, as though she rarely encountered violence. Her dark eyes looked friendly and kind. While I would not rate Mel's chances in a fair fight, I knew I could handle both of you without breaking a sweat.'

I ignored the threat and remembered the first time I'd entered Powell's room and felt her careful study of me without sensing that an ancient intelligence was curled inside the inmate's skull. *Ancient intelligence? Hang on Wanda!* Only yesterday, I swung back and forth like a metronome, doubting my senses, believing I was Melissa Powell who dreamed of being Wanda Jones, then moments later, convinced I was Wanda, and would wake from this nightmare, and describe it to Steph over coffee. Now, I was acting as though Harrokabis was not only real but also my friend. Was that the power of stories? Did they teach us to accept things we were previously unable to conceive?

I turned my back on my parents' religion long ago. My concept of the world did not allow for demons. I didn't even believe in the healing power of crystals. But if demons and monsters didn't exist, did that mean I was somewhere safe, working through my trauma, creating a monster to represent my parents' all too human evil? Or did the monster represent a part of myself, something I needed to forgive before I could move on? Why couldn't things be simple? Why did my dreams insist on using metaphors? Was it just to confuse me? Another trick of my treacherous mind?

My internal debate did not prevent Harrokabis from continuing his tale. 'You were patient with us. Did you consider Melissa a child? You asked who cut her hair, and Melissa told you it was a guard. Dawson changed the subject, complimenting Mel on her photos.'

I heard the call for dinner. The food would be awful, and I wanted to hear the rest of Harrokabis' narrative, but compliance would prevent them from beating or drugging me, or throwing me back into Psych.

I excused myself, feeling like a sinner confessing on their death bed in case God existed. 'I won't be long,' I said. 'I want to hear the rest.'

But he was not in the cell when I returned from dinner.

'Harrokabis!'

Nothing.

'Shit!'

Unable to settle, I pulled myself up to the window and stared at the strips of light leaking from D block, then pushed myself away and stormed out of the cell, shivering as I gripped the guardrail and ground my teeth.

I stormed into the bathroom and found Amos covertly indulging in a cigarette.

'Give me one,' I said, although I hadn't smoked since I left university.

She pulled it from her shrivelled lips and handed it over without complaint.

'Thank you.'

'Are you okay?' she asked.

I coughed as the smoke hit my lungs. 'I don't know.'

'Take it easy,' she said.

I smoked the rest of the cigarette, my mind welcoming the drug, while the librarian stayed by my side, eyeing me carefully.

I flushed the filter, washed up, and headed back to my empty cell, my head feeling lighter than air. I fumbled under my pillow until I found the photo again. The lights went out while I was staring at the house, impotently.

CHAPTER EIGHT

STEPH and I entered a tiled lobby and made our way to the reception desk, which wore the deep glow of regularly polished wood. An old-fashioned brass bell resounded a single note when pressed. Elegant fingers intertwined with mine, and Steph's scent lifted the base notes of bees' wax and coffee.

'This was a good idea,' she said.

I tilted my head and returned her smile. 'Better than dirty London and a bunch of psychopaths.'

'Definitely, and just what you need,' she said.

'You're right. The atmosphere at the prison was intense.'

'Good morning, Powell.' Miss Zane stood in the doorway.

Shit! What had felt beautiful before I was jarred awake now seemed like the cruellest of jokes. My entire body ached. Still in the cell, curled like a foetus on a lumpy mattress, desperately clinging to the dream, squeezing Steph's fingers, begging her to keep hold and never let me go.

'Don't forget to go to the library after breakfast, Powell.'

I called Harrokabis' name after closing the cell door. He did not reply.

I dressed on autopilot, ate a tasteless breakfast, then found Amos surrounded by boxes. We organised the book delivery, matching some to names, and creating a separate pile for those which would be added to our shelves.

'Do you want to do the deliveries or sort the shelves?' Amos asked.

I chose the latter because it offered solitude and time to think. Solitude meant loneliness or boredom for many, but I needed to be alone for a while.

It was hard to keep my mind on the work. I kept imagining Steph in a metal box, pounding on the lid, or drugged and asleep. Why had Harrokabis not returned? Was he with Melissa? What would I do if he never came back? I would wait for Laney Dawson and try to convince her to believe my incredible story. That was the true hell of prison, waiting.

After lunch, I returned to the cell and tried again. 'Harrokabis, take me to Highgate.'

'Now?' Harrokabis asked.

I held the photo in front of me like a talisman and concentrated on the red front door. My eyes crossed as I stared through the image, doubling everything beyond the diamond of my distorted nose. 'I can't do it without you.'

'Take my hand,' Harrokabis said.

Dark wood floorboards scuffed and pitted; a staircase and three open doors, and beside me, a table, telephone and notepad. I reached for the pen, but my fingers passed through the plastic. The house was warm and filled with the delicious scent of baking. Animated voices wafted through the doorway on my left. I glided forward. A dozen people sat around a massive dining table. I did not recognise most of them, but my body sat at the head near the far wall, and beside it was Steph. It was strange and disorientating to glare at my own face and watch its eyebrows dip towards the bridge of a nose I used to see in the mirror. Melissa appeared unaware of my presence. Was my spirit, *astral body* Harrokabis had called it, invisible? I thought she, of all people, would see me.

Sharp nails pressed into my shoulder. A female voice seethed. 'You don't belong here.'

A tunnel of air shoved me out of the front door, across a park, and downwards into Melissa's frail body, on the prison cot where I'd left it. 'Who…?'

'Onyx,' Harrokabis said. 'She's screaming at me. I cannot take you back there.'

'Don't go,' I pleaded as the demon's body faded. 'I don't want to be alone. Tell me more. Dawson and I were with Melissa, and Laney complimented the photos. Stay, please…'

I covered my eyes and wept. Fur tickled my throat as Harrokabis patted my shoulder; the one Onyx had gripped like a bird of prey before expelling me from the house. At least I'd seen Steph nibbling a croissant, healthy and unafraid. It ended too soon for me to read anything from Steph's body language or notice any doubts she might have that the person sat beside her was not me.

What would happen to Steph, alone in Highgate, without me to protect her? I had to warn her. They might be planning another ritual. Would they all die like before? Or would they sacrifice Steph to ensure their survival?

Who was Onyx, and why did she see me when Melissa did not? How did she throw me out of the house, and why was Harrokabis afraid of her? The questions roiling inside my head were too muddled to vocalise. He continued his story, distracting us both, and distancing us from Onyx's wrath.

'When Melissa held the new photograph up, the colour faded from your skin and your face looked waxy, like the candles in the cellar. Sweat glistened on your brow and dripped down your nose.'

It was an unattractive image. Did I look like that now, sat on the cot, hyperventilating, desperately trying to figure some way out of this impossible, insane situation? My body was there, and my mind here, my partner there, and Melissa's here. My head throbbed and my stomach churned. I had no point of reference, nothing familiar, not even the pain in my skull. As much as I wished for death when migraines struck, their blinding familiarity might have been reassuring. If my pain did not belong to me, nothing did.

'You fled the cell, followed by Dawson. I knew the photo was connected to the retrieval of the hair, but not why it spooked you?

'Eventually the block grew quiet, and Melissa headed to a tropical beach to sleep under the warm sun, while the sea whispered a lullaby. I stayed behind, wanting to uncover the photo's significance, to know whether it put Melissa in danger. I overheard you talking to Dawson. I am sorry we scared you, Wanda. Wanda? Can you hear me?'

The muscles in my neck moved in unfamiliar ways when I tried to nod. The idea of speaking made my stomach churn; I hated my new voice and the awful way it wheezed through my nostrils, too light and sibilant. Eyes shuttered against his strangeness, I untangled myself from his embrace, and lay on my side. Harrokabis sat beside me, his forearm resting against my shoulder.

'Lily Masterton woke Melissa the following morning. Another woman hovered near the doorway, her soft but rapid breaths communicating anxiety. Beads of sweat clung to Lily's arched eyebrows, hinting at a nervousness we had not glimpsed the day before. Her half-sneer appeared cold, nonchalant, as if Melissa was far beneath her contempt, and we should be both flattered and terrified by the impromptu visit. "I asked you a question, freak?" Lily's voice boomed, her low register projecting masculine power.'

I imagined the scene: Masterton towering above Melissa, her expression carefully crafted to intimidate while sacrificing none of her beauty; pale fingers splayed over slender hips; torso jutting forward in a conscious demonstration of power and dominance. In a parallel universe, Lily Masterton would have been the star of stage and screen, adored by millions. Instead, she had killed children and filmed herself gloating.

'While her audience was small in cell forty-eight, she did not forgo theatrics,' Harrokabis said.

I shuddered. 'Can you hear my thoughts?'

'Sometimes. The Asian woman shrank against the wall. "*Nǚ wū*." Witch in Mandarin. Masterton strode forward to absorb our gaze. "Wilson was screaming your name last night in her cell. What did you do to her?" She saw through our projected innocence because she spent years mastering the same look. Masterton clicked her tongue, eyes widening as she considered what mischief she might cause, pushing past us to tug open the top drawer of Melissa's desk and inspect its contents. "You have almost as much mail as me. I suppose you think you're some sort of big shot." She threw a fistful of letters at her companion. "Tear them to shreds."

'Lily had an arm around Melissa's throat before we could lunge at the Chinese inmate. Pieces of letters were scattered like confetti, carpeting the concrete floor. Miss Zane stood in the doorway. "What's going on? Masterton and Lee, get out now."

'"We've been discussing Wilson, Miss Zane," Lily said.

'"Well, the conversation is over." After the inmates left, Zane scooped up handfuls of torn paper. "Is this yours?" Melissa did not cry. I would not let her show weakness. "I'll take them to the post room. I'm sure they can be repaired." Miss Zane studied the wall of photos. "You got them all up." We asked if she had a favourite. Zane pointed at a postcard of the Taj Mahal, and we suggested she sit down and look closer. Does it bother you that Zane was our first choice?'

'You think I want to be stuck in Melissa's body?' I snapped, then softened my voice. 'Why did you choose me?'

'You were a better match, and Miss Zane said she was too busy. We enquired after the guard who cut our hair, and Zane's forehead creased between her brows. She asked Melissa's lunch plans. "I thought I would try the cafeteria, Miss Zane."

'The guard nodded and left, cradling scraps of paper. I separated from Melissa, and she curled up on her cot. The cell door was not locked, and I refused to leave her body unprotected. "How dare that woman enter our space, threaten us, and cause chaos?" Melissa whispered. Her eyes darkened, and I wondered whether she was remembering Brother Dennis, the man who hurt her and was killed in the cellar. "Find out what she values most and destroy it, Harrokabis. Rip it to shreds." Melissa never chose violence. I should have remembered... before I... well, it isn't time to tell you that yet.' Harrokabis paused, and a soulful sigh escaped his jaws.

'What happened to Melissa's other letters? There must have been more.'

'I took them to Highgate, out of reach,' he said.

'Can you bring them to me?'

His eyes widened. 'They're hers.'

'Please,' I said. 'If I knew more of her past.'

'I am telling you everything you need to know,' he said.

I hoped that was true. 'I'm sorry, please continue.'

He sat silently for a moment. Was he considering my request, or had he lost his place in the story?

I reminded him. 'Melissa wanted you to teach Masterton a lesson, but she did not want you to use violence.'

His eyes were misty when he spoke. I hadn't noticed such nostalgia when he described the happy times in Vinnie Green. Perhaps, now I knew Harrokabis better, I could discern the nuanced emotions he expressed.

'That's right, but Mel needed to clear her mind first, so she explored the prison. I guarded her physical form while her astral body moved around the compound, discovering its secrets. I had already visited the other cells in this block, studied photographs dominated by the smiling or sullen faces of loved ones; watched inmates gather on the ground floor to play games and chat; roamed the grounds, sports facilities, and walled vegetable garden; followed the high perimeter fence beyond scrubland and visited the summits of the six guard towers to enjoy views of the entire prison complex; stood beside guards as they drank coffee from flasks and watched inmates harvest vegetables, run along a terracotta-colour track, or play basketball. I had explored the red-brick mansion where ancient screams echoed behind barred windows and ghosts of long-dead patients haunted abandoned rooms – a place of nightmares, ice baths and electro-therapy, which would never know peace; where pain still vibrated through the mortar, and visceral anger launched spiteful attacks on anyone who strayed too close.'

'I heard their voices sometimes. I thought I imagined it,' I said.

Harrokabis cocked his head.

I recalled one night, sitting on the toilet, listening to muffled weeping. At first, I thought it was a burnt-out guard. Ours was a difficult, challenging job, and many women could not cope. After flushing, I knocked on the stall door. It swung inwards, revealing only the porcelain toilet, high cistern, and chain. A quick glance into each of the other stalls assured me I was alone, and that the sobs which echoed around the tiled room were disembodied memories. Another time, I'd been called to Reynolds' office. Standing outside her door, I felt fingers stroke my hair; again no one was there. Even when I dismissed it as imagination, the discomfort remained, the feeling of being watched, followed, as if someone or something was desperate to communicate their deep and unending misery. Recently, the voices had seemed more insistent. Were they a symptom of my heightened anxiety, or had they been trying to warn me about Melissa's trap? The shadows moving in empty rooms, the voices and touches; if they did not belong to ghosts, then I was seriously disturbed.

'You are sensitive to the activity of spirits,' he said.

Tears burned my eyes. Whenever I mentioned voices, shadows, atmospheres, or ghosts, people told me my perceptions were flawed; that I couldn't trust my own senses because of undiagnosed c-PTSD, migraine symptoms, or exhaustion. Being believed, having someone accept my words at face value, made me feel respected – loved. I realised how much it hurt to have those who claimed to love me constantly dismiss my feelings as falsehoods.

'Melissa returned to me an hour later, eyes wide. "Spirits haunt the trees of Witchwood, and I watched entities dance and heard fairies sing. Ghosts of executed women promised their help whenever I need it," she said. "But I was too afraid to explore the old building. It holds only darkness and pain. It reminds me of home."'

Ice filled my veins. It reminded me of my childhood home too. A cloistered sadness too traumatised to leave.

'You shuddered,' Harrokabis said.

'A memory. My mother and father.'

'Tell me.'

'I'd prefer to hear Melissa's story.' I felt unable to articulate my childhood trauma without falling apart. I'd endured so much and feared my mind could not survive the retelling.

'You are afraid.'

It was not phrased as a question, but I tried to answer. 'It was difficult, the powerlessness. If I was not stuck in someone else's body, powerless again, then maybe…'

'You've been silent for a long time. Too long.'

'Give me time. I'll muster the strength to tell you, but I need to find the right words. What did Melissa do after sensing all that pain and darkness? How did she move past what happened to her?'

'I held her tight, and she wept until the inmates were called to lunch. She dried her face before she left, and I stood guard in her absence, promising no one who entered would keep their sanity. I used the time to decide the best way to punish Masterton.'

I wiped a tear from my eye and forced a smile. 'Clever, destroying her clothing. But how did she know it was Melissa?'

'It was an obvious parallel. Masterton made Lee tear up the letters and someone tore up her clothes in the night.'

'The guards did not think those events were linked. They thought Masterton did it herself.'

'You suspected,' Harrokabis said.

'Yes, I suppose I did. I suspected a lot of things, none of which I could prove. Laney thought I was paranoid.'

'After lockdown, we were handcuffed and escorted to an interview room where two plain-clothes police officers introduced themselves as Detective Smith and Detective Michaels. They asked the guard to wait outside. Detective Michaels gave us a polystyrene cup of milky coffee.'

'The night Wilson's cell was torn apart. Was that you as well?' I asked.

'Do you want a summary, Wanda, or a story?'

'Sorry, I'm listening.'

'Detective Smith asked Melissa how she was settling in at Witchwood Prison. "We were told a guard gave you the… pixie cut you're sporting, and now Miss Patterson is missing." The detective sounded agitated. "You know something." We denied all knowledge, of course. Detective Smith's mouth twitched. "You showed a photo to a guard yesterday." He checked his notes. "Ms Jones. We believe it was taken at the same place the missing guard's car was discovered."

"'That's a strange coincidence," we admitted.

"'We don't believe in coincidences, Miss Powell. In our line of work, they're called circumstantial evidence. When did you receive the photograph and from whom?"

"'I promised I wouldn't tell. I wouldn't want anyone to lose their job.'"

I forced myself to be quiet so he could continue uninterrupted, but I wondered whether Powell's talent for lying came from Harrokabis. If it did, why should I trust anything he was telling me now? My stomach churned and my head felt like a tangled ball of yarn. He expected me to trust him, but I was often too gullible for my own good.

"'Where is Moira Patterson?" Detective Smith asked.

"'I have no idea, detectives."

'The men looked at each other. Michaels went to the door and spoke to the guards. "Take her back to her cell and bring the photo to the supervisor's office." The guard gripped Melissa's arm too tightly, but we distracted ourselves from the discomfort by replaying the short conversation. "It was different before," Melissa communicated silently. "When I was thirteen, the police bullied and shouted at me, and interviews lasted for days. Did you influence them, encourage them to treat me gently?"

"'No, my love. It's probably because they have nothing to threaten us with now. Where could they send us? Nowhere worse."

I stiffened. I always tried to treat inmates with respect, but in the days since the body-swap, I learned many of my colleagues did not. Harrokabis was right. There was nowhere worse than here, but I couldn't give up hope. Somehow, I would leave this awful place.

'We handed the requested photograph to the guard and waited for them to leave before separating. Melissa crossed her legs, ready to travel. "Welsh coastline, I think. It's a good place to unwind," she said. I told her I had things to take care of and would join her later.

'Stuck in a colourless concrete and steel block, surrounded by dull and ugly people, I felt certain Lily's primary concern was her physical appearance. She wanted to be seen, revered, and feared. I knew what would hurt her most.

'I enjoyed ripping and shredding Lily's clothing and did not want to stop. I turned Betty Wilson's vacated cell upside down before flooding it. It was pointless destruction; the ex-nurse was already broken, whimpering in her sleep in the psych ward when I last checked, but it was fun, and I was still giggling to myself when I found Mel paddling in the Irish sea. "Two down, one to go," I said.

'I heard shouting and knew one of my tricks had been discovered. Would the guards want to speak to Melissa? They could not prove it was us, but I thought it sensible to return. "Powell are you awake?" a woman in a business suit asked. She, you, and Dawson were in our cell when we opened our eyes and forced a smile.

'"Powell, I'm Miss Reynolds, but you may call me Ma'am if you prefer. How are you? Can't you sleep?"

'"I heard noises, Miss Reynolds, Miss Dawson, Miss Jo-ones."' Harrokabis mimicked Melissa's elongated pronunciation of my name. 'Do you want me to skip this part?'

'I remember. She refused to tell us who gave her the picture, and Miss Reynolds threatened to take all her photos,' I said. 'But a few days later, she told us it was a guard.'

'I brought the photo back from Highgate. Presumably, whoever kidnapped Patterson and recovered the hair had sent a digital copy of the location to *The Friends*. The wonders of technology. Like magic. A plan was forming which involved Miss Zane and a photograph of the Taj Mahal, but your boss is a stubborn woman.'

Melissa and Harrokabis had discounted Miss Zane and stolen my body and freedom instead. I should hate him, but lounging beside Harrokabis, listening to him weave his intriguing, fantastical tale and mimicking Melissa's voice, was indescribably wonderful.

'Reynolds is fierce, but not stubborn,' I said. 'We needed to know the significance of the photo. We hoped it would help us find Patterson. She would have done the same for me or Laney. It's what strong leaders do.'

Harrokabis seemed to consider this, then shrugged. 'As you know, Melissa refused to discuss the photo, so they took them all the next day, all but the one I advised her to hide.'

'I need to use the bathroom,' I told him. 'I won't be long.'

Amos was there again, and despite the currency tobacco represented in the prison, she offered me a cigarette.

'Thank you,' I said.

'Thank you for dealing with Masterton.'

I felt my cheeks flush. 'I didn't…'

She threw her cigarette in a toilet and left. I brushed my teeth and emptied my bladder before returning to cell forty-eight and slipping under the covers, no longer noticing how they scratched my skin. It was amazing what discomfort a person could get used to.

'May I sleep beside you?' Harrokabis asked. 'It comforts me.'

'Yes. I think it'll comfort me too.' I felt his warmth against my back as I drifted off to the rich sound of his voice.

'Screaming, shouting, yelling. Melissa's name with a death threat attached to it. I left our cell and watched as Lily Masterton was wrestled to the ground by four guards. Her baby-blue silk negligee was torn, and her small left breast was exposed when she was pulled to her feet. "She tore up my clothes. Fucking Powell. I'll kill her."

'A guard snapped handcuffs around the prisoner's wrists as the Chinese inmate rushed from her cell. I could not catch what the prisoners said to each other, but Lee glared across at Melissa's cell as she was pulled away.

'Another guard hurried through the gate with an orange jumpsuit. "I'm not wearing that!" Lily yelled. Despite her protest, they got the garment over her legs; their efforts to protect her modesty were repaid by kicks to heads and chests. They tied it around her waist as if too afraid to remove the handcuffs. Inmates emerged from their cells, wiping sleep from their eyes to gaze at the scene. A few cheered. Lily Masterton was pushed and pulled, her cheeks glowing red, like my eyes…'

CHAPTER NINE

As we stood at the cliff's edge, two dark clouds draped above the horizon like theatre curtains or gates. A briny breeze ruffled Steph's hair, whipping it against my ear and cheek.

'It will rain soon,' Steph said. 'We should head back.'

'I want to stay,' I told her, absorbing the details of her freckled face. 'Have I told you how much I love you?'

She smiled. 'Not in the last five minutes.'

Hand in hand, we followed a gentle footpath, winding through woodland where trees stood respectful of each other's space, rather than crowding shoulder to shoulder as they did in Witchwood. Sunlight speckled the path and grass, which had been trimmed neatly by non-human gardeners too shy to reveal their presence. It was idyllic – a beautiful place, warm and flower-scented – the light to Witchwood's darkness.

'Good morning, Powell.'

After breaking the spell of my dream, the guard slipped out before I opened my eyes. It was funny how quickly I had grown accustomed to being called Powell. Was I losing my self-identity or simply learning to survive?

If I managed to get Miss Zane alone, I might be able to find out whether she had been sent to a strange land on Powell's wall. It was a long shot; Harrokabis and Melissa may have abandoned the idea before things went that far, but it had to be worth asking. If Zane knew what Powell was capable of, she might believe my strange tale.

Zane would return, even if today was her rest day. In the meantime, there was more to learn from my cellmate. His soft fur tickled my neck.

'I fell asleep as they took Masterton away,' I prompted.

He understood my cue and continued his tale. 'Melissa ate breakfast in our cell. An hour later, three guards arrived. I warned Melissa not to resist, but they countered our passivity with aggression. "Maybe we should burn these," said a guard whose blonde hair was pulled back in a bun, laughing when we bristled. Miss Zane was not among them. They did not offer their names, and we did not ask. The quicker they finished, the better.

'"Where's Patterson, bitch?" A wide-shouldered woman with short grey hair strode across the cell and leaned forward until our faces were centimetres apart. Her breath stank as she rolled back creased lips to expose tan and yellow teeth. We maintained eye contact while I held Melissa's body steady. My beloved wanted to back away, but I refused to show weakness. This tactic seemed to confuse the guard. Eventually, she straightened her back and towered over the cot. "I asked you a fucking question, inmate!" The other women grinned and pulled pictures from the wall, creasing and ripping Melissa's treasures.

'The grey-haired guard drew back her arm, then a huge fist hurtled towards Melissa's chest. We fell backwards, hitting our skull against the wall as our spine bounced on the mattress. Melissa bit her tongue. A crimson river poured from her mouth as we spat out a chipped tooth. The guard launched a globule of spit that landed on our face. "We done?" she asked her colleagues, who acted as though this was normal.

'The last guard to leave had brown hair, short at the back and spiked on top. She looked a little older than Melissa, early twenties perhaps, and stole a final glance at the defenceless body sprawled across the mattress. Our red-toothed smile made the woman recoil and hurry away, carrying the box of photos, leaving us alone. Only yellowed scraps of sticky tape remained on the wall.

'When the door was shut, we sat up and touched the base of

our throbbing skull. We probed the swelling, and a white-hot poker of pain sliced through our head, forcing us to hobble to the stainless-steel toilet and empty our stomach. The foul smell filled the airless room, and we vomited again, tasting bile. The bitter jus, produced by Melissa's liver, burned our throat as it rose. I pulled the last photo from her pillowcase. "Spend some time in Highgate," I told her. "While I deal with this."

'I swilled blood and vomit from her mouth, held a wet flannel against the bruise and folded her tiny body as small as possible, concentrating my healing powers on her head and spine. I could not understand what pleasure the hag gained from punching a defenceless inmate and promised myself I would find something suitably terrifying to destroy the guard, and any future aggressors, until no one dared hurt my beloved again, but Mel inflicted her own revenge.'

'The guard she claimed gave her the photo?' I asked.

Harrokabis grinned.

'Was she fired?' She must have been disciplined at least. It made no sense that smuggling a photo to an inmate, or informing police about letters, earned a harsher punishment than physical abuse, but that was the world we inhabited.

'I haven't seen her since,' Harrokabis said.

Inmates were heading to the cafeteria. After breakfast, I worked alongside Amos in the library, busying myself with a damp cloth, first cleaning and then filling the shelves until lunchtime. Eager to hear more of the demon's story, I skipped lunch and raced to the cell. 'Harrokabis?'

He appeared near the window.

'Where were you?' I asked.

'I visited Melissa. She wants me to stay there, fears for her safety.'

'But you came back?'

'You need me.'

'I do. Thank you. What's happening? Is she still in London?'

'They're preparing another ritual. Melissa is not sure she will survive this one.'

'Tell me everything,' I begged.

'But the story will be out of order.' The idea seemed to cause him pain.

I relented. 'At least tell me whether Steph is still there.'

'She is, and she's fine.'

'Are they sleeping together?'

'Who?'

'Steph and Melissa. She thinks it's me.'

'I did not ask. Do you want me to find out?' His lips curled, revealing sharp fangs, but he was no longer monstrous, and I feared him no more than a pet dog.

Did I want him to find out? Only if he brought back the answer I craved, that they were in different rooms and had not slept side by side or, worse still, made love. If I knew they had been intimate, I would obsess about them day and night, unable to concentrate on anything else, hating Steph for it, even though she could not have known it was a betrayal. Perhaps it was better not to ask rather than to risk hearing an uncomfortable truth.

'No. Continue your story. We must be near the time Melissa sent me into the photo.'

'There's a lot more to cover first. Melissa returned after a few hours. I had healed her body during her absence. A tray of food was on the desk, meaning someone had entered while I was unconscious. I moved our limbs tentatively, relieved to discover no further damage. The headache had dissipated, and our back felt warm but not painful. Only the rotten taste in our mouth and the sharp edge of a broken tooth proved the attack was not a dream we had shared.

'"I have good news," Melissa said. "Someone connected to *The Friends* knows a guard; Onyx assures me she will be easy to manipulate, turning her interest in me into an all-consuming obsession. She could be our way out of here if your plan does not work out. A photo of her home is on the table at Highgate." I left her body and stretched my limbs, touching the ceiling, then the rough concrete floor. "What do you think?" she asked. I said it was great news.'

It did not stretch my imagination to connect the photo of my house to this good news. My interest in Melissa had betrayed me. If I'd done as Laney urged and ignored my curiosity, Melissa would be inside Zane's body. 'Who is the connection? Who gave them the photo?'

'She did not say, and we could not risk putting the new photo on the wall, so Melissa hid it with the image of the Highgate house. "Won't you eat?" I urged. "You'll waste away." She complained her mouth hurt. "You'll need a dentist. Mending a tooth is beyond my skill set," I said.

'I spent the day in our cell, not daring to leave Melissa unprotected until I glimpsed you and Miss Dawson at the gate. I checked the whereabouts of our enemies: the vicious, grey-haired guard had already left; Lily Masterton was trapped in a windowless cell, growling and muttering between sobs, and Betty Wilson was in Psych. One other inmate needed my attention. Chow Lee had torn Melissa's letters to shreds, and a lesson must be taught. I thought it might help Melissa's self-confidence if she were party to Lee's punishment.

'"Isn't revenge your thing?" Her accusation confused me. Vengeance had never been my motivation; everything I had done was to protect her. "One day, you may need to solve your own problems," I warned.

'She grabbed my hand. "Are you leaving me?" I never meant to imply I would abandon Melissa, but her fear vindicated every decision I had made. "Of course not, but you can learn to resolve conflicts without me; it takes training and practice, like everything else I've taught you."

'What she said next made me bristle. "I prefer to stay pure." It was the first time she cast judgment on what I did, and she must have been shocked by my reaction, because she apologised, "I'm sorry. I'll come if you want."

'Melissa's astral body entered Lee's cell first. The woman gasped, and her high voice repeated the same phrase. *Nǚ wū*. Witch. The Chinese woman's mouth grew wider when I appeared beside Melissa. Like Onyx, Chow Lee saw both of us. Before she could scream, I dragged her downwards, through the cell floor, the room below, the earth. It was not Lee's flesh I gripped, but her consciousness – her astral body, the same incorporeal energy which allowed Melissa to travel through photographs and fly unseen around the prison complex. Lee struggled and tried to hold her breath, not knowing her lungs remained in her cell. I took her to the cellar. Although, from the look on her face, she thought we were in Hell. Her whispered prayers denied me. Shadows rustled below the vaulted ceiling; the borderland creatures were excited. "Do you want to play?" I asked.

'Their arrival was the only answer I needed. They pulled Lee's hair and bit her limbs. When she opened her mouth to scream, their fingers sought entry. Terrified, she bit down and whimpered, lips trembling but never reopening. She jerked her head to avoid seeing what surrounded her, things she glimpsed even when she screwed her eyes up tight. I punched through the facsimile of her ribcage, tore out her heart and ate the fluttering organ while she slapped her chest, unable to believe she was still alive.

'Melissa left before I returned Lee's spirit to her body. In the gloomy cell, Lee blinked and screamed. Madness made her eyes shine. The inmate was a broken shade, no longer any threat to my beloved.

'I watched you and Dawson from the skylight as you handled Lee, then followed you and the others into cell forty-eight. You stood by the wall while Reynolds and Dawson sat on either side of Melissa. You wanted to know about the cellar.'

'I dreamed about it… before Lee… Did you take me there?' I asked.

'You visited the cellar without my influence… both times, but Melissa tried to convince you it only existed in Lee's head.'

'I remember. I thought I was going crazy. Am I? Zane can't see or hear you. No one else can. Are you really here? Am I?'

'Do you doubt it?' Harrokabis asked.

'I don't know what to believe. How can I trust my senses when they aren't even mine? This nose, this mouth… It's all wrong. Everything! Isn't it more likely that I'm dreaming or experiencing a psychotic break? I don't know of anyone who has body-swapped or met a demon. People who claim things like that are diagnosed with schizophrenia.'

'I'm as real as you are,' Harrokabis said. 'And I already told you I'm not a demon.'

'I'm starting to doubt whether I am real. Maybe I'm someone else's nightmare. And if you aren't a demon, what the hell are you?'

'I'm a borderland creature; just a different species from another dimension parallel to this one.' Harrokabis rested his paw on my shoulder and squeezed gently. 'I need you to accept me, and you need a friend.'

I nodded weakly. Whatever this was – delusion, dream or reality, I didn't want to be alone.

'You promised not to reject me.' His eyes flashed like warning beacons. 'Don't push me away like Melissa did. After you, Dawson and Reynolds burst into the cell, I wanted to curl up inside my beloved's skull where I could guide and protect her, but when I approached, she repelled me. The exclusion made me feel cold and my fur stood on end. No one noticed me or my distress. I moved to the window and sat on the desk, hugging myself.

'You wanted to know everything: the cellar, the photo, Patterson. "What we perceive when we look at something isn't always objectively true," Melissa said. I sensed a dual meaning in my beloved's words. She was questioning our friendship. Once, she believed I was her only friend; now, when she looked at me, she saw yet another monster.'

'She was referring to the photo,' I said. 'My mind interpreted it as a familiar landscape. She made me doubt myself. Is that why I'm stuck in this prison cell? Is my mind creating another familiar landscape?'

'You are not insane. You are really here with me, but I understand why you have doubts,' Harrokabis said. 'Did you taste the food at lunch? Was it familiar too?'

'Lunch had no flavour at all. No proof either way.'

'An impasse.' He shrugged. 'Do you often doubt reality?'

Tears burned behind my eyes. 'I've always been taught not to trust my memories. Mother and Father stretched the truth to breaking point, always claiming I was wrong, mistaken, even crazy. If the people you rely on assure you your mind cannot be trusted, you believe them. Steph does it too, but I don't think she wants to hurt me; she probably thinks she's helping me. Whenever I'm angry or upset, she tells me it's because of past trauma, things I've locked away rather than facing. There are times when I think she's right, but sometimes I'm angry at her and it feels like she's deflecting rather than accepting responsibility. She's cleverer than me. I've never been able to explain my feelings without her twisting my words and muddling my thoughts. My parents trusted in God, Steph in science, but none of them ever trusted me enough to let me decide for myself what was real. I take nothing at face value now and second guess everything. If I see something, I want to know whether others see it too – test its reality. Does that make sense? No one sees you, apart from me. Does that mean you aren't real? If I asked my parents or Steph, they would say I'm psychotic and you're a symptom.'

He cocked his head, and his eyes moistened. For the first time in my miserable life, someone empathised, cared without judging me. More than anything, I wanted that to be real.

'I'm okay,' I said, willing it to be true. 'Please, continue.'

He nodded. 'Your boss, Reynolds, urged Melissa to name the person who had supplied the photo. My beloved claimed it was the grey-haired guard, the one who punched her. She was learning the ways of revenge. Did she still feel pure? Perhaps, compared to me.

'When I tried to put my arm around Melissa, she shrugged me off. She would not talk to me. I gave her space, leaving her cell, chased away by her glare. I considered returning to the borderland, knowing the others would crowd around me for tales of my adventures. But I wanted, no, I needed, to hang around a while longer.

'Lee and Wilson were both on the psych ward, and I overheard

Betty Wilson's attempts to engage Chow Lee in conversation. I am sure you can guess the subject – yours truly and my mistress, assuming Melissa was still that. Lee did not respond intelligibly to Wilson's questions. The Chinese woman seemed virtually catatonic. I had promised to break her, and I had. Knowing Melissa was troubled by my actions made me see the woman through my mistress's eyes, and I felt guilt like a toxin, freezing my blood. I stayed behind the curtain, not wishing to cause further trauma.

'Lily Masterton seemed as fiery as ever, making the prison-issue jumpsuit look good as she strode around the grey box. "How did she do it?" Lily asked herself. "She didn't, I did." My answer went unheard. "I don't deserve this," Lily muttered. "I'm the victim here… Everyone on the block saw me fall apart… they'll think I'm vulnerable. If I don't do something, the fucking witch will replace me; she'll be the one they look up to, the one they fear… even the bloody guards treat her with reluctant respect. Whatever I do, it must be big. Think. Think!" She wrung her hands, stamping across the rough floor, wearing plastic slippers two sizes too big. Her hair was unbrushed, and smudged makeup created shadows beneath her eyes. Was she my best hope to keep hold of Melissa? I had planned to free my beloved from the prison, but I feared her rejection when she no longer needed my protection. It sickened me to admit I needed Lily Masterton.

'"I know you're there," Melissa said as I entered our cell. I asked whether she was ready to talk. She moaned and bent double, holding her head between her hands. "She's inside me!"

'I rushed to her side. She did not shrug off the arm I wrapped around her bowed shoulders. "Get her out!" she pleaded. "I'm full of her." Tears drenched her skirt while trembling fists kneaded her temples, as if she could squeeze the intruder from her mind. Her body rocked back and forth, nose bouncing off her thighs before rising again. Lilac and pink blotches covered her face while her twitching lips turned white. I stroked her hair, trying to calm her. "Stop!" she growled, and I withdrew my hand. "Don't kill them." She was somewhere else, not growling at me but at whatever or whoever was inside her mind. To protect my beloved, I became mist and entered the arena inside Melissa Powell's skull, knowing I didn't have her consent to do so, but fearing what might happen without my help. Through her eyes, I saw the carnage in the cellar. Borderland creatures were everywhere, ripping and shredding flesh, tearing apart limbs. Melissa and I sat at the centre while hot blood arced across the room, soaking our skin and her white dress, and tormented screams rang in our ears. It was Hell. Five years ago, she stayed in the borderland, only waking when men pulled her from the aftermath. Now she witnessed the massacre first-hand. I sensed another consciousness filling Melissa from her toes to her antebellum. We could not move, not even to close our eyes and block out the horror.

'I knew Melissa would never forgive me. She had requested freedom, and this had been my answer. A Pyrrhic victory, and what had she gained except fear, pain, and further imprisonment? The only creature in the world who loved her was the monster responsible for this nightmare.

'When the carnage ended and the flies descended, we were jolted back into cell forty-eight. "You are a demon," Melissa said, shaking her head, making me dizzy. I knelt before her; my empty palms proffered in supplication.

'When she invited me to join her at Vinnie Green, I believed we would be together forever. I thought I could hide the price of her freedom; I never wanted her to know what happened to her guardians; the burden would be too great for her to bear. Now she knew it all, and the rage in her eyes, the twist of her mouth, felt like daggers in my chest.

'She pulled the drawer from her desk and threw it at the window. It bounced off the bars and shattered when it hit the floor. She tore off her bedding and mattress, pulled clothes from the wardrobe, and shredded them with nails and teeth. I watched in horror. Was this how I looked when I wrecked Wilson's cell? Manic? Insane?

'The door opened, and someone called for help. Melissa was tackled, handcuffed, and marched from the room. It was impossible to intervene without making things worse, so I stood aside and watched, impotent. "I'll save you," I promised. "I can make it better." "Fuck off!" she screamed.

'I took the two remaining photographs to Highgate house, wanting to see Onyx. I waited in an armchair, unobserved by *The Friends* who wandered the rooms, chewing pastries, gulping coffee, and glancing out of windows. I sensed something was happening. Something big. The bustle made me feel small and inadequate. Again, I considered leaving this world, but I postponed the decision, hoping I could still make things right. Melissa was a victim before she was born. I had promised to protect her and owed Melissa her freedom, even if it meant losing her.

'A knock on the door announced Onyx's arrival. She strained under the weight of her bags. I rushed to help and took her burden, making *The Friends* gasp. Onyx assured them it was only me, but it did not ease their anxiety. She led the way to the dining table, thanked me, and opened the briefcase. I expected magical items, but she pulled out and opened a shiny laptop, then asked whether everything had been prepared. A man nodded. The medium's fingers danced across the keyboard and a page opened – *Find my Mobile*. More keys were pressed, and we waited. "Here," she said, tapping a dot on the screen. "She's on her way. She'll reach the forest in three minutes."

'The man pressed a button on his phone. "ETA three minutes." I did not understand what was happening but knew I must wait until Onyx was free. "Two," Onyx said. A woman delivered a pot of tea, a bowl of sugar cubes, a cup, and a silver spoon to the table in front of the medium. "Thank you," Onyx said. "One." The telephone rang, and the man answered. "Target has been sighted. And we're go." Onyx told me you were being led to the missing guard.'

'They wanted me to find Patterson. Why?'

'I asked the same. Onyx scowled and said it was for Melissa.'

'How did they track me? How did they know I would be there?'

Harrokabis hung his head. His mouth twisted as if he was chewing his words. The chill of dread made hairs bristle across my body. The single blond hair, which had been wrapped around my throat after the terrible nightmare; was it the strand I gave to Steph? My girlfriend, who was obsessed with serial killers, had pushed me to become a prison guard and apply for the promotion to C block, claiming it would mean more time together, a way to synchronise our working hours. The money was enough to support us while she studied, but was it the only reason, or did she plan each stage of my career, leading me to this moment? Was it Steph who helped Onyx track my mobile?

No, Steph loved me, and she was in danger because of me. Everything else was paranoia, albeit with good reason. Someone was out to get me, but not my partner, Melissa Powell and her friends in Highgate, but not Steph, never Steph. She wouldn't, couldn't…

'I walked away. The laptop snapped shut and soft steps followed in my wake. I smelled patchouli and knew Onyx was behind me. A dozen anxious faces met us in the dining room. A man bounced his fists against the table. Onyx told me to grab her briefcase. "We'll find somewhere quieter."

'The red room was empty. After setting up her crystal ball, Onyx asked for my hand. "Tell me what's wrong." I told her someone had invaded Melissa's mind and revealed to her the horror of that night. My fur tingled as she stared into the reflective sphere. Her eyes rolled back, and a thread of drool oozed from the corner of her mouth. "Wanda Jones." Although the name was formed on her lips, the voice did not belong to Onyx; it was far deeper, more like mine.

'Detective Smith had told Melissa he did not believe in coincidences, called them circumstantial evidence, but this felt more like synchronicity.

'Onyx released my hand, wrapped the crystal ball in a velvet scarf, then lowered it carefully into her case. "The guard would make a fine vessel for Melissa."

'I asked Onyx not to tell Melissa it was you who invaded

her mind, requesting she leave it to me. The medium smiled and nodded, not sensing any reason I might betray their trust. Duplicity was an ugly idea. I wasn't convinced that I could keep your identity secret. I knew I should tell Melissa as soon as possible, but... "Of course. It should be you. You've always looked after her." Her eyes shuttered, and I heard the gentle purr of a snore.

'I would lose Melissa the moment she left prison; the thought weighed on my chest, but could I keep my secret, knowing eventually she would discover my betrayal? I did not want to be her gaoler; I wanted to be her friend, her beloved, the one she could rely on, no matter what happened. Keeping her trapped was heartless and cruel. What right did I have to prolong her misery?'

Inmates were moving towards the gate. Dinner time. My stomach grumbled. 'You'll be here when I get back, won't you?' I asked.

Harrokabis nodded and curled up on the mattress. Did the monster need sleep too? Did he eat? If so, what?

While forcing slimy spinach down my throat, I decided not to repeat my question. Either Harrokabis did not know how *The Friends* tracked me, or his answer would confirm my worst fear. When I got free, I would find Steph and ask whether she betrayed me. Would I sense the truth if she lied, or would I accept her version of events as I'd been trained to do? The world was crammed with lies and half-truths, it was exhausting, but I trusted Steph, and my belief in her gave me the strength to keep living. It would destroy any vestige of hope if Harrokabis told me she had been complicit in my imprisonment.

CHAPTER TEN

BY the time I returned to C block, my question was locked away, and I was eager to hear the rest of the demon's story. Masterton glared at me from the mezzanine. So, they had let her out of solitary at last. As a guard, I was protected by my status and colleagues; now, I needed to fend for myself. Eyes narrowed, I stared at my cell door, urging Harrokabis to push the serial killer down the stairs. Melissa had never chosen violent solutions to her problems; that probably meant she was better than me.

The borderland entity did not appear. White knuckles wrapped around the handrail, I ascended, expecting a fight when I reached the top. Had the prison guards not noticed the threat? They were at the gate, concentrating on the prisoners returning from the cafeteria.

'Masterton,' I said when I reached the top.

She stared at me for a moment before jabbing her elbow into my shoulder. 'Not now, but soon,' she threatened.

By the time I reached the relative safety of my cell, I was panting.

Harrokabis waited on my cot. 'Are you okay?' he asked.

If I revealed Masterton's threat, he would deal with it, but the violence I envisioned as I climbed the stairs now seemed like overkill. It would be better if he concentrated on his tale while I considered my options. 'Did you tell Melissa I was inside her mind?'

'I lay on warm slate tiles, feet butted up against a Victorian red-brick parapet interlaced with lead drainpipes, feeling peaceful, and enjoying the sunshine, while deciding what to tell my mistress. This sense of well-being ended the moment I saw Detective Smith and Detective Michaels exit their car.

'I followed their progress through the prison. If they interviewed Mel, she would need me by her side. The men were escorted to a room marked WARDEN, and their guide knocked on the door. A middle-aged woman in a powder-blue blouse and navy skirt greeted them and handed over a heavy-looking plastic bag stuffed with brown envelopes, before sending them on their way.

'I could not bear the thought of their sweaty hands opening those envelopes and riffling through whatever the sleeves held. While I saw nothing to identify the contents, I smelled the subtle perfume of my mistress' fingers. It was Melissa's property they were removing from the prison; I was sure of it.'

'Her letters,' I said.

Harrokabis had watched the detectives leave. On their way back to the station, the same officers were involved in a fatal car crash. My lips moved, but the words to silence him were stuck in my belly, and covering my ears seemed pointless, because I saw it unfold in my mind's eye.

His words only confirmed what I knew. 'The detectives flung their ill-gotten gains on the back seat, nosed their way through two gates, and swung left onto the main road.'

I sat in the back of the squad car, as I had when they escorted me home from the forest. Michaels chatting and smiling, and Smith driving, blissfully unaware of what would happen, eager to discover what secrets the bag would hold, wishing they had not placed them out of reach, wanting to flick through the envelopes, but knowing they should wait until they reached a sterile environment where evidence would not be polluted or lost.

'Be careful. Slow down,' I said. Neither Smith nor Michaels heard. This had already happened, and nothing I did could stop it.

'Maybe I should have spoken to Melissa or contacted her friends in Highgate, but the metallic taste in my mouth told me there was no time to waste. I hurled myself into the air and followed.'

Imagining the huge, leather and fur-covered, many-limbed monster airborne was a horrifying vision which threatened to crack open my skull.

'The densely packed trees of Witchwood Forest lined the carriageway. The men chatted to each other and laughed as they progressed towards town. I spotted a sharp bend ahead and swooped, allowing myself to become visible, plummeting towards the car bonnet and obscuring the driver's view.'

Panic, disbelief. The two men must have been terrified.

'Detective Smith tugged the steering wheel to avoid hitting me and wrapped his car around a giant oak. Metal screeched as it tore open, and glass exploded.'

It was like a scene from *The Matrix*. Glass rotated in slow motion, making rainbows as it soared outwards from the point of impact. The detectives lunged forwards as airbags inflated. Bones snapped like dry twigs. Weak gurgles from Detective Smith's pierced lung as he fought to breathe. Michaels' neck was broken, and he appeared to be looking over his shoulder, watching Harrokabis as he removed the bag from the back seat.

'I knew neither would survive their injuries, but I felt no guilt. I hid the bag in a blackberry bush so no one would find it accidentally.'

You are a monster, I thought. *How could I allow myself to forget?*

'When Melissa returned to our cell the following day, I kept my own counsel and did not discuss the detectives' accident, certain she would be appalled and distance herself further from me. But this was why she needed me. I protected her while allowing her to keep a clean conscience.'

Harrokabis' bulk suffocated me. He was too close. My chest burned, heart and lungs working too hard, too fast, adrenaline flooding me, paralysing me. Fight and flight both impossible – complete surrender to my horror.

'Melissa wanted to talk. It felt like aeons since she had shared her thoughts, made plans. "Harrokabis, I've been thinking. The guard, Jones. How did she get inside me?" She knew already, sensed it was you. There was no point trying to deny it, instead I offered my opinion, "I think the two of you are connected somehow. I see the same sadness in her eyes."'

My mind was too full of screaming to process his words. My eyes were sore and dry, but I could not even blink. He continued, paying no attention to my despair, perhaps oblivious, lost in his memories of her – his friend, his beloved. The girl who fled this monster and left me here.

'Melissa pulled a photo from her pillowcase, sat silently on her cot, and sent her consciousness to the Highgate house. I could have followed. Before Lee, she would have expected me to join her, but things had changed, and I did not feel welcome. I tasted salt water and realised I was crying. Why do the people you love hurt you the most?

'Knuckles rapped against the cell door. I hid Melissa's photograph and pinched her wrist, warning her to return. Miss Ives entered the cell and perched on the desk. She held an electronic device. "You've been here for a week," Miss Ives said. "And it's part of my job to settle you into a routine to make your prison term more productive and support your emotional well-being." Miss Ives wanted Melissa to list the medications she had been prescribed at Vinnie Green. She offered educational opportunities and suggested a job at the library. "You're allowed time outdoors, but because of the animosity you've received from some of the other inmates, we'll ensure you're closely monitored. We can stroll around the grounds after our meeting if you would like some fresh air."

'"I would love to go outside. I'm sorry I messed up my cell. I was angry because of my letters and photos, and reacted without thinking, but it won't happen again."

'"We're aware of the circumstances. I'd like to tell you it'll get easier, but I can't make any promises. If you want to keep your privileges, you cannot rise to provocation. Do you understand?"

'Witchwood might feel more like Vinnie Green if Melissa

socialised and learned to fit in. Things had gotten very dark, and I yearned to see her smile again. I glimpsed it an hour later as the box of photographs was handed to Melissa. As she put each on the wall, I recounted memories of when we visited those places together. "We swam with dolphins there; they were always laughing… I wonder whether the worshippers ever found their shoes… The sand and the sun's blue-white glare made you squint and blink, but it was worth it, don't you think, when we perched atop the pyramid and saw all of Cairo spread out beneath us?" She shrugged and contributed an occasional sigh to my soliloquy. When I complained she was being unfair, I glimpsed hate in her glare. "You killed those people." I protested my innocence. "Not me. I stayed by your side, protecting you. I'm still protecting you."

'She spun away from me and held a photo to the wall, hands trembling. "You should never have taken me to Lee's cell. I thought you were gentle, but you ripped the poor woman's spirit through concrete. It was violent, horrible. I watched as the light left her eyes."

'I did not understand Melissa's anger. We had never argued before. Once, I saw my beauty in her eyes. Now, it was as if she could barely tolerate the sight of me. "Do you think you would survive here without me?" I asked. "I won't be staying much longer," she replied. The thought chilled me. I knew she intended to leave me behind, but she couldn't leave, could she? Not without my help.'

'Why did you kill Michaels and Smith?' I asked.

'To protect Melissa.'

'I thought you were kind,' I protested. 'I thought you were my way out of here, but all you do is kill.'

'That is not fair.' He lurched away, and I gained the distance I needed. 'You sound like Melissa.'

'That's because she was right. You make unilateral decisions without understanding what Melissa or I need. Maybe you don't even care.' Anger overcame shock, and I had no intention of backing down. 'You have this idea of who I am, but it isn't real. I am not her, and I doubt she's who you imagined. My father claimed he was protecting me, keeping me pure, innocent, good. He had a thousand inconsistent, petty rules; maybe they made sense in his head, or perhaps they were an excuse to take out his frustration on me. His solution to every problem was violence too. You don't get it. How could you? You aren't even real, just some shade, a composite of hope and fear. I thought I was dreaming of Steph, but what if my dreams are reality, and this is a feverish nightmare born of nervous exhaustion, or maybe my scars are too deep, and I'm psychotic?'

'Calm down, Wanda.'

'Oh, calm down, you say. A demon tells me to calm down when I'm trapped in a prison cell wearing someone else's body. Calm down? I'm not panicking enough. Stuck here, forced to listen to an ode to your obsession with a little girl who outgrew you and moved on. I'm sure Freud would have a field day.'

'It might help if you talked,' Harrokabis said.

'Talked?'

'Talking will help you process your childhood.'

My laughter was sardonic. Only I could have a demonic therapist. I realised how much I held back from everyone. Perhaps he was right, this borderland creature, dream, projection of my ego, or whatever Harrokabis was. Sharing my pain might be the first step towards healing, and I had nothing left to lose.

I'd never opened up to Steph even though she begged me to do so. The fact that I trusted Harrokabis with the information I'd denied my girlfriend, caused a sliver of guilt as I told him about my childhood. 'Father was a miner before the pits closed. He brought the darkness home with him each night. Mother, a devout protestant – deeply religious – tried to heal him with gospel, and made excuses for him, lied for him, as if truth was subservient to loyalty, but it only made him worse. He caught the bug, the virus of repression, from her. She filled his head with shit, told him religion made him a better man, until he believed the coal mines were the pits of Hell from which an angel had freed him. He claimed he wanted more for me, but the only things he gave me were more bruises and more fear. I'd cower at night, staring at shadows, knowing they were demons, half-hiding around my room, when really it was my parents who terrified me, and now, here you are – a demon formed from shadow.'

'I am not a demon,' he said.

'Liar. You dragged Chow Lee to Hell, and you've taken me there too. I liked Smith and Michaels.' My shoulders shook as I sobbed. There seemed little point in pretending to be strong. Whatever I did, my fate was no longer in my hands. Had it ever been? Apart from leaving home, my decisions had always been made for me, from Steph telling me where to work, to Onyx and her friends delivering me to the box in the forest.

Harrokabis drew closer. His arm wound around my back, pulling me against his leathery chest. Hating him but having no one else, I toppled sideways, head landing gently on his lap, and stared into the forlorn features of an abandoned old dog with a fierce and warped sense of loyalty. With my legs stretched across the mattress, and my eyes struggling to remain open in case I dreamed of my father or the dead detectives, I prayed desperately for dreams of Steph.

He interpreted my submission as his cue to continue the story. 'Melissa spent the next day doing all the things prisoners were supposed to do, while I sank into despair. To Melissa, it may have looked like I was sulking, but I was full of a powerful darkness which consumed everything good. I huddled in the corner of the cell, invisible head resting on my invisible knees.

'She did not return until the sky turned silver and the shadows deepened. Then she sat on her mattress and stared at her photos. We did not talk. What could we say? If I was not dulled by self-pity, I might have returned home, leaving Melissa to fend for herself. She seemed capable enough without me. Happy if the sly smile on her face was any sign. It was the night you came to the cell and entered the photograph, and Melissa left.'

His words clogged my veins. Goose pimples decorated my arms, and the monster's soulful eyes flashed as I blinked. Behind those crimson orbs lay a code I needed to decipher, but I was afraid of what I might learn.

'Do you have any questions?' Harrokabis asked, his tale complete.

Without tearing my eyes away from his, I managed to shake my head.

'Do you believe me?'

I lifted a thin arm and traced Melissa's elfin features with my fingertips. 'Yes, I believe you. I don't seem to have a choice.'

'What will you do?'

Tears filled my eyes and snaked over his thighs. 'What can I do?' I remembered the two photographs, lifted the pillow, and shook it until it shed them like dead leaves – my house and hers.

'At least you know Melissa's power is not absolute. Everything you thought she did was through me.'

'Take me there again,' I said, reaching for the image of the Highgate house.

He took my hand. One moment we were in the cell, and in the next… people filled the hallway and adjoining rooms. Too many to count. There was no sign of either Steph or Melissa among them. A cornucopia of accents and languages bombarded my ears.

'What's going on?' I asked.

'The ritual. They're here for the ritual.'

'What's going to happen? Why do they want this? Aren't they afraid of dying?'

'They believe my siblings can give them power and riches beyond their imaginings,' Harrokabis said.

'What are they offering in return? I presume there is some sort of bargain. These people want money and power, but what do the demons… sorry, I mean Borderland creatures, want? There must be some trade. They cannot expect to receive everything without giving something back. A sacrifice? Steph?'

'I don't know,' Harrokabis admitted.

'Then we must find Melissa and ask.'

Conversations halted and silence settled. Movement on the stairs, a woman descending, dressed as ornately as a Catholic priest and wearing my face – Melissa.

'There she is. Ask her!' I demanded, spinning on my heels.

Another figure filled the space Harrokabis had occupied moments before – a young man with a deep tan, whose dark eyes brimmed with resentment.

Melissa wove between bodies. I reached for her shoulder, but my fingers slipped through her skin as if she was a hologram. The others followed; their heads bowed in reverence. Many passed through my body as if I was vomiting them forth, giving birth to these greedy men and women who made deals with demons.

Melissa halted at the end of the hall. People formed semi circles around her, tightly packed so all could see and hear, many leaning over the banister and from doorways. A woman knelt before the priestess and held out a ceramic cup as if it were the holy grail. When Melissa took the offering, the woman retreated to find her place among the worshippers.

'It is time,' Melissa said before drinking.

Two men took her arms and guided her into the room. The gathered throng filed through a large kitchen and into the cellar.

Melissa's voice rang out from below. 'Bless the souls gathered today as I, Melissa Powell, open a portal between two worlds, the material and the esoteric. We raise our voices in songs of devotion to prove our love and respect for all that is hidden and shall be revealed. We offer ourselves willingly, expecting no reward greater than knowledge. Protect your loving children as you birth us into this new life and surround us with power beyond our mortal imaginations. We would taste your greatness and offer freedom to roam where you will. Amen.'

Something brushed my arm.

'Time to leave,' Harrokabis said.

'But Steph…'

He gripped my wrist and pulled me back to the prison cell.

CHAPTER ELEVEN

At the edges of my consciousness, I heard screaming. I opened my eyes, expecting a prison riot, or Masterton wielding a knife. Instead, I found myself in the cellar. There were sixty or more people, sat cross-legged in circles like ripples in a pond. I scanned their faces and spotted Steph in the second row.

Dark limbs bulged from the shadows above my head. Marbled creatures dropped from the ceiling, then danced and skipped across the flagstone floor. Veins of pulsing colour gilded their gyrating bodies, and ebony tongues waggled at the congregation as the creatures weaved playfully between the entranced. No one was touched, but misshapen shadow-cloaked torsos wiggled before unseeing faces.

Harrokabis called them his siblings, but there was little familial resemblance between these dark entities except each belonged to nightmares. Even the most humanoid female, whose exaggerated breasts bounced against a distended belly, had birdlike legs and feet. One had mandibles instead of a mouth and insect eyes bulged in a face which looked like moulded jelly. Another had a goat-skull head and hollow eye sockets.

I pushed myself to my feet and staggered towards Steph. The weight of my body, the strength of my legs, and the width of my shoulders seemed unfamiliar for a few disorientating moments until adrenaline flooded my system, preparing me for anything. My mind had returned to where it belonged – my body, and despite the strange surroundings, I was grateful. I did not know how or why I was in my own flesh; I was just happy the nightmare was over.

Over?

The cellar full of demons was nightmarish, but now I had the tools to overcome it – a body which was toned and ready for battle – I could face whatever happened. My priority was to save Steph. What had she been thinking, allowing Melissa to keep her in this awful place? I tugged her arm, trying to lift her. She seemed sluggish, drugged, perhaps.

'Steph,' I said, shaking her shoulders.

Her eyes flickered open before heavy lids shuttered them again.

Dislodged rubble tumbled around us. A sharp stone sliced my cheek. I lifted my girlfriend and carried her towards the stairs. Demonic hands and scimitar claws grasped the air close to our faces, threatening yet avoiding contact.

'What's happening?' Steph asked, stirring in my arms.

'Demons,' I said.

She wriggled, and I put her down. Steph scanned the room. Her expression was difficult to read; it seemed to flicker between fear and awe.

'Come on,' I urged, dragging her up stone stairs, through a warm kitchen, along a hallway, and out of the building, which creaked and cracked behind us. As if guiding a sleepwalker away from a precipice, I pulled her beyond the railed gate, across a road, and into a park where she finally broke out of her trance-like state. We stood shakily on the damp slats of a bench and watched the town house from what I hoped was a safe distance.

Three people stumbled down the front steps and into the small garden, blinking and coughing. They swayed on the path while slates tobogganed down the peaked roof and smashed around them. One headed back up the steps, presumably planning to rescue others. The remaining pair seemed rooted to the spot, mouths agape and chins resting on their shoulders as they craned their necks to keep the front door in sight. Walls and ground shook. The escapees toppled, their palms meeting the path, but this time they did not linger in the shadow of the trembling walls. Instead, they crawled towards the road.

'Wait here,' I said and sprinted back to the house.

The two men had sought dubious shelter beside a luxury car. More slates fell, smashing in the front garden. Mortar crumbled in zigzagged cracks down the front of the four-storey house. It was going to collapse. We needed to get further away. I grabbed the men's wrists and guided them to the road. They moved without purpose, probably in shock. The roof collapsed before we reached the park. Billowing clouds of rubble obscured my view as I searched for a gap in the privet, eventually finding it further to the right.

The men looked dazed when I dumped them on the nearest bench, propped shoulder to shoulder in a Gothic arch. Before I returned to Steph, I took a moment to study them. It felt important to remember their faces.

'We should leave,' she said, gripping my hand. 'Thank you for rescuing me.'

Dust itched my eyes and tickled my nose. 'Did they hurt you?'

Steph shook her head. 'I don't understand what happened? We came to Highgate like we planned, but when we arrived, you were different. I don't remember what happened after.'

'It wasn't me,' I said as we hurried away.

Sirens. A neighbour must have phoned the emergency services. How many of those grand homes would remain standing at sunrise?

'Powell switched bodies, leaving me stuck in the prison. I wanted to warn you, but they wouldn't let me phone. I am so sorry, Steph.'

'I'm okay. It's okay. We can discuss it later. The car isn't far from here. Unless it's been towed.'

We found her jeep on a parallel street, a plastic envelope stuck to the windscreen. Steph tore it off and pushed it into her pocket. 'Are you up to driving?' she asked. 'My head is groggy.'

'Of course,' I said. 'Do you have the keys?'

She patted her pockets and shook her head. 'Can you hot-wire it?'

'Do you think I spent my youth boosting cars?' I laughed as hysteria threatened to overwhelm me. 'We have no money, no keys, no phone. Maybe we should go back and talk to the police.'

'No!'

I studied her face, shocked at the force of her refusal. 'Why?'

'How in hell are we supposed to answer their questions?'

'We could claim they kidnapped us both. The police are already looking for me. Melissa left my car at the prison, and the other guard, Patterson, will verify our story.'

'I can't,' she said, trembling. 'Please, don't make me go back there.'

I stood beside her, hands on hips and legs astride, what Harrokabis had called my fighting stance, trying to formulate coherent thoughts; my masculine pose juxtaposed with the floaty gown Melissa had been wearing.

'Wanda…' It was the voice that once woke me from my dreams, led me through Witchwood, and to the cellar. *You're not getting back in my head*, I told it.

'I have an aunt in London. She'll help us,' Steph said.

'Can we walk there?'

She nodded.

I wrapped my arms around myself to keep warm as we marched. For ten minutes or more, the voice pestered me and invisible fists battered my skull, trying to gain entry. I concentrated on my body, refusing to let go. Eventually, Melissa gave up.

Despite the cold, neither Steph nor I reached for each other. It was strange to be so close yet feel so distant. The streets were busy despite the hour, and the air stank of car fumes. A stark contrast to the quiet, companionable scenes I had dreamed while in prison. Was this yet another dream? Every time I heard footsteps, I glanced over my shoulder, expecting to see Harrokabis behind us, but I only saw strangers.

After thirty minutes, during which we remained distant from each other, never breaking the silence that became more oppressive and awkward with each passing moment, we reached our destination.

A woman, wrapped in a satin dressing gown, opened the door. 'Stephanie, what are you doing here?'

'Can we come in, Aunty Lana?'

Lana eyed us carefully before stepping aside.

'This is Wanda,' Steph said. 'We need your help. We've locked ourselves out of my car. Do you know any locksmiths?'

Lana frowned. 'A search engine would be more useful.'

It was late and undoubtedly, she felt inconvenienced, but her frostiness seemed deeper. I guessed she and Steph were not close.

'Our phones are… in the car,' Steph lied.

'Are you with a breakdown service?'

'Yes. Can I borrow your phone?' Steph pasted a sweet smile onto her features. Would Lana notice it was fake?

Lana lifted her hand to stifle a yawn. 'Go ahead. Do either of you want some tea?'

I followed Lana to the kitchen, apologising for the intrusion.

The woman glared at the door, then leaned towards me, conspiratorially. 'Are you two… together?' Her thin mouth twisted. Was that her problem? Was Lana homophobic? 'Be careful. She's trouble,' Lana whispered. 'Always has—'

Steph appeared in the doorway. 'Sorry, Wanda, we have to go. They need us to wait at the car.'

It was a relief to be leaving. 'It was good to meet you,' I said.

☽⬠☾

'We're home, Steph,' I said, four exhausting hours after we left London.

I had thought about things as I drove. Steph was the only good part of my life, but the thought that she was in the cellar of her own volition nagged in the back of my mind. Maybe, I should have asked her outright, but whatever she said would be turned over and analysed by my deep paranoia, and I still would not know the truth. Part of me regretted not asking Harrokabis while I had the chance.

At least I was out of prison, and soon I could get dressed in my own clothes, lie in my own bed. I doubted I would sleep well, always wondering when Melissa might push me from my body again. What would I do if the woman I loved was complicit? I stared at her slowly awakening face with dread. The sky was growing lighter, and according to the clock on the dashboard it was 7:30 am.

'I could sleep for a year,' Steph said.

'I'm not sure I'll ever sleep again,' I replied. 'What if she gets back in?'

'How did she do it last time?' Steph asked.

'A photo.'

'Don't look at photos,' she said.

'That's not funny.'

The house was locked, so I shuffled next door to ask for our spare key.

'Did you have a good holiday?' the neighbour asked.

It seemed easier to say yes and thank her than argue.

When I pushed our front door open, Steph stumbled inside, shaking off her shoes as she headed to the stairs.

'Don't you want to eat?'

She shook her head.

I padded to the kitchen to brew coffee. The bread was mouldy, but I found a packet of crispbreads and added butter. After munching the crackers, I made a phone call. A door closed upstairs; it sounded like the bathroom.

'Can I speak to Detective Inspector Lewis, please?'

'Who shall I say is calling?'

'Wanda Jones.'

The inspector said he would arrive within half-an-hour. I waited for him on the front lawn. Lewis and Marrs arrived in an unmarked car. I led them inside and gave them coffee. They did not seem surprised by my tale of demons and body-switching, but I doubted they believed me. They asked to speak to Steph, and I found her asleep on the toilet. She grunted when I rocked her shoulder.

'The police need to ask you a few questions,' I said. 'Have

you got a numb bum? You've been here for over an hour.'

'What? Did you call the police?' Her eyes flashed angrily before she looked away, sighing. 'Give me a minute to make myself decent.'

I waited on the upstairs landing while she flushed and washed up.

She sat in her usual spot on the sofa, frowning.

'I made coffee.' I placed a steaming mug of coffee in front of her while sighing inwardly at my awkwardness – the Queen of Pointless Announcements.

Steph and I sat close to each other, but our bodies didn't touch. Her scent combined with the smell of coffee made me feel like I was finally home, that the nightmare would soon be over. There was one last hurdle to face – convince the police of my innocence.

'Miss Walker, I'm D.I. Lewis and this is W.P.C Marrs. We understand you have had quite an ordeal, but we need to ask you some questions.'

Steph nodded, and the interrogation began.

'Miss Walker, tell me about your trip to Highgate.'

'Wanda and I went to London to check Melissa Powell's old house. When we arrived, Wanda seemed more interested in the park. I left her there while I looked for somewhere to ditch the car. I found her by the swings. I remember thinking it was odd, but I assumed she was nervous or overwhelmed. She had been stressed at work, and I figured she needed to relax.

'She took me to the house, a four-storey terrace. The front door was unlocked, and people rushed at us from all directions when we crossed the threshold. I wanted to run, but Wanda stood firm; she's always been the brave one. It felt like they had been expecting us. Despite my desire to leave, I followed a tall woman to a small room on the top floor with five mattresses. Wanda was taken to a different room and joined me in the dining room an hour later, washed and changed, her hair still damp.'

'They welcomed you?' D.I. Lewis's brows arched.

'It felt like they did, but in the way of dreams, where you

cannot question what's happening. They called Wanda priestess, like she was their leader,' Steph said. 'It doesn't make sense, but at the time, I accepted it…'

'How many people were there?'

'Dozens, I think.'

'At least sixty,' I interjected.

'Thank you, Miss Jones, but we already have your statement. When did you arrive at the house in Highgate, Miss Walker?'

'A week, ten days ago, maybe. We went on Friday, but after we got there, time seemed to ebb and flow, and I couldn't follow what was happening, not until Wanda dragged me out.'

'Did you see the building collapse?'

'It started shaking when we were still inside, but Wanda saved me and rescued two others. She's a hero.'

'Why didn't you stay and give statements to the police?'

Steph paused, glanced at me, then stared at her hands. 'I wanted to get far away. It felt like the house, the people… like they would grab hold of my mind again. I begged Wanda to let me leave, to take me home.'

☽⛤☾

'Do you think they believed us?' Steph asked after the police left.

'I'm sure they will when they check on the house and confirm it fell down.'

'But the body switching, I mean?'

'We didn't have time to agree a story, so I thought the truth was best.' I had told the police she had been kidnapped, but privately I remained uncertain on that point. Had Steph been abducted or was she one of *The Friends*?

'Have you phoned work?' Steph asked.

'No.'

'Do you plan to go back?'

'I'll phone them tomorrow. Turn on the news while I butter some crispbreads. You need to eat something.'

When I returned, the Highgate house was on the television. Firefighters sifted through rubble while the flushed faces of the two men I saved, and a reporter, reflected flashes of blue. The surrounding houses remained intact, and the view made me think of a tooth torn out of an otherwise healthy mouth. I sat beside Steph and placed the plate in front of her.

'No evidence of explosives or a gas leak have been found. However, viewers may recall that this is the spot where, five years ago, Melissa Powell murdered and dismembered thirty-six people. Melissa Powell was transferred to Witchwood Prison recently, and it remains uncertain whether a bizarre coincidence or a conspiracy caused that prison to be destroyed only one hour after firefighters were called to Highgate. Mateo Ignacio and Thomas Lloyd managed to escape before the house collapsed. Mateo, tell us what happened.'

It was impossible to drag my eyes from the screen. Steph's shoulder pressed against mine, and her hand squeezed my fingers.

Mateo's accent was Mediterranean – Italian, probably. 'It was late when I heard the walls groan. I knocked on bedroom doors as I left, but only Thomas met me outside.'

The journalist tilted the microphone towards himself. 'Did you hear an explosion?'

'No, but we felt the walls shake.'

'How many people were in the house?'

Mateo shrugged. 'A few, I think.'

The reporter touched his earpiece. 'We have learned that the building was leased to an organisation calling itself *The Friends of MP*. Are you members of that group?'

Mateo shook his head.

'We have also uncovered a familial connection between Thomas Lloyd and Melissa Powell. Tell our viewers how well you know the Highgate Priestess.'

'I'm her great uncle.' Thomas smiled at the camera. 'My organisation has been trying to overturn her wrongful conviction. She is not a killer.'

'What are your thoughts on the disaster at Witchwood Prison?' the journalist asked.

'I have no knowledge of what happened, but I pray Melissa

is safe, and I offer my condolences to the families of any victims.'
Thomas nodded gravely.

'Thank you, Thomas and Mateo, now over to our correspondent at Witchwood.'

I leaned forward. 'Why didn't the police tell us anything?'

The Victorian fascia appeared intact, but when the screen switched to an aerial view, vast piles of rubble lay where four prison blocks once stood. The camera view returned to the front, where a reporter stood with a maturing man in a tailored suit.

'Emergency services are searching for two guards and twenty prisoners. We remain optimistic that they'll be found alive. I am here with the custodial manager, Mr Jefferies. Sir, can you tell us what happened?'

'I am proud of the emergency services and the way prison staff responded to this disaster. If not for the quick thinking of my team, many lives might have been lost.'

'Why did the buildings collapse?'

'The investigation is ongoing, and a statement will be made when we have answers.' Mr Jefferies looked calm and professional.

'Did any prisoners escape?'

'The public has no reason for concern. The perimeter is secure, and there is no evidence to suggest any inmate has left the grounds.'

'Is Melissa Powell among those still missing?'

'No comment.' The manager blinked a few times before regaining his calm demeanour.

'What is your response to news that this disaster happened an hour after Powell's previous residence in London collapsed?' the journalist asked.

'No comment.'

'Thank you, Mr Jefferies. This is Horton Matthews for News North, on location at Witchwood Prison in Lancashire where last night four cell blocks were destroyed. Now back to the studio for other news.'

Steph switched off the television and grabbed a buttered crispbread from the plate.

'What the fuck?' Laney Dawson was on holiday, but what

of my other colleagues? Which guards were missing? Which prisoners? Melissa Powell must have planned this and would be far away by now. My fingernails dug into Steph's shoulder. 'I need to ask you something, and I need the truth, however much it hurts.'

The colour drained from Steph's cheeks.

'How well do you know Melissa Powell?' I asked. 'I've been putting everything together, and I reckon you met Powell before I did.'

She shook her head. Her wide eyes glimmered. 'Do you think she escaped?'

I stood up and marched towards the front door.

'Where are you going?' Steph asked.

'I have to find out.'

'I'll come with you.'

'No,' I said. 'They won't let you in the prison. Stay here and work on your alibi.'

Driving Steph's jeep, I approached the spot where I discovered Patterson's car, and glimpsed a blonde figure sprint across the grass; my foot hit the brake, and the car jolted to a stop. After shoving the door open, I clambered out and gave chase – she was one-hundred-metres ahead, but my stride was wider, and it did not take me long to narrow the distance between us.

'Melissa!' I shouted.

The girl did not stop; she pushed herself harder.

I needed to reach her, catch her, speak with her, find out what she had done and why. I chased my prey like a wolf pursuing a startled deer. Chest tightened, head emptied, and thighs and calves burned, but I gained ground. I did not see Harrokabis but presumed he would be close. When I was a metre behind her, I lunged and grabbed her waist. She toppled and hit the ground.

My knees pressed on either side of her spine, pinning her in place. 'I'm taking you back.'

'I didn't kill anyone.'

'Not my call. I'm a guard, and you're my prisoner.' The world had righted itself, and I was back in control. The waif beneath my arse had tormented me, and I enjoyed some well-earned payback as I pushed down on her spine, forcing air from her lungs. I did not plan to kill her, only scare her, make her feel powerless.

'Wanda.' I would recognise that growl anywhere.

'Don't try to stop me, Harrokabis,' I warned. 'Why are you here?' I asked Melissa. 'Running from the forest like a common thief.'

She mumbled something.

I clambered off her back and let her sit beside me, keeping a tight hold on her wrist. 'What was your plan?'

'I only want to be free.'

'Your followers are dead,' I said. 'Another mass slaughter.'

'They promised…'

'Who promised? Your demons?'

'The borderland creatures. They promised not to touch the worshippers.'

I snorted. 'They didn't touch them, Melissa. The walls crushed everyone. Nice loophole, huh?'

'I suppose both of us have been betrayed. Did anyone survive?'

'Three. Four, including me.'

'Who?'

'Steph, Mateo and Thomas. Tell me about Steph.'

'Will you let me go if I do?'

Although the strength was seeping from my limbs, I shook my head. 'She used me, didn't she? You both did.'

'Come with me. We could be a family,' Melissa said.

The adrenaline, which kept me alert during police questioning and allowed me to outrace Powell, deserted me now, making me doubt my ability to drag even Melissa's feather-light body to my car. My world was crumbling, and nothing made sense. I should have known Steph was involved; she never hid her obsession with killers, so why was I surprised to hear she plotted with one of the most infamous mass-murderers in recent history?

Blind to Steph's faults, it was no wonder I had been trapped in the web of her lies. She had gaslit me for weeks. The hair around my throat, Steph must have placed it there while I dreamed. She did not want to return to the Highgate house, not because she was traumatised, but because she feared someone would reveal her part in it all. Her aunt tried to warn me. Harrokabis told me Steph was being treated like an honoured guest. Had he imagined that would be enough to undo her spell on me? Feeling like an idiot, I shook my head again, slower this time, wanting to curl up on the grass and sleep; wake up in another time or place, or not wake at all.

Harrokabis lifted me from the earth and cradled me in his arms. His eyes blazed with sympathy. I did not struggle or ask where we were going; I had no strength left, was barely aware of Melissa, marching by the monster's side, away from the prison.

CHAPTER TWELVE

I WOKE, lying on a pile of straw, surrounded by filthy, raw wood walls and floorboards.

A vivid dream about Steph clung to my skin, refusing to dissolve upon waking, lingering – painful and poignant – because I wished more than anything it was real.

We sat at a table on a patio surrounded by dry stone walls. Steph smiled at me and lifted a glass of red wine.

'Cheers.' Her smile brightened the air, like a halo around her face, so loving and innocent.

It felt like a beautiful memory, but it had never happened.

I swatted a fly away from my glass, making it buzz disdainfully before rushing off to bother another diner. Her gentle laugh lifted me, and for a moment I imagined soaring around the tables like that persistent insect. Perhaps my eyes glazed as I thought about it, that wonderful freedom she had given me, because her mood suddenly changed.

She peered at me, grabbed my hand, and stroked her thumb against mine. 'I lost you again, didn't I? Wanda, what's going on with you? You seem distant.'

But it was only a dream. Reality was dark and grimy, full of magic and monsters. I blinked back tears and chewed my lip. For one blissful moment, we had been happy, Steph and I, holidaying together as though she never betrayed me. It felt like waking from a nightmare, knowing you're safe, then seeing the monster at the foot of your bed.

Giant paws had left a trail of prints in the dust, leading to and from my makeshift cot. Beyond the doorway, yellow light flickered. My head spun, my stomach too, and an acidic burp burned my throat. My knees wobbled violently when I tried to stand unaided, so I placed my palm on the wall, impaling myself with splinters. I staggered across the room and paused at the doorway, trying to understand what had happened and where I was. If someone told me I had left one world and entered another, I would have believed them. It would have made as much sense as everything else.

Harrokabis knelt by a wood fire, stoking the flames. Melissa was curled by his feet. He glanced at me, held a claw to his mouth, then rose, unbending joints until he filled the room. The girl did not stir. He gazed at her lovingly before lurching towards me.

'How are you feeling?' he whispered.

Rubbing my head, I stepped back.

'It's cold. Come closer to the fire.' He supported my elbow, tightening his grip when I stumbled.

Although I saw Detective Michaels' broken body standing behind him, I was too weak to push him away. Tears stung my cheeks. 'Leave me alone,' I begged.

He bowed his head but did not let go of my arm. Melissa looked peaceful, almost angelic. The demon settled me beside the rustic fireplace.

'I'll get more wood,' he said.

It was the first time I had seen her horizontal. Her tiny chest rose and fell – no cares, no guilt; secure in her freedom, knowing Harrokabis would protect her, and I was no threat. Envy slunk like ice through my veins. I had never known such peace and doubted I ever would.

Harrokabis returned and added logs to the fire.

My blood thawed, and my eyelids grew heavy. 'Where are we?'

'An abandoned croft. We'll move again in the morning.'

'The authorities, they'll know she's missing. They'll hunt

us down.'

A sharp snap echoed around the room. My eyes darted to the window, half-expecting to see a malevolent face peer through the filthy pane. What did Melissa say when I caught her? *We have both been betrayed.*

'It's the noise of the fire.' His soft growl was soothing.

My anger seeped away, although I tried to cling to it. *Harrokabis is not my friend. He'll kill me too if I threaten Melissa.* But his kind eyes belied my thoughts, assuring me I had nothing to fear.

'I'll protect you both,' he promised.

'What happened to the prison? Why did it collapse?'

'My siblings freed Melissa.'

'Where are they now?'

He was quiet for a moment, staring at the dancing flames. 'I do not know.'

'Steph lied to me, didn't she? Why didn't you tell me?'

'And rob you of hope. I could never be so cruel to a friend.'

Was that what we were? Friends? Could this monster, this killer, be my friend – my only friend? How could I see any goodness in his strangely proportioned face? Yet, I did see goodness there, despite what had happened to Smith, Michaels and Chow Lee. Harrokabis cared more for me than my parents, Steph, even Laney. He took care of me, protected me. Was this Stockholm syndrome, or did I love him? He stroked my head, and I felt at peace. Nothing could be done until morning. It was safe to rest.

My dreams returned me to the cellar where demons danced with headless humans whose intestines dangled like magicians' scarves from their open stomachs, while great chunks of stone rained from the ceiling.

'Steph!' I screamed, looking for her among the waltzing dead.

Blue lights flashed from an unseen source, filling the room like sheets of lightning. The devils' discotheque. Unlike the wallflower from my past, who preferred to stay outside the crowd, I crept between bodies both alive and dead, weaving across flagstones, determined as ivy to cover the ground. Steph was dancing with her arms around Melissa's shoulders. She leaned forward to steal a kiss from the priestess.

The croft was warm, and the fire threw shadows around the walls. Visions of the grotesque ball lingered as my mind straddled the line between sleep and consciousness. When they eventually faded, I realised the room was empty. Low voices talked outside. I considered escape, but where would I go?

The front door swung inwards, and three humans entered, followed by my monstrous friend. The two men were the pair I had left on a park bench, and later seen on the news. I reached for their names.

'You're awake,' Melissa said.

'Bad dreams,' I replied.

'This is Thomas and Mateo. Onyx sent them here. Thomas has somewhere we can stay until everything dies down.'

'Things are never going to die down,' I said. 'Do you think people will forget?'

Her head bowed, and I felt inexplicably cruel despite her having single-handedly destroyed my life.

My cheeks felt tight and sticky. Had I been crying in my sleep, or was this empathy for a woman who would never be free? I should feel anger and hatred, but these contradictory emotions shoved my justified rage aside and made my head spin. The edges of my vision shimmered. If I did not calm myself, I would be blinded by a migraine strong enough to make me wish for death.

'Come with us.' Melissa's smile was crooked but warm.

'It's a thirty-minute trek to the car,' Thomas said. 'But we brought coffee and cake in case you're hungry.'

'I can't walk far,' I said. 'Leave me here.'

Harrokabis lolloped towards me.

'Eat. It'll make you feel better.' Thomas passed me a plastic beaker and filled it with a coffee that smelled of nuts and vanilla.

I dipped a croissant into the dark liquid, and crumbs skated across the surface. 'Do you have water?'

He retrieved a bottle and passed it to me.

'Thank you.'

Harrokabis rubbed my temples, making the pain retreat.

'Can the men see you too?' I asked.

'No.'

His answer made me feel extraordinary… like Melissa; *they told her she was special*. No one had called me that, not my parents nor my teachers, not even Steph. But Harrokabis chose me. If I went with these people, I might find out why. If I refused, would they force me? It was a moot point. Returning to Steph was not an option, and where else could I stay? Not with my parents, I left their home at eighteen, promising to never return. A promise I'd kept for nine years and would not break now. Laney might take me in, but she was still on holiday and had a full house; I would be an added burden. What had Detective Michaels said about wanting adventure? Whatever his exact words had been, I felt such desire, not only for adventure, but also to know these people better. Melissa was enigmatic, and I was stimulated by Harrokabis' company. My grief for Michaels and Smith, the innocent victims of an intrigue I'd encouraged, did little to counter the thrill of being with these strange people.

The coffee, the croissant, and the calming touch beside my eyes combined to strengthen me. Now, I could walk for half-an-hour, run if needed, fly perhaps, and I did not wish to be parted from my demonic companion nor his priestess.

'You're right, Thomas. I feel better,' I said.

☽⛤☾

We arrived at a mansion with sprawling grounds, entering via a gate which was lower than those at the prison, but no less intimidating. I imagined or glimpsed sniper rifles in the gatehouse windows. The main building was old, Georgian maybe, with tall windows and towers at each corner. Unlike the historical dramas I'd watched on TV, there were no servants to greet us.

'Is this yours?' I asked, mouth agape.

'A friend's.'

'One of the dead?'

Thomas did not elaborate. Instead, he unlocked the double

doors on the ground floor and led us inside. It smelled damp. Clouds of disturbed dust danced in the shards of early morning sunlight, which penetrated the narrow gaps between shutters. Harrokabis stood tall under the high ceilings. His bulk inspired awe, making my heartbeat quicken as I watched him move.

Thomas pressed buttons on a bleeping alarm panel. 'Leave the shutters closed. We'll only open the ones in the rooms we use. No one will find us here, but I'll show you the cellar and escape tunnel, anyway.'

I studied my companions' responses. Only Mateo displayed the amazement I felt, his eyes wide, scanning the walls, absorbing every detail, reminding me of a thief tallying up everything worth stealing. Even here, in the shadows of the ground floor, there was plenty to choose from: a billiards table, Wurlitzer jukebox, shelves of whisky and brandy, tapestries with risqué designs, depicting fairy folk in various stages of undress, frolicking in forests with deer and hares. A playboy's paradise.

Thomas led us to a kitchen. There was food in the chest freezers, and tins in the pantry, but nothing in the fridge. He turned on a tap and let the water gurgle and splutter until it ran clear. The next door he opened reminded me of the cellar door in Highgate, the one I'd burst through, dragging Steph in my wake. Bitterness burned my chest and tongue. She betrayed me. Did she regret what she had done? Was she searching for me or Melissa? She would never expect to find the two of us together, protected by a demonic bodyguard.

The staircase was wooden and led to a well-stocked wine cellar. Not abandoned then. Probably a second home for someone based in London or overseas, protected by their vast wealth yet wanting more, while I struggled to support myself and my partner financially, doing whatever it took to get by. The unfairness of it made me shake.

We weaved between shelves of dusty bottles until we reached a Welsh dresser that reeked of mildew. Thomas grasped one of the drawer knobs and twisted it anti-clockwise until we heard a loud click. The cabinet shuddered and the patterned porcelain crockery chimed like bells, then the entire thing glided left to reveal another door. Thomas placed a black key into the lock.

'There are two sets, so I'll leave one set under the cabinet and keep hold of the other. There's a second gate halfway along the tunnel.' He twisted the key and opened the door. 'I guess the original owner was a smuggler or some sort of dissident.'

I smelled brine as chilled air rushed towards us.

'There's a torch in the left-hand drawer,' he said. 'The tunnel leads to a cave. There's a cord on the right to close the entrance behind you.' He turned to me and held my gaze. 'Don't use it unless you and Melissa need to run. If you want to leave, please use the front door.'

Melissa answered. 'She won't run away, not from adventure.'

Thomas nodded, then closed and locked the door. He turned the knob clockwise, and the dresser slid back into position, then he pushed one set of keys under the cabinet.

Melissa waited until the men's footsteps faded. 'Thomas is okay, but I don't trust Mateo.'

'Harrokabis could watch him,' I suggested.

'I shall. I sense greed and an overwhelming desire for power in the boy,' Harrokabis said.

'What do we do now?' I asked.

Melissa touched my cheek. 'I'm really sorry. I know I hurt you. Now that we are both free, what do you want to do?'

'I don't know. Before Steph betrayed me, I wanted to grow old with her and become a vet, but now...'

'We could explore the house.' Melissa bit her lip.

I am not a spiritual person. Any belief in a benevolent God had been cut from me by the buckle of my father's belt, and New Age folks seemed like con artists to me, but I swear the aura of Melissa's excitement radiated around her in clouds of yellow and orange. She was like a child. I corrected myself; she was still a child, barely eighteen and with no experience of taking care of herself, no independence or autonomy. I saw her in a new light, no longer the manipulative witch of Witchwood Prison, inspiring fear, but a puppy, delighting in a world of unfamiliar smells and learning through play. She was my baby sister, and it was my job, as the experienced sibling, to guide her.

I smiled and said, 'Okay.'

Melissa's movements were fluid, while mine were solid. My footsteps were heavy, hers light. She was ethereal, and I was chained to the ground like Prometheus. An eagle had devoured the Titan, but it was doubt that consumed my heart.

'You were never really a prisoner at Witchwood,' I said.

'I have been locked up all my life.'

'Those photos allowed you to escape whenever you wanted. Do you want to know how many times I have slept on a beach? Never. Why did you tear the walls down? Surely, the demons could have let you walk out.'

She chewed her lip and did not hold my gaze. 'The others.'

'The other prisoners,' I said. 'They were all bundled up and sent elsewhere. They're crowded into tiny cells with less freedom.'

'You don't understand.'

'Melissa, you feel sorry for yourself. You think the world revolves around you. By the time you reach my age, you'll realise you're a tiny cog in an uncaring system.'

'My mother sold me.'

'My mother hated me,' I said. 'I often wished she would give me away.'

Melissa's fingers stretched elegantly towards me like a dancer's pose. Her affection was too self-conscious to be genuine. I turned from her and marched up the stairs. The more distance I gained from her, the less power she held over me. She was not my sister, and I bore no responsibility for her. At the top of the stairs, I headed towards the front door. Light footsteps sprinted behind me.

She caught up with me as I reached the billiard table and grabbed my hand. 'Don't go.'

I let her lead me through the rooms, studying her face more than the house. We found a staircase, ascended to the first floor, and entered a dining room. Even with the shutters closed it offered a sense of the infinite. The ceilings were at least five metres high, and windows dominated most of one wall. Angels in each corner of the plaster ceiling held the ends of festooned garlands of flowers. The table was dark, but everything else was light – pale walls and rug, a white fireplace – it resembled a wedding cake with dust frosting.

I paused at the doorway of a cosy sitting room where the men lounged on leather sofas. Not desiring their company, I let Melissa guide me away.

We were silent until we reached the next room. It was empty except for a piano, four side tables and decorative lamps. A hundred metres square of parquet floor spread out between these items. Plenty of space for dancing – probably the room's original purpose. There were no rugs, and strange shapes were painted on the wooden floor, suggesting it was used for ceremonial magic rather than entertaining guests. I tramped over the designs and shivered as electricity coursed through my veins.

'Be careful,' Melissa warned.

'Where's Harrokabis?' I asked.

She shrugged.

'Do you think they used these circles to summon demons?'

'Maybe. Or perhaps they were trying to reach the borderland without my help,' Melissa said.

'Harrokabis said anyone can go there if they free their mind.'

She looked doubtful, and I noticed a slight quivering of her chin. 'Then why did they…'

'Lock you up and torture you,' I said when she seemed unable to complete the sentence.

She nodded.

'I don't know. It's possible the creatures refused to give them what they wanted, so they made you their ambassador, but that's speculation. Who can really know why people are cruel to each other, especially to the children they are supposed to protect?'

We entered a library filled with leather-bound books on walnut shelves. Only a few spines included titles, and those were not written in English. Latin was my best guess.

'Do you think there's a secret door to another room?' she asked, examining books, and running her fingers over each knot in the wood.

She did not tire of looking. Long after I realised there was no secret door, she continued stroking wood and pulling out books. If I did not distract her, she may have spent days at this task.

'Are you free now?' I asked. 'Do you finally feel free?'

'Uncle Thomas promised to take me to another country where no one will recognise me. Then I'll be free. Where will you go? You can come with me if you want.'

'I don't know. I'm still trying to figure everything out.'

'Do you want to be with Stephanie?'

'No, it's not that.'

'What then?' she asked.

'Sit down for a minute.'

Her constant movement exhausted me. Impossible to believe this was the same woman who had sat for hours on a prison mattress unless, like me, you knew that while her body seemed frozen, her mind wandered through the landscapes on her wall.

'Harrokabis told me our childhoods were the same. It's time you understood; everyone's life is hard.'

'You think I don't know? I've listened to the stories of prisoners at Witchwood and Vinnie Green. I'll bet you don't even know why Stevens killed her children.'

'She was crazy.'

'Her abusive mother got custody. Stevens didn't want that life for her children. She thought it better for them to have no life at all.' Melissa's shoulders pressed against the books, arms crossed over her chest, as she stared at me, icily.

Was her expression a challenge or a rebuke? I'd always tried to stay neutral, treat every inmate with respect, but I judged them all and, the moment I saw Melissa cross-legged on her cot, I assumed she was guilty. Despite my best intentions, my mind had been colonised by the institution.

Did I become a prison guard just to meet Melissa and aid her escape? Had Steph or fate mapped my life out for me and controlled my choices? Was that why I felt as trapped as the prisoners? Autonomy was an illusion.

'Some of the women were evil,' I countered, clinging to a fleeting sense of righteousness. 'Masterton and Wilson.'

'Two out of how many? The rest deserved to be free. I escaped while others stood around, stunned, awaiting instructions. They've always been told what to do; it's what prevented them from leaving. Obedience is a hard habit to break.'

☽⛤☾

'Here you are.' Mateo sauntered into the library.

Melissa glanced up. 'What do you want?'

'Thomas is cooking. Lunch in twenty minutes. What are you two doing? You look, what is the phrase? As thick as thieves.'

'Nothing.' Melissa pouted. 'We aren't doing anything.'

'Don't you talk?' Mateo asked, staring at me.

I held his gaze until he looked away, shrugging. He wasn't much older than Melissa. The two of them were kids. 'How do you know Melissa?'

He glanced at her before answering. 'I'm her *sostitutu*… her understudy.' His mouth twisted. He glared at each of us then marched out of the room.

'Seventh child envy,' Melissa said after he left.

'I think he wants to hurt you.'

Steph giggled as she filled my plastic glass with pink fizz. We were on a beach, dressed in jumpers and coats to protect us from the chill. The sea was dark periwinkle blue ridden by white horses. The roar of waves calmed my soul. Steph's hair was down, whipping her cheeks. I leant towards her and pulled errant strands from her mouth before kissing those upturned lips, sweeter than the sparkling wine.

I was at the kitchen table, a fork in my right hand, and chewing soggy pastry. 'What the…'

'Sorry, it's not the best. We only had tins. I'm defrosting a joint for dinner, though,' Thomas said.

My eyes darted around the room – Thomas, Mateo, Melissa,

175

lunch on the table, fork in my hand. None of it made sense. We were in the library. Mateo stormed out. I searched my mind to understand what happened next but found nothing bar the traces of a happy dream.

'How did I get here?'

'Are you okay?' Melissa asked.

'We were in the library…'

Melissa patted my hand. 'Don't you remember leaving the library?'

'No, I… I mean… I…' The chair legs scraped a tragic refrain as I pushed away from the table. I'd never lost time before. Was the gap in my memory caused by stress or the house? The former made more sense, but it felt like a malevolent, external force was messing with my mind.

'Wanda. It's okay,' Melissa said. 'It's understandable if you forgot. It's not the most exciting thing to happen to either of us.'

Edging backwards until my spine pressed against the doorframe, I shook my head. 'We walked to the kitchen together?'

Melissa nodded.

'No one carried me… Harrokabis?'

She touched her bottom lip with the tip of her index finger. 'We walked.'

I needed to get away, spend time alone, figure out what tricks my mind was playing. 'Which room is mine?'

'Whichever you want,' Thomas said. 'Eat first. You might have low blood sugar.'

I knew I could not sit quietly and finish the meal. 'I'm not hungry. I just need rest.'

'I can escort you,' Mateo said.

'I'll find my own way.'

'There's clean bedding in the second-floor closet,' Thomas said.

I chose a room on the second floor, far from the stairs, and locked the door, hoping to avoid company. Disturbed dust caught in my nose and throat when I threw myself on the quilt. The healthy choice would have been to change the bedding or at least open a window. Instead, I lay there while the motes floated over my body.

Desperately, I tried to recall leaving the library, searching the twists and turns of my memories, without finding any trace. If they'd carried me from room to room while I slept, they would have told me, and that would not explain why I was holding a fork and eating when I regained consciousness.

'Harrokabis,' I called.

He did not appear even though he had promised to protect Melissa and me, and I needed his wisdom.

My eyes shuttered.

Silk tickled my inner thighs. I reached down and stroked my lover's hair. Cupping her chin, I guided Steph across the landscape of my body. Her kisses tasted of sex.

'Is this real?' I asked.

She nodded, stroking my cheek.

'I love you.'

My foot dropped, and I stumbled. Hands flailed as I tried to balance, grasping what felt like a pipe. My eyes snapped open. I was on a spiral staircase, and what had felt like a pipe was a wrought iron banister. My toes hung precariously over the edge of a triangular step. I descended anti-clockwise and entered the ballroom, then recoiled, unable to face those weird circles and pictograms. In my haste to leave, I lost my balance again and clung to the banister to stop myself tumbling head over heels down the narrow stairs. Having no desire to explore where those steps led, I headed upwards until I reached a narrow landing with two doors. The one on the left opened onto a balcony. Wind kissed my cheeks as I leaned over the balustrade, gazing at the paving stones far below. Afraid of losing consciousness again and falling to my death, I withdrew and checked the right-hand door, which led to my bedroom. When I pushed it closed, it merged with the wall, with only a small and easily overlooked brass handle to differentiate it. I wedged it shut with a chair before checking the rest of my room. Certain I was alone; I sank onto the bed and wept.

My door opened, soft footsteps, then the bed dipped behind me.

'Are you okay?' Melissa asked. 'Did you really forget going down to the kitchen?'

'I lost time,' I said, drying my face with my sleeve. 'But it's never happened before.'

'It is a strange house…' Her voice trailed off.

I shifted position to face her, but no one was there; no one in the hallway, or in any of the rooms on the second floor: five bedrooms, a bathroom, and a linen closet, all empty. Limbs flailing, I hurtled down the stairs and stumbled into the kitchen where Mateo was filling the dishwasher, and Thomas and Melissa sipped coffee.

'Were you in my room?' I asked, already knowing it was impossible. My door had been locked, the key on the inside. Before chasing the phantom, I had to unlock the door.

She stared at me blankly.

'I'm leaving. This place makes me ill.'

She frowned.

'I expect it's all the stress of the past week,' Thomas said. 'Not the house.'

'Let her go,' Mateo said. 'We do not need her.'

Melissa guided me to the table. 'Please stay, at least for tonight.'

'There's food left,' Thomas said. 'Or would you prefer coffee?'

'Coffee.'

Melissa grabbed my fingers. 'Did something happen?'

'I don't know,' I said. 'I might have been dreaming. Where's Harrokabis?'

'Is that the name of a demon?' Mateo asked. 'If so, they tore down the house and went home.'

'They didn't go home,' Melissa said.

Mateo strode to the table. 'What deal did you make with them? We got nothing we asked for.'

'Mateo!' Thomas roared, reminding me of Harrokabis.

'She betrayed us. You might not see it, but I do. You should never have let…'

'That's enough, Mateo!' Thomas brought coffee to the table.

I leaned back and studied the three faces. Melissa looked as tranquil as ever. Mateo's dark stare seemed almost murderous, and Thomas sucked his cheeks anxiously.

'Okay,' I said, squeezing Melissa's fingers. 'One night.'

She smiled. Was I being manipulated again?

'Want to explore the garden?' Melissa asked when I finished my coffee.

I followed her outside. The house was impressive. Balconies ran between the corner towers on the first and second floors, and the sandstone shimmered like gold in the sunlight.

'Do you know who owns it?' I asked.

'Lawyer, politician, businessperson… does it matter? They're dead.'

'How long was Stephanie a part of your coven?'

'Coven?' she asked.

'That's what they called it on the fan site.'

We reached the grass. I picked my way down a gentle slope while Melissa spread her arms, running as if she might take off and fly. All the flower beds were dormant or empty. I hurdled the dirt, skidding as I hit the yellow-pebbled path, but staying upright. After spending so much time indoors, the exercise invigorated me.

'Do you really want to know?' Melissa asked.

'I need to know.'

'She came to Vinnie Green to give me the tea. The one I used to reach the borderland.'

'When?'

'Four years ago.'

After I started working in Witchwood Prison, but before Steph and I signed the rental agreement for our house. 'Why did she join *The Friends*?'

'The promise of riches, like the others.'

'Or a chance to meet you, to be part of your world.' My theory fit better with the Steph I knew.

The grass grew longer the further we strolled. Red and orange wildflowers supplied relief from the dark green. Stones shifted under foot; the sound reminded me of waves breaking on a pebble beach, and I forgot all my worries: the oppressive house, the prison, everything.

'I met her nine years ago,' I said. 'When she and I were both eighteen. We were long distance for a while, and I only saw her during holidays. How did she know you would be arrested and end up in Witchwood? We're not the only high-security prison. Did *The Friends* arrange the transfer because I was there?'

Melissa shrugged. 'They moved me because I turned eighteen.'

'She knew. Somehow, she knew and pushed me to apply there.' I felt no pain, picking through the details of Steph's betrayal as if we were discussing someone I hardly knew or had known long ago.

I glimpsed water ahead and followed a dirt track to a beautiful lake. A rowing boat was moored beside a boathouse made of glass and wood. Ducks and swans waddled down the bank of a small island and swam towards us, perhaps hoping for food.

'What are we going to do?' I asked. 'I don't want to stay at the house.'

'We'll only stay a week.'

'And then?'

'Another country. We could go to France or Thailand.'

We followed the curve of the lake until we reached the boathouse. I removed my shoes and sat on the jetty. The water was cold, but I enjoyed dipping my feet, swirling them around, and watching the ripples. It was peaceful, being in the moment, and I would have been content to sit there for hours. It was Melissa who said we should head back.

'If Thomas has keys for the boathouse, I'd be happier here.'

'I'll ask him,' Melissa said.

Melissa strode ahead, while I meandered, letting blades of grass tickle my palms, stopping to smell flowers, with only the sky above my head and wispy stripes of clouds. I imagined horses galloping across the fields, excited hounds racing at their heels.

The mansion loomed ahead, and I saw my worries reflected in its shuttered windows, biding their time until they could overwhelm me again. The moment I stepped through the door, I heard raised voices.

'Your niece betrayed us all!'

'None of this is her fault. You and Onyx, arranging things behind our backs. You should have come to me, Mateo!'

'I did nothing wrong. Onyx promised me the world, but what did I receive? Nothing! I never should have come to England.'

'You came, like the others, because you wanted something and did not have the skills to obtain it alone.'

'The others are dead.'

'That is not Melissa's fault. They betrayed us, the angels, not my niece.'

'Angels!' Mateo yelled. Glass shattered. 'You still believe they are angels?'

I slammed the front door and heard someone scamper up the stairs. Thomas was alone in the kitchen, sweeping up shards of glass. He said he didn't need any help, and the oven made the room stuffy, so I returned to the billiard table for a solo game.

As I leaned over the green felt to take my first shot, a hand gripped my wrist. 'Wanda, what do you think you are doing, displaying yourself like that?'

Every muscle in my body strained to pull free, but the grip was too strong. I was six again, and Mummy was dragging me along the street.

'Don't tell Daddy,' I begged, knowing what would happen if she did, remembering the sting of his belt.

The hand released my wrist and slapped me. My cheek vibrated, then burned. The street faded and the games room surrounded me again. Translucent grey shapes, like diffused shadows, hung around the walls. The silent audience of featureless faces mocked me before fading into the ornate tapestries. I was bent at the waist, leaning over the rim of the billiard table, cue in hands, balls in a triangle, half-expecting to be grabbed again, accused and shamed again. I dropped the cue and raced upstairs. Someone called my name, but I could not tell whether it was Melissa or a voice from my past.

Without a fixed destination, I ran until I reached the ballroom, bursting through the double doors, my hair wet with sweat and prickling my earlobes and cheeks. Mateo's back was towards me, and he seemed unaware of my intrusion, sitting cross-legged in a painted circle. He was the last person I wanted to talk to, so I retreated and shut the doors. Tired. Drained. Afraid to return to my room in case I wandered again, or Melissa visited me without ever leaving the kitchen.

Voices radiated from the dining room, accompanied by the chinking of knives and forks against plates. A glance assured me the room was empty, so I told myself I imagined the noises, blaming it on frayed nerves rather than ghosts.

Tiptoeing down dark wood stairs cushioned by carpet, I returned to the ground floor. Thomas and Melissa were talking in the kitchen. I stood near the door and listened.

'Onyx?' Thomas asked.

'She wanted Mateo to take over when I failed.'

'Wanda worries me more.'

'What do you mean?' Melissa asked.

'She's here against her will. We've kidnapped a guard whose body you borrowed. If anyone wants to hurt you…'

'I trust her. She's a pure soul. While I was in Highgate, a brother said they were planning to sacrifice me to save themselves. It's why I changed the deal, Uncle Thomas.'

My nostrils itched. A sneeze tickled my sinuses. I sniffed and entered the kitchen. 'Have you seen Harrokabis?'

'How much did you hear?' Melissa asked.

'You were discussing Onyx. She's the medium, right? Harrokabis told me. He likes, I mean liked, her.'

'She's still alive,' Thomas said. 'Onyx wasn't in the cellar, and she told us where to find you.'

'Would Harrokabis have gone to her?' I asked.

Melissa approached me. 'You look pale. Did something happen?'

'It's this house. Unless someone is drugging me. Are you drugging me, Thomas?'

The old man blushed so hard his grey hair looked pink. He denied the accusation. I let him bluster for a while, enjoying his discomfort. When he recovered, he leaned towards Melissa and whispered loud enough for me to hear. 'Who told you they planned to sacrifice you? What did he say exactly?'

Melissa threw me a half-smile, which I interpreted as a request for patience while they finished their conversation. 'You don't need to know who. The important part is what he said. "When the shadows descend, Mateo will intervene and offer you as sacrifice."'

'Did he have proof?'

'We were interrupted,' Melissa said. 'I don't want Mateo here.'

'We can't send him away,' Thomas said. 'At least while he's with us, we know what he's doing.'

'Right now, he's sitting in a magical circle in the ballroom,' I said.

Thomas glared at me, then rushed out of the kitchen. Melissa sprinted after him, and I followed them both up the stairs and along the corridor to the ballroom. Mateo was not sitting now. He lay on his side, curled up tight. As we got closer, I smelled blood.

'Wanda, what did you do?' Thomas knelt beside the boy and placed fingers on his throat. 'He's still alive, but he's been badly beaten.'

'It wasn't me,' I said.

'He needs an ambulance. Melissa, they cannot find you here. Hide in the cellar.'

Melissa nodded and grabbed my hand. 'Let's go.'

'I need to see,' I said, pulling away.

I skirted the body and stared at the previously pretty man. His hair was matted with blood from a gaping wound in his cheek. His nose was flat; his lips were swollen, and his arms were folded around his head to protect his skull. If Thomas had not told me otherwise, I would have assumed Mateo was dead.

Only ten minutes earlier, I'd rushed into the ballroom, pausing at the door when I glimpsed Mateo. He was sitting in a circle, unaware of my presence. After that, I left, didn't I? Or had I lost time again? Did I cross the room? Did I attack him?

If the circles were used for summoning demons, had Mateo been trying to conjure his own Harrokabis to challenge Melissa?

Did he succeed? Did that demon attack him?

A jumble of images flashed through my head – I was both beside his unconscious form, *and* I was by the door simultaneously. Innocent *and* guilty. Flashcard glimpses of missing memories lingered without unfolding. Was my mind suppressing what happened? Thomas glared at me, trying to see the truth in my eyes. Accusing me. If I could not remember whether I did this, how could he expect to find any truth behind my unfocused gaze?

'Come on,' Melissa urged, stretching her hand towards me.

I searched for a weapon, anything I might have used to cause such terrible injuries, but I found nothing. Lamps were still on the tables, undamaged. My hands were not bruised. If I'd pounded someone with my fists, I would feel pain. I remembered the cue, its weight in my hands. If I brought it with me… but it was not here now… 'I hate this fucking house,' I said.

Melissa took my hand and tugged me out of the room. We hid in the wine cellar, crouching behind shelves while shadows blossomed around us. It felt like hours before we heard the pounding of feet in the hallway above. Once the sounds of frenetic footsteps started, they did not stop. How many paramedics arrived, or was the house full of police as well? We held each other, shivering from fear and cold. My mind begged Harrokabis to come and protect us. His continued absence felt like a missing limb.

'They're still moving around up there,' I whispered. 'It must be the police. They're bound to check the cellar.'

'You're right,' Melissa said. 'We'll take the tunnel.'

We scuttled from our hiding place like disturbed cockroaches and retrieved the keys and torch. The grinding of gears and screams of wood being dragged across stone had not seemed this loud before. Someone would hear and come rushing down. The door opened, and Melissa dragged me into the tunnel. I found the cord and pulled it. Echoes from ancient machinery bounced off the stone walls, filling the narrow darkness, and the door closed before anyone burst into the cellar to intercept us.

CHAPTER THIRTEEN

MELISSA was already fifty paces ahead, and the shimmer of her outline was getting smaller, dense air swallowing the light of her torch. How long was this tunnel?

'Wait, I need to get my breath.' Invisible fingers squeezed my throat, cutting off air. Was it a panic attack, or was the oxygen too thin? Melissa seemed fine.

'Harrokabis.' The unanswered plea wasted scarce energy, and I imagined dying here alone, abandoned by my temporary friends. At least it would be an end to the insanity.

Cobwebs clung to my hair and eyebrows. The tunnel's smell reminded me of a diseased mouth, repulsive and sickly sweet. The distant rhythmic splashes of dripping water were my only consolation, promising an eventual release from the dust, which filled my nose and clogged my throat.

Melissa's silhouette stabilised, and the glow around her stilled. She had stopped moving. If I rose to my feet and forced myself to walk, we would be together again in minutes, seconds perhaps. She turned and the torch's eye glared at me. The brightness forced me to avert my gaze. A spotlight that was never mine. There would be no fifteen minutes of fame for me, not that I wanted it; I was fame adjacent, and the distance between Melissa and I remained a treacherous chasm. I should never have come here. How many opportunities had I been given to walk away? Yet I kept following her, and now I would suffocate in this tomb.

Laney had warned me not to let Melissa get inside my head – told me my obsession and fear were ephemeral glamours. Although she could not have predicted this, perhaps my colleague foresaw a different fate for me – a padded cell, broken relationships, broken mind. My march towards danger in Witchwood Forest, sitting beside Melissa in her cell, staring at a photograph and allowing myself to be overwhelmed, was that madness?

Is this?

It was not too late to retrace my steps, find the authorities, and give myself over to their mercy. Melissa did not have the strength to stop me. Physically, I was stronger. Mentally, emotionally… that was the problem.

Melissa had broken me; or was the damage older – the legacy of parental abuse? The violence, the isolation, the constant questioning of my reality: '*No, that did not happen. You're a nasty little liar. You must have dreamed that. You're crazy.*'

The pool of light closed around me as Melissa approached.

'Wanda? We should keep moving. What's wrong?'

Everything.

Her fingers hooked my armpits, and her willowy body tensed with effort. I'd worn her insubstantial frame and knew she could never lift my weight, so I helped. I borrowed strength from the Highgate Priestess, the witch of Witchwood Prison, and stood up. Then it was a march, a stumble, a crawl towards fresh air. I smelled salt when we finally reached the second gate. Melissa inserted and turned the key, then pushed against the browned metal.

'It's stuck,' she said.

I dedicated my remaining strength to our mutual freedom. Using my body weight, I leaned against the gate. Melissa grabbed my arm as it gave way, trying to stop me from falling. Instead of preventing my descent, I pulled her with me, trapped myself beneath her, until she found her feet and locked the gate against pursuers.

Pale light glowed between rocks, forming a Z; a symbol of the sleep I so desperately needed. We found a gap large enough to squeeze through and emerged in a cave. Leather twitched and dark jewels flashed above us. A dormitory for bats. The ground was soft. Decades of guano muffled our footsteps. Melissa angled the torch to the floor so we would not disturb the creatures which hung above us like the murderous shadows of the now buried cellar. The chamber was an almost perfect circle, broken in three places, one high and wide, the others low and narrow. We chose the largest opening, hoping it would lead us to sunlight.

Luck was on our side; the carpet of shit thinned and soon we were trekking over shifting granules of sand. Water dripped on my head, stagnant and viscous, stinking like rotten vegetables. Ten minutes or two hours later, we clambered from the cave onto a beach. Still on my feet, but ready to collapse, legs shaking – or was the ground moving – I bent double, resting hands on knees, and emptied my stomach.

As I stumbled from the steaming mess, I saw Melissa. Her back was to me, but her pose was so familiar – crossed legs, straight spine – it could be no one else. She sat in the shallows with her dress floating like seaweed above her narrow hips. Beyond her, close to the dark stripe of the horizon, I saw the impossible. A pair of black gates above the edge of the ocean, held open by strands of pale blonde hair. While the scale made no sense, I knew it was Melissa's hair tied around the metalwork.

As I stared, the land beyond the gates became visible. Dark and marbled with glowing red, like Harrokabis. His home? The landscape was barren, unwelcoming, but the desire to explore it made my limbs tremble. I hobbled down the beach, determined to reach the gates; I was exhausted, but I would swim if necessary, certain my salvation depended on getting there.

'Wanda, no.'

Icy water suckled at my breasts. Behind me, Melissa shouted my name. I bent my knees and stretched my arms towards the mirage while water lapped my face. How far was it? A few miles or thirty? Shaking arms held me back, feverish spasms from the cold, fear, or excitement. I ground my molars to stop the chattering of my teeth.

'It isn't real,' she whispered.

'Let go.'

'Look again,' she said.

I planted my feet, my fighter's stance, and lifted my head from the water. The gates had vanished, and in their place, storm clouds striped the sky.

'Bring them back,' I begged.

Melissa bobbed in the water, saying nothing, arms arcing in circles around her while her chin rode the waves. Her face was squeezed by my open palms, as the desire to crush her skull consumed me. But her beautiful, oceanic eyes, so loving, generous and innocent forbade me from hurting her. I released her head and gripped her shoulders before wrapping her in my arms. She was so tiny my elbows met at her spine, and her toes brushed my thighs as she treaded water. When I kissed her wet skin, she didn't respond. My affection wasn't returned, but at least she didn't push me away.

'What should I do?' I asked, breaking the embrace, losing myself in her eyes.

She shook her head. 'I don't know.'

I rested my chin on her crown and gazed at the beach while waves buffeted my shoulders. Dry dunes, spiked with long grass and gorse bushes, created a border between the tranquil beach and the world beyond. As I stared, two figures appeared on a ridge.

'There are people here,' I said.

Melissa and I swam back to the shore while the newcomers skated down the dunes, their arms stretched like wings. The distance was too great to see their faces clearly. Broad strokes preserved their anonymity, like an oil painting – the suggestion of human life depicted by Monet.

We met in the middle; we were soaked while they were dusted with sand. I'd not expected to see Steph again, yet here she was with a woman who reminded me of Greer. Although, out of uniform, I was not certain it was the young prison guard. Steph passed a bag to Melissa. The priestess dipped her hand inside and pulled out platinum coils. Déjà vu.

'We made it into a wig,' Steph said.

As Melissa pulled the wig onto her head, my mind snapped, and everything turned red. I pounced. I did not know who was pinned to the ground as my arms drew back, and I pummelled a face with fists, landing a flurry of blows.

'No!' Strong arms grabbed my waist and pulled me away.

We wrestled each other on the sand as hands gripped my wrists and tried to pin me in place. I glared at the frown, the set jaw and flinty eyes, then rolled onto my hands and knees, shedding the woman's grip before crawling to where Melissa kneeled over what looked like a pile of clothes. The fabrics were covered in a filthy paste of blood and sand, and within them was Steph. She looked deflated, curled in a protective comma, face swollen and red with blood. I stared at my bruised and bloody knuckles, unable to grasp the concept of cause and effect. Had I done that to Steph? My mind had not caught up with my actions, but my body understood, and ice dripped through my veins.

'Is she dead?' I asked.

Melissa put fingers to Steph's throat. 'She's breathing. I can feel her heartbeat. Why did you do that?'

Steph and Mateo. Had I attacked them both?

The other woman fished a mobile phone out of Steph's jacket. 'I'll call an ambulance, then we'll get out of here.'

'I'm staying,' I said. 'I can't keep running. Mateo and now Steph.'

'Let me help,' Melissa said. 'Come with us.'

'I'm staying with Steph.'

The other woman was already fifty metres away. 'Melissa, come on,' she called.

'Are you sure?' Melissa asked.

I nodded, expecting it to be the last time I saw her.

Steph coughed, and blood bubbled on her lips.

'It's okay. The ambulance is on its way,' I said.

How many heartbeats before I heard the distant wail of sirens and collapsed beside my erstwhile lover?

I woke abruptly in a room that was too bright. Metal bit into my right wrist when I moved. I sensed someone beside me and made a canopy of my wrapped left hand to shield my eyes from the glare as I stared at the familiar face.

'Miss Jones,' D. I. Lewis said.

'Is Steph okay?' I asked.

'She's in surgery. Fractured skull. The second person to be brought in with those injuries. You've been busy.'

'Will she be okay?'

'It's too early to know. Tell me what happened.'

My knuckles felt hot under the bandages – patched up and chained up. 'Was it me? Did I hurt them?'

'It appears so,' he said.

'And Melissa?'

'What about Melissa?'

'Did you catch her?'

His brow creased, as if there could be any doubt which Melissa I meant.

'Melissa Powell,' I said.

'She's still at Witchwood in solitary confinement in the original building, but you must already know that.'

'She escaped. I found her.'

His glare softened. 'You're confused.'

'I'm not!'

'Miss Jones, you're mistaken. Powell, Masterton and Wilson were moved to solitary after the wings collapsed. No one escaped.'

'But… that's impossible. I remember…'

'Get some rest. I'll return in the morning,' D. I. Lewis said.

'Wanda, there's a visitor here to see you.'

I opened my eyes and focused on the ruddy faced nurse beside my bed.

'Wanda!' I'd not heard my mother's voice in almost a decade, except in nightmares. 'How are you feeling?' A clammy palm checked my forehead.

She settled on the chair which D. I. Lewis vacated seconds or minutes, hours or days ago? What was she doing here? How did she know where to find me? Squeezing my eyelids shut, I wished her gone – not caring whether she was real or a hallucination – willing myself to lose time again; anything to avoid experiencing this reunion.

'What have you been up to? Your father and I always knew you were no good, but this?'

'Fuck off, Mum. Demons are real, and my father's the worst one of all.'

Her face shrivelled as she sucked her lips between her teeth. Her eyes narrowed in a cold, hard, disbelieving stare. My hate made me shake with the thrill of imagined violence. Red mist revealed her face and my father's pummelled by my fists. All those years of powerlessness, cleansed with their spilt blood.

Melissa never chose violence. But I was not Melissa, could never be Melissa. Violence was on the syllabus long before I slithered from Mother's womb, and I'd learned the lessons by heart.

'Why did you let him beat me?' I asked.

'He would never hurt you. He was protecting you, keeping you safe. The world is cruel, and evil surrounds us. A father protects his family from dark outside influences, temptation, and sin.'

'He broke my wrist, and you didn't even take me to a hospital. What sort of mother are you?'

'Stop telling lies, Wanda. This is her, isn't it? She's poisoned your mind. You would never have spoken to me like this before.'

'Her?'

'Stephanie… awful woman.'

'It has nothing to do with Steph. Why do you think I haven't seen you for years? I have no good memories from my childhood. None. How did you even find out I was here?'

'Lesbians,' she spat. 'Cursing, dressing like a man.'

'Give me strength…'

'No point asking God for strength now. You abandoned him long ago.'

'Leave, Mum. Go. If I see you or Father again, I'll kill you both for what you did to me.'

CHAPTER FOURTEEN

'WANDA, eat something.' A nurse shook an old-fashioned glass thermometer between her thumb and forefinger, as if conducting an orchestra.

'How long have I been asleep? When did my mother leave?'

'My shift started ten minutes ago,' the nurse said. 'Would you like me to check?'

'It's not important. Is Steph okay?'

'She'll be fine. She regained consciousness last night and told the police everything. Can you sit up?'

I raised my right hand, expecting to rattle the handcuff and thus reveal the absurdity of her question, but my arm moved without restriction. I pushed myself to a seated position and stared at the tray of food. The tea and toast were no better than they served at the prison, but the orange juice was deliciously sharp.

Stomach full to bursting, I sank into unconsciousness.

The door swished open with a whisper that, to my anxious mind, sounded louder than a battle cry. Fear jolted me awake.

D.I. Lewis sat beside me, smiling this time. 'How are you? Do you remember anything? Can you describe the man who attacked you? What were you and Miss Walker doing in Porthmadog?'

'Where?'

'Don't you remember coming to Wales?'

'A lot of what's happened recently is very fuzzy, detective,'

I said. 'Did Steph tell you what happened?'

'I would rather you tried to remember.'

'Honestly, the last thing I remember clearly is you telling me the detectives were in a car crash. Everything since is confused. If we're in Wales, why are you here? Isn't it outside your jurisdiction?'

He crossed his legs and scratched his chin before answering. 'I placed a note next to your name. The local constabulary called me when they identified you.' I opened my mouth to yell at him, but he pruned my words at the root. 'Miss Walker says you came to Snowdonia to get away from the stress. She thought you were heading for a nervous breakdown, but says you grew calmer once you got away from the prison. She claims a man attacked her on the beach, and you dragged him off, saving her life, punching him until he ran away. We would like you to identify him. Can you remember his height, his hair colour, anything?'

'I'm sorry. I don't remember. Did you tell me Melissa Powell never left Witchwood Prison?'

'I did.'

'Have you seen her?'

'No, but…'

'Why would the prison lie?' I could imagine a few reasons, but all would sound like paranoid conspiracy theories. 'Did you also say another person was admitted with similar injuries to Steph?'

'Yes.'

'Man or woman?' It had to be Mateo.

'Man. Unfortunately, he was not as strong as your girlfriend.'

'He died?'

'Yes.'

Poor Mateo. I did not understand why Steph lied. Why would she protect me after what I did to her? While I couldn't remember killing Mateo, there were vivid flashes of memories from the beach. I'd punched someone, and Steph was unconscious. Occam's Razor – I assaulted her, but could I have blanked out the presence of a male attacker? I had not recognised Steph's face as I lashed out, but I doubted I was a hero. If I attacked Steph on the beach, she was lying to protect Melissa, not me. 'Did the same person attack both?'

'We don't know yet.'

'But you don't believe in coincidences.'

D.I. Lewis' smile made him look years younger.

☾⛤☽

The hospital discharged me before Steph and gave me the address of a local guest house, so I could be near her while she recovered. When I phoned the prison, I was told to take extended leave, they didn't even offer full pay, just a retainer, and suggested I look for another job. They didn't tell me whether it was because the prison collapsed, because I went AWOL, or because I took time off for stress? Maybe I should have asked, but I felt too tired and bitter to argue. I needed to hear a friendly voice. Laney was home and sounded sympathetic on the phone. She asked me to call round, and I promised to visit her when I got back.

There was nothing online to suggest Melissa Powell escaped on the night Witchwood Prison fell. How could I trust my own memory when faced with such evidence? What I remembered was impossible. Confused snippets whirled around my head, making me feel nauseous.

The room felt suffocating. I grabbed my jacket and room key then wandered around a city which, as far as I could tell, was entirely suburbs and retail parks. Hills surrounded me. The city was a depression in the landscape, a grave to clamber out of the moment Steph was fit to leave.

Anxiety crushed me, muddling my thoughts and making it difficult to breathe. I had no clear memory of how I had spent the past weeks, only the nagging feeling that what I had experienced, tasted, heard, lived was a lie, pure hallucination. What if reality was even darker and more sinister? Had I created a friendly demon to block out something far worse?

Sat on the uncomfortable shelf-like bench of a bus shelter, I pushed my mind back in time, hunting for any vivid, incontestable memory. Anything tangible and undeniable I could use as an anchor. D.I. Lewis did not deny visiting me after the detectives died. It was something, but was it enough to test my other memories? Or was it too brittle and ungrounded to use as scaffolding? Years ago, while trying to coax me from the edge of a meltdown, Steph explained how memories worked, and why they were not objective snapshots of the past, or reels of film waiting to be accessed like reruns on the BBC.

'We reconstruct events each time we access them, piecing together disparate fragments to create an image or pattern we can understand, but which is always coloured by what we have learned since. We interpret our memories through the lens of our present selves.' Were those the words Steph used?

Memories were jigsaw puzzles, like the ones Laney and I pieced together from Melissa's torn letters, separating scraps by colour and quality, then judging which pile each belonged to. Steph had always encouraged me to keep the fallible nature of memory in mind when I recalled painful events from my childhood. Parents' words and actions, which made no sense, might fit into a context I had not included in the pile. She wanted me to see a therapist, and recent events would lend weight to her argument, but I preferred to leave my trauma in the past, do my best to forget, and patch up cracks when they appeared. A mountain of cement wouldn't fill these fault lines. Was that why I created a demon?

If I accepted the past two weeks had not happened exactly as I remembered them, if the truth was less strange but more painful, how could I uncover the actual events? If I created Harrokabis to protect me, should I accept some things are best left undisturbed?

Steph would offer her own version of the events, and if past arguments were anything to go by, she would expect me to accept hers as truth, but if my memories were flawed, why should hers be definitive? I had always let her rewrite events, walked the easy path, maintained harmony in the house by discarding anything counter to her wisdom, and I feared I would do so again. I bristled when I imagined shedding my memories of being imprisoned and befriending a demon. Even if my memories were wrong, could

I trust her? I was convinced she had betrayed me. If I was right, I would be a fool not to uncover the truth for myself. I delved deeper until pain shoved me back, resisting my constant probing, and warning me to stay in the present or risk another blinding migraine.

When Steph was released from the hospital, I drove us home in her car. My Renault was still impounded.

I collected Steph's jeep from a grand hotel, which she claimed we had been staying in before she was attacked on the beach. The shiny surfaces and scent of beeswax seemed familiar. It was not the same mansion where I remembered hiding from the authorities with Melissa. It looked older and was granite rather than sandstone, but equally impressive.

'I can't wait to sleep in my own bed,' Steph said.

Our journey weaved through miles of beautiful countryside, and the music on the radio calmed me. We both hummed tunes from the sixties, sharing relieved smiles. I dared to dream of finding a better job, something I might enjoy, which involved caring for animals. Even if it meant drastically reducing our expenses, we agreed it was worth it to protect my health.

I felt happier than I had for weeks, wholeheartedly embracing the false sense of security, until the universe smashed it with a song: the one I heard when I discovered Patterson's car. The first few bars of the Zombies' track triggered dark memories of helplessness and confusion. I saw the bearded man loom in front of the windscreen and had to pull over.

Steph's hand stroked my shoulder as I rested my forehead against the steering wheel. I felt the hair around my throat, saw the cell door close with me trapped inside, Thomas sweeping up shards of glass, and Mateo's broken face.

The pressure of Steph's fingers grounded me.

'They never found the man who attacked you. Did you lie to the police to protect me?'

'You still don't remember?'

'I remember things differently.'

'What do you think happened?' she asked.

'I punched you. I would have killed you if Greer hadn't pulled me off.'

'And why would you try to kill me? Be sensible, Wanda. We were having a lovely holiday, no stress, no night shifts. What made you see red in your version of events?'

'You gave Melissa Powell a wig.'

'Wanda!'

'What?'

'I thought you left your obsession behind. I never met Melissa Powell let alone gave her a… what did you say?'

'A wig. Was it in the bag in the attic? The one you said was my birthday present.'

'Wanda, hush. You're scaring me.'

Her eyes dampened with concern, but I could not believe she was worried for me. Was she anxious about Powell, stuck in prison without a vessel to use for her escape?

'Did you go to London?' I asked.

'You know we didn't. We came to Wales instead.'

'I don't… I can't believe you. You were there when the house collapsed. I met your auntie. She told me not to trust you.'

In my peripheral vision, I saw her shake her head. A kernel of doubt became a shrub of prickly needles, piercing every neuron simultaneously. 'Pass me some painkillers. I need something to ease this pain.'

'Are you okay?' Judas concern again.

I clambered out of the car without checking whether the road was clear, sat on a grass bank, put my head between my legs, and used my knees to squeeze my temples. It did not relieve the pain.

Steph handed me a bottle of water and some paracetamol and sat beside me. The road was deserted. If she planned to kill me, this would be the perfect place. Instead, she stroked my hair and told me everything would be okay.

Steph busied herself in the kitchen when we arrived home. For once, she would feed me. I snuck upstairs and pulled out the ladder and torch as silently as I could. Music wafted up the stairs, masking any sound I might make, allowing me to relax a little. The bag was not in the attic. If I asked her, she might claim she had wrapped my present and hidden it elsewhere in case I was tempted to peek. She had an answer for everything. I put the ladder away and flushed the toilet to provide an alibi in case she asked why I went upstairs.

After lunch, I stood in the back garden while she stared through the window, studying me while her hands were busy with the washing up. I convinced myself she was trying to decide whether I was a threat to her or Powell. Her chosen role of sweet and worried girlfriend was almost believable, but I knew better.

Steph came into the garden an hour later and told me she had booked an appointment with a therapist. I had no choice but to agree to attend. If I had not beaten my girlfriend unconscious on the beach, how could I be sure I had swapped bodies with a mass murderer or made friends with a demon? I wanted to forget it all, but those memories lingered, stronger and more real than the reality Steph described as she tried to rewrite my recent history. I needed professional help.

)⊕C

I visited Laney as promised a week after we returned home from Wales. I had already had my first appointment with the shrink who did not believe me, but never explicitly denied my version of events. She said we would discuss my childhood next time.

Laney made me a cup of tea and we sat in her garden.

'Me sorry about yuh job,' she said. 'Most of the guards relocated. Me is based in the old building for now.'

'How was your holiday?' I asked.

Her face brightened. 'Wonderful, but me sorry me wasna here when yuh was having such a hard time with everything.'

'Did they tell you my car was left in the carpark?'

She nodded. 'Me worried. Me glad yuh ring and put me mind at rest.'

'You were right. I was obsessed with Powell. I should have

listened. Did Reynolds tell you what happened?'

'Only that yuh have a breakdown. Me surprised them no treat you like them treat Humphries. Time off.'

'They gave me time off, but nowhere near full pay. I'm not sure I want to go back.'

She squeezed my shoulder. 'More tea or lemonade?'

'Tea please.'

I wandered around her garden when she retreated to the kitchen. It was a beautiful space full of flowering bushes and bird song. Peaceful. A cat sunned itself on the path, too content to hunt the chaffinches in the apple tree.

Laney confirmed Melissa Powell was at Witchwood Prison but could not fill in any other blanks. I had hoped she might give me a definitive version of what happened.

Being with her was the medicine I needed. I trusted her, which made me realise I did not trust Steph at all. Our relationship was doomed; there would be no growing old together. Once, Steph had been my world, but here in the sunshine with my best friend, I understood things change. It was okay. I trusted my strength.

Instead of telling Steph it was over, I built a wall around myself to shut her out. The therapist fought Steph's corner, not overtly, but implicitly, telling me how important emotional connections were and that decisions made in a period of mental distress were rarely correct. I argued my depression was situational, and only after leaving the toxic environment could I get better. Perhaps the shrink was as conservative as my ex-colleagues and did not believe in throwing things away.

Whenever I saw Steph, I saw her betrayal; the manipulation and manoeuvring to ensure I would be close to Melissa Powell and could aid the priestess's escape. It did not matter whether it was the truth. Love became mistrust, then resentment. I knew I had to leave. It took me twelve months to break free.

CHAPTER FIFTEEN

Almost two years have passed since I left Steph and Lancashire behind. Three years since both the Highgate Murder House and the wings of Witchwood Prison fell into rubble. They rebuilt the latter within a year, but my healing has taken longer, delayed by frequent self-sabotage. A least my mind is clearer, and day-to-day life has gained a stability, which allows me to confront my anger issues from a healthy distance. Most of my time is spent in the company of dogs whose simple loyalty grounds me. I can look back with the objectivity of a dreamer now awake. I have accepted the fault lines in my psyche and mended the cracks with something stronger and more beautiful, like the Japanese art of Kintsugi.

I would like to say I am well now.

I cannot.

At least I am not around people who insist my memories are lies and my decisions are mistakes. No one here knows my history, and the dogs I care for look at me in the same way Harrokabis once did, with absolute devotion.

I wake in swampy sheets again, knowing I have had a nightmare without remembering the details. Kabis stirs beside me. An elderly bitch I rescued from the pound, who charmed me with her big eyes and long lashes.

'Good morning, girl.'

Kabis is instantly alert and races to the door, eager to be fed. I move more slowly, picking my way across the carpet and wrapping myself in a dressing gown. I spot mail on the doormat but feed my companion before collecting the pile of bills and a handwritten manilla envelope that makes me tremble when I hold it. I pop it in a drawer, afraid of its contents. Something to face after work or never.

I love my job. I still patrol cages, but the inmates are happy to see me and whine for my attention. If I could, I would adopt them all. As things are, I can only care for them at the pound, see to their needs, teach them to trust humans again. I understand betrayal by loved ones and know it is a long journey to recovery.

I leave at five and go for drinks with one of my colleagues, a young woman called Amy. Sometimes I catch longing in her gaze, but I am not ready to love again and pretend not to notice.

These days, dinner for two means a microwave ready meal for me and a bowl of meat for Kabis. I cannot help but remember cooking for Steph all those times I returned from work before her, afraid she would fade away if I did not fill her belly. I suppose it is the same with Kabis. It feels great to be needed without wondering whether I'm being lied to or manipulated. There is no duplicity in a dog.

Is it strange I named her after my demon companion? Harrokabis is the only thing I cling to from that period of my life. He may have done terrible things, but he gave me a safe space to be myself when no one else did; he let me scream at him and never retaliated, healed my injuries, and never caused them. It is hard to reconcile such goodness with the awful things he did to other people: those worshipers in the Highgate house, the detectives, and Chow Lee; yet I cannot remember him without smiling. I have not seen him in three years. Often, I suspect I dreamed him into existence. Did I do the same with Melissa?

After dinner, I pop open a can of beer and retrieve the A5 envelope, trembling as I open it, tempted to rip it to shreds, but curiosity trumps destruction. Inside is a letter, a photograph, and a plastic bag. I glance at the image first, but only from the corner of my eye, still afraid of the power of photos to suck me through a gateway. The edge of Witchwood Forest and a river. I am not surprised. I expected something like this when I saw the envelope this morning. How did they find me, and why did it take them two years?

Dear Wanda,

If you want to know what really happened, mix these herbs with your menstrual blood and boiled water.

Onyx.

I throw the envelope and its contents in the bin, imagining the cloudy concoction in my favourite mug, and recoiling at the thought of drinking blood, pinching my nose to down the bitter brew. Not sure whether I am dreaming or remembering, I see gates; the same black gates that hovered over the ocean, held open with strands of Melissa Powell's white hair. Walking between them, I feel the same compulsion I did while being guided by torchlight to Moira Patterson. I wonder how my colleague is doing. Did she recover and return to her job at the prison?

My thoughts turn to Laney Dawson, and I see her in the distance. The ground between us is striped with veins of lava. I stride towards her, smiling. The closer I get, the taller and stranger she appears, until it is not Laney but Harrokabis who opens his arms to embrace me. I am full of love as I sprint the final metres to throw my arms around his furry form.

'I thought I dreamed you,' I say, forgetting this too is a dream.

'Welcome to the borderland.'

Floorboards appear beneath our feet. We stand in a circle of strange markings and candles. He bows, then leads me around the room in a waltz. Others dance together: Steph and Melissa, Thomas and Greer, D.I. Lewis and Officer Marr, Laney and Masterton. We are joined by the shadow demons from the cellar and their dead dance partners.

'It's not real,' I say, spinning on the balls of my feet.

'What we perceive isn't always objectively true.' Melissa's

whisper reaches me even though she and Steph are far away, at the edge of my field of vision.

A brown faeces-like substance oozes through the gaps between floorboards and solidifies into a male body curled up, tight as a snail shell, bruises mottling his skin. Crimson taints my vision, and I ball my fists, pulling back my foot, ready to kick the knobbled spine.

My monster steps away and Steph rushes into my arms, pushing me from the body. 'You were protecting me from a stranger on the beach. You can't keep blaming yourself.'

Something punches me between the shoulder blades, thrusting me into wakefulness. I sit up, sweating. Kabis is beside me, ears twitching, grumbling in her sleep.

)⊕(

The following day feels as dreamlike as my nightmare. One moment I am spooning food into a bowl for Boris, a blind Rottweiler, and the next I am sprinting across the borderland fleeing an unseen presence. While bathing an ugly but friendly mongrel, I return to the borderland to hunt for my demon. By five o'clock, I know I must face my past before I can move on.

'Witchwood Prison.'

'Good evening. This is Wanda Jones. I worked as a guard on C block. Can you tell me whether Melissa Powell is still an inmate there?'

'She is.'

'I would like to visit her.'

'Are you family?'

'No. I worked with her.'

'You can write to the inmate, and she can request a visit… or not.'

'Thank you.'

My handwriting is awkward, but readable.

Dear Melissa,

I am not sure you'll remember me. My name is Wanda Jones. I would like to visit you at Witchwood. If you are happy to meet, please let me and the prison know.

Wanda.

I post the letter the following morning. Perhaps it is the promise of closure which prevents me from remembering my intervening dreams. Days return to normal, with no unscheduled visits to the borderland. A week later, I receive two letters, one written in the same hand as the manilla envelope, which brought painful memories hurtling back, and the other with a stamp from Witchwood Prison.

Dear Wanda,

I remember you and give my permission. Please arrange a day and time.
Yours sincerely,

Melissa Powell, Witchwood Prison.

Wanda,

We should meet. Call me on 020 79460814 to arrange a convenient time and location.

Onyx.

I phone the prison and arrange to see Melissa this weekend, feeling frightened yet strangely excited. I stare at Onyx's elegant handwriting until I leave for work.

Two young dogs are adopted today. It's my favourite part of the job, pairing lonely animals with loving families. I exercise, feed and groom the other canines in my care. Three are due to be euthanised next week. It isn't fair, but it's part of the job. Unlike human criminals, abandoned animals are on death row. If I were wealthy, I'd adopt them all.

If I'm not insane, and Onyx's missives suggest at least some of what I remember is true, I have access to the most notorious murderer in history and could write an insider's account. After I meet with Melissa and check my facts, I'll decide whether to call Onyx. The medium is unlikely to have my best interest at heart, but the risk would not have stopped the old me, and the new me has more to gain. If I wrote a bestseller, I might have enough income to give the dogs a real home.

Should I reach out to Steph? It'll be an awkward reunion, and I can't trust anything she tells me. While painful, it might be cathartic to see her again. I call her after dinner.

'Hello.' Steph's voice. She hasn't changed her number.

'It's me.'

'Wanda? How are you? I didn't expect to hear from you.'

I wonder whether even that is a lie. Does Steph know Onyx wrote to me, and I arranged to visit Melissa? A rabbit hole opens around me, and I feel myself hovering in the air above it. Where is my solidity now?

'I'm okay,' I lie. 'Are you still living in our old house?'

'Yes.'

'I'll be in the area on Saturday. If you're free, we could meet up.'

She pauses, and I listen to her soft breath. 'I'd love that. What time?'

Visitation is at two. 'Half-four?' I ask.

'At the house?'

It's a risk, but it would be easier to talk in private. 'I'll be there.'

'I miss you.'

I hang up then bend double, head on my knees. Kabis licks my hand. I want to take her to Witchwood with me, but they would not let her through the security gates. I'll have to be strong without her. I can leave her in the pound for the weekend. Will she enjoy catching up with old friends, or fear abandonment? When I collect her on Sunday, I'll assure her she's loved, and I'll never abandon her. 'I need you to be brave this weekend, but you'll be home again soon.'

She barks once, and I stroke her brow, hoping she understands.

One-thirty. A dog sniffs my car. I recognise one of the two OSGs, but there is no hint of friendliness in his eyes. Thousands must have come through these gates since I last drove this route. At least my spare tyre is in good repair this time.

I head towards my old parking space before remembering to use the visitors' bay. I queue with family members. After an efficient search, we are led to tables. The Victorian room, its wooden framed windows, ancient and noisy radiators, high ceiling and rows of tables and chairs remind me of my school days. In some ways, this is not so different. I will face an intimidating teacher, hoping to pass the exam.

Ives escorts Melissa to my table. The guard's face throws me back in time; for a moment, it feels as though I'm locked in cell forty-eight, wearing Melissa's flesh again. My hands shake. I want to flee the room and memories, but force my body to sit still, grounding myself with the sounds of mumbled conversations and squeezing the flesh of my thigh to feel the muscles beneath until I know I am still Wanda.

Melissa lowers herself into the chair opposite. Those eyes. Looking at her is like drowning in tropical waters. My soul lunges towards her. My shoulders shake and rusted metal coats my tongue, forcing me to tear my gaze away.

'Hello, Melissa.' I glance at her mouth rather than her eyes, passing her first name across the table like a baton of friendship. 'How are you?'

No reply.

'It's Wanda. Do you remember me?'

She rubs her slender fingers together, nervously. She seems different. I expected an insolent Miss Jo-ones at least. I want to reach across the scarred plastic tabletop, cup that pointed chin and force her to face me, but that no contact is allowed has been drilled into my brain.

'Was any of it real?' I ask.

She lifts her lashes, revealing glistening turquoise. A confused frown makes her cheeks droop.

'Did you use my body to escape? Did you summon demons? Were we in the mansion with Thomas and Mateo? Or did I dream it all?'

'You too?' she asks. 'No one believes me. New photos arrived: an animal shelter and a concrete building that looks as ugly as this place. Is that where you live and work now?'

I swallow hard. 'Onyx wrote to me.'

'The duplicitous bitch!' Melissa's aggression and adult language shock me.

'How did they catch you?' I ask.

'Officially, Melissa never left Witchwood.'

'Unofficially?'

'Heathrow Airport.' She reaches for my hand.

Ives stiffens, ready to stride towards us. I pull away so Melissa will not be punished further.

'Help me,' Melissa whispers.

'I can't.'

'I heard rumours. No one believed them, not even me, not until… She switched with you too. How did you get your body back?' Her eyes drill into mine, fear magnifying her pupils. 'I'm afraid, Jones.'

Ice trickles down my spine.

'You don't believe me either,' she sighs.

'What's your name?' I whisper.

'Greer… Elaine Greer.'

'You were at the beach with Steph.'

Her head droops as if her neck cannot carry its weight. 'Onyx sent us. We were supposed to take Melissa back to London.'

'Where is she now?'

'Help me?' she pleads.

'Elaine, I can't.'

Can I help her? I doubt it, and if I'm honest with myself, I wouldn't if I could. I feel vindicated. She is stuck here, not me. I'm certain she knew it was me when she slapped my face, pulling me from the cave behind the waterfall and into Melissa's body. She isn't innocent. At best, she was a paid pawn; at worst, she enjoyed tormenting me. I want to leave her here. I believe she deserves this.

'Five minutes,' a guard announces.

'It's not long enough,' I say.

'You can come back. I'm not going anywhere. They all think I'm making it up or crazy.'

'Why did you come to the beach?'

'I already told you… Onyx.' Greer grabs my wrist.

I stare at the fragile hand. 'Where does Onyx fit into this? What does she want?'

Ives marches across the room and towers above us. 'Visiting time is over, Powell. Come with me.'

'A few more minutes,' Greer pleads, releasing her grip and tucking her hands under the table.

'Now, Powell.'

'Help me, please,' Greer says before Ives leads her away.

The shaking muscles in my legs make it hard to stand up, so I watch the other visitors leave before pushing myself onto unsteady limbs and stumbling outside. From the privacy of my ancient Renault, I glare at dark bricks and shadowy windows while wondering whether Greer or Melissa spoke to me, trying to untangle meaning from the events of the last three years, a sickening carousel which never stops turning. I press my temples, then swallow two tablets. I shouldn't have returned. My visit has left me with more questions, and I hate the feeling of confusion that whisks around my mind.

I wind down the window and gaze at the slate roof, half expecting to see Harrokabis crouched on the parapet, either real or a figment of my disturbed imagination. My eyes scan the malevolent walls of time-blackened bricks and narrow, barred windows, behind which the shadows of long-dead lunatics lurk. This confusion, this madness, belongs in the past. If I pursue this mystery, I will drown in magic and demons again. But if I drive away, return to my new life, will I always wonder who is watching me, taking photographs of my home, and sending them to the prisoner in cell forty-eight?

I start the ignition and drive out of the carpark. When I meet the road, I turn right towards Steph. Woodland makes walls on both sides, making me feel like a sheep guided through pens. I drive through the forest where I found Patterson in a box. I am sure that happened. Fairly sure, at least. Dense canopies hide the sky. A sharp bend ahead where the detectives crashed and died. I pull into a layby and imagine hunting for the bag of letters Harrokabis buried under a blackberry bush. Finding them will prove the monster is real, not a symptom of psychosis, but if I search every inch of the forest and find a sliver of plastic caught in the thorns of some flowering shrub, will I squeeze between sharp branches, endure deep scratches, shed blood, and still find nothing because there is nothing left to find. Years of rain and wind could have removed every trace of evidence. To go through all that, and still not know, would make my mind crack again.

I check my rear-view mirror and accelerate onto the road. I pass the meadow where Patterson's car was abandoned, the grass where I leaped onto Melissa's back and forced her down. Both feel like traces of a half-forgotten dream. I drive until I reach the housing estate, and park in front of the one-bedroom house I shared with Steph before I lost my body or my mind.

She's at the window, smiling. I turn off the engine and step out of the car as the front door sweeps inward, and she rushes into the garden, arms wide. I sleepwalk towards her and let her engulf me in an embrace.

The nutty scent of coffee fills the house. Steph guides me to the sofa and brings me a mug.

'How have you been?' She sits on the couch opposite, on the other side of the coffee table, brushes hair from her eyes, then reaches for her cup.

The room wobbles and blurs and she is staring at the television while a reporter announces Melissa Powell's arrival at Witchwood Prison. The scene is from a lifetime ago, yet not long enough for me to forget her lies or trust her double-exposed smile.

'Why me?' I ask.

Her lips flap, but instead of Steph's voice, I hear Harrokabis. 'You and Melissa are the same, Wanda.'

I shake my head. 'What did you say?'

'I asked how you are?'

'Better than ever.' I did not add *now you're out of my life*, although I think it.

'Did you visit Melissa Powell? How was she?'

'She claims she's Elaine Greer.'

Steph purses her lips. 'Don't let her drag you back there. You look good. Have you been… getting… help?'

I rise, desperate to leave, and drive far away from this place and this woman.

'You don't need to go. Drink your coffee. We can discuss other things. I've missed you. Is there anyone new?'

I sit down again. 'Kabis, my dog.' Her smile warms me. 'How's work?'

'I qualified. My hours are more reasonable these days.'

'Anyone new in your life?'

'No. I keep hoping…' Her voice trails off.

'What?'

Her cheeks redden. 'That you might come back.'

'I can't.'

She lifts her mug but cannot hide her frown. 'What do you remember from that time?'

'I'd rather forget it all.'

'Unless you deal with your trauma…'

'And what trauma is that?' I do not disguise the anger in my voice.

She places her mug down and leans forward. 'Babes, you were attacked.'

I stare at her. 'No…'

'I know what you believe happened, but none of it was real.'

Shadows congeal on the wall behind Steph while she wrings her hands and stares at me with a mixture of pity and concern.

'Go,' I whisper.

Her eyes widen. 'Wanda?'

'Run!' I yell, aiming my mug at the shadows. It shatters as I sprint towards the door.

Watching the house from my car, I wait for Steph to appear. Either she thinks I'm crazy, or evil forces within the house prevent her from leaving. I'm sane enough to realise which is more likely, but afraid I will find two detectives in my living room when I get home, waiting to tell me my ex has been torn apart. They might even arrest me. It would be the ultimate irony to return to Witchwood Prison as an inmate, although they might decide a secure hospital is better suited. Better to grab Kabis and run. Go somewhere new. Change my name again. Find a better place to hide. I'll be more cautious, choose somewhere remote, a place no one will look. I start the car and drive.

I don't need to break in, I have keys for the kennels. Kabis is delighted to see me, but am I doing the right thing? Life will be hard on the run, but at her age, the chances of adoption are low. People prefer young dogs. Considering all she has done for me and what she means to me, I can't leave her there to die nor the three dogs who are due to be euthanised. After ushering them onto the back seat, and with Kabis sitting proudly at the front, I start the engine then ruffle the fur between her ears. She licks my wrist.

Although it would be easier to live out of a car than on the streets, keeping my trusted old Renault would be equivalent to holding a signpost saying, I'm here, Onyx. I abandon it outside my apartment, leaving my phone in the glove compartment.

Releasing the death-row trio anywhere is a risk, and chances are they will be recaptured, but it buys them more time, and they might be clever enough to avoid detection. I open the car door and tell them they are free.

I retrieve cash and bank cards from my apartment, feed Kabis and bundle warm clothes into a satchel. I will have forgotten something, but it is time to leave. Time to disappear.

☽⛥☾

Living without a fixed income is possible, but difficult. You trample over lines you never expected to cross, treating each day as if it is your last, knowing it might be. I'm afraid to settle down. The moment I do, Onyx and my past will catch up, and I'm not ready to face them. I need more time. Know your enemy – isn't that the advice we're given, but how can I know the unknowable? Memories twist inside my head, refusing to be unpicked. I feel Harrokabis beside us every time Kabis and I curl up in a doorway or under a bridge to catch a few hours of sleep. Is he taunting or protecting me?

I could run for the rest of my life and never escape.

Six months of shoplifting and selling blowjobs is what it takes to hit rock bottom. The only way is up or prison.

I remember a book, part of Steph's collection, with black and white photographs: images of the Highgate house, and a group photo of the residents before they died, wearing hooded robes, their faces obscured by shadows. If I look again, will I recognise some of them?

There are no copies of *An Insider's Tale* in the library. I steal a magnifying glass and a copy I find in a second-hand bookstore. When I first started stealing, I felt a strange fission each time I took something without paying, as if a part of me was elsewhere, but now I am calm. No one notices me. The homeless are invisible.

It is a fine day, so I take my loot to the park. When I magnify the face, I know why it seemed familiar. The entire group is presumed dead. The sole survivor, Melissa Powell. So, why is my ex in this photo? Steph, what did you do?

Kabis whines, sensing my distress. Reassuring her helps calm me.

I need to return to Witchwood and face the woman I once loved, the person who betrayed me most. Both Steph and Melissa were in the cellar when the demons descended, and both survived. What if another borderland creature attached itself to Steph? Harrokabis claimed he was different from his siblings. If something else gained possession of my ex, it might be cruel and manipulative – the darkness to Harrokabis' light.

Kabis rests her head on my lap. I scratch behind her ear. The photo is grainy, but I am sure it's Steph. Melissa remembered Steph from a visit at Vinnie Green, but maybe they had met earlier. With thirty-six people in the cellar, would Melissa remember every face? A lump the size of an apple fills my throat. Part of me fears I am teetering on the edge of madness, but its warnings are quiet enough to ignore. I develop my theory further – a demon forced Steph to betray me because it wanted to be reunited with its siblings. How can I find peace while Steph is at the mercy of a cruel and manipulative demon? I loved her once. She was my universe.

Pain cleaves my skull, and my stomach bubbles with acid. Kabis' tongue warms my trembling fingers.

'We have to try to save Steph,' I say, hoping Harrokabis is listening.

He appears beside me, my beloved guardian. A monster whose sins I have forgiven. I reach up and stroke his throat, awed by his terrible beauty. He clutches my hand as we walk towards the bus station.

CHAPTER SIXTEEN

KABIS and I reach the town of Witchwood at sunset the following day. After the first bus journey, I resorted to hitchhiking, standing for hours at the roadside while my thumb turned purple, bruises heating my right forearm and thigh where dozens of affectionate or predatory hands squeezed circles into my skin. We have a long walk ahead, past the prison and forest, but I dare not sleep rough in a place where I am so well known. My stiff muscles ache, and my head is full of conspiracies and poisonous hope.

While the thought of knocking on Laney's door is tempting, answering all her questions would exhaust me. Much easier to switch off my mind and hike the final five miles. I pretend I am protecting my friend, not wishing to embroil her in my mess, and manage to half-convince myself this is true, even though I know it is not.

I retrieve half a sandwich from a bin and share it with Kabis as we head out of town. The hood of my sweater obscures my face, and though I glimpse familiar figures, no one recognises me. Three-hundred metres from town, the streetlamps end, and I rely on Harrokabis' supernatural vision to guide me. A few cars pass, but when I stick out my thumb to hitch a ride, no one stops. Kabis trots by my side, happy to be anywhere if she is with me.

Steph. It has been a long time since I saw her. Has she changed? I know I have, but I also know she will recognise me despite the grime and straggly hair. As I visualise her lightly freckled face, and the strawberry curls I used to tuck behind her ear, my chest tightens and my heart races. What will happen after we save her? Will she fall into my arms? Will her pupils dilate with love and burning desire, or will her eyes narrow in cold hatred and resentment?

Assuming I am right, and Steph survived the first massacre because a second borderland creature bonded with her, then Harrokabis, at my request, will take something from her without her consent, but it is pointless asking what she wants, knowing it is more likely the demon will answer.

I hate Steph, and I love her.

Hating is easier.

Love makes me vulnerable. But I'm not trekking towards her house out of hate. I believe, beneath all the lies and betrayal, she is someone worth saving. And I'm not doing this for me. I'm doing it for her, and for all the times she pulled me out of darkness and brought me into the light. She convinced me I wasn't a monster and loved me when my parents couldn't. Her love made me strong, not vulnerable.

And Harrokabis is with me.

Whatever happens at the end of this journey, I will face it.

My limbs prickle. I shudder, not because I'm cold, but because, despite my strength, I'm afraid. I reach for the source of this fear, but it is undefined, diffuse, and I can't grasp hold. I'm not afraid of death, although I know the battle might kill me. It can't be disappointment I fear; I have no preconceptions, no idea how Steph will react once the parasite controlling her is torn out, and you can't be disappointed when you expect nothing. The reason for the icy worm which wriggles down my spine isn't death or disappointment. What then? It hits me like a high-speed train smashing through my skull. I'm scared Harrokabis will not return from the borderland.

'If this works, and you take the borderland creature home, but somehow can't return to me, I want you to know…'

He gazes at me expectantly, and I brush his waist with my knuckles. The words make my throat bulge. Can I force them over my tongue? Do I need to, or does he already know what I want to say?

'I want you to know…' Tumorous language slides further down my gullet, and my mouth makes strange clicking sounds as my lips open and close impotently.

Why is this so hard? Is the feeling too big or complicated to express with mere words?

He nods and stoops until his chin rests on my head. The lump behind my oesophagus dissolves. He knows.

☽⛤☾

The bright halogens surrounding the prison make a strange haze in the sky as they glare at me, accusingly. *You're a criminal now,* they shriek; *you should be in here, not out there.*

'I did it to survive,' I reply.

They laugh. Most of the women inside Witchwood Prison could make the same claim, but no one cares. Kabis growls, sensing my distress.

'Is she in there?' I ask Harrokabis, meaning Melissa, of course.

'If she is, she's shielding her thoughts from me.'

Could Greer still be trapped in cell forty-eight? Maybe she deserves to stay there; she accepted *The Friends'* money, and I suspect it was that sharp slap which drew me from the photograph into Melissa's body.

The wind picks up, and I hear misery in the howling air – centuries of the stuff. I shrug and walk faster, but it's a long hike, and when I reach the shelter of trees, I slow to a more leisurely pace. My stomach cramps painfully. When did I last eat properly?

I must look terrible. If Steph isn't home when I arrive, I can't risk waiting outside. A nosy neighbour might call the authorities. I push this new worry to the back of an exceedingly long queue. For now, I must keep moving, one foot in front of the other. Ignore everything else; focusing on worry and pain has never helped me before.

We round a bend and see a thumbnail moon shining brightly in an indigo sky, low enough that birds could make their nests on it. It steals my breath, the huge white rock hanging amid innumerable stars. A witch's moon. As cold as death.

Harrokabis points beyond the treeline to a black abyss where the moon's icy glow cannot penetrate. 'Wait.'

A chorus of voices, high and soft. If the song has words, I can't discern them, but the melody is so achingly beautiful that tears swell between my lashes.

'Where's it coming from?' I ask.

'Shall we find out?'

I nod before remembering the last time I trod through these woods in the dark and was drawn towards a metal coffin. Is it another trap? A trick?

'Maybe we shouldn't.' I resist and pull away, releasing my hold on my guardian.

Yellow light flickers in the distance like a tiny sun. The scent of woodsmoke tickles my nostrils – a bonfire. It's probably a party of teenagers escaping their parents' gaze for a few hours of freedom.

His mouth droops, and I realise he wants to delay the coming battle. How great a risk does Harrokabis face? Is he afraid? Bubbles in my gut whisper a warning, and my skin tingles as if an army of ants are marching across my limbs. I don't ask what he fears. If I know I will lose him, I might not have the strength to continue, and I must confront Steph or lose myself again. What Harrokabis sacrifices is his concern, not mine. It is up to him whether he joins me or follows his curiosity into the forest. I will love him either way.

Moonlight silvers the grass verge, and I see enough to continue alone. The distance between the demon and me grows, stretching our connection until it's thread thin. I know, without looking, that he is still gazing at those golden flames, entranced by the ethereal melody.

Every step makes me wince. The strap of my satchel digs into my shoulder, and blisters compress under my weight as if I am treading on pockets of acid. The heat of my feet does not offset the chill in my fingers. The hike is torturous, but I'm half-way there. Heaviness in my knees and calves, like I'm wading through mud even when I ditch the kerb and switch to tarmac. Harrokabis is far behind. I ask whether he is coming, and he assures me he will catch up.

The river bubbles on my right, chattering like an excited child. I wish I could feel like that. Anything is preferable to the cold dread weighing on my shoulders, bending my neck until I see only the path under my feet. A thousand fears whirl through my chest; pain slices behind my eyes, and my knees click and bend in unnatural ways, jarring my hips. Perhaps I should stop and rest while Harrokabis catches up. But if I stop, I will find some excuse not to see Steph, so I push on, massaging my temples to disperse the pain. Not far now. I have passed the spot where Patterson's car was abandoned, and where I tackled Melissa and knocked her to the ground. The land holds many memories. Why are none of them good? Do we only recall things that hurt us?

I search for happier memories, but they are pale and without substance, merely an absence of pain. I thought Steph and I were happy, but as I remember the years by her side, I convince myself it was never love, never joy, only the dim hope that she would continue to tolerate me. I doubt Steph and I even liked each other; we are too different. Wanting love and acceptance, I had pandered to Steph's needs while ignoring my own, pushing every doubt aside, believing what we had was better than I deserved. It's no wonder I didn't notice my girlfriend was possessed by a demon when I closed my eyes to anything that threatened my equilibrium.

Streetlights ahead assure me we're almost there. My tongue swells in my desert-dry mouth. Muscles protest every step. I must go on. If I turn back now, I'll eke out a cowardly, shameful existence, but if I do this, I'll prove my worth to myself, and that is what counts.

When I reach my old house, a car is parked outside, not Steph's jeep, but she might have exchanged it for a newer model. Light speckles the closed curtains with pinpricks of white. Where is Harrokabis? I give myself a minute to control my breathing before striding towards the door with Kabis at my heel. After ringing the bell, I hear movement. The door sweeps inward, and she is there, exactly as I remember her. Her hair is pulled back in a loose ponytail, and rebel curls, unwilling to be tamed, soften the lines of her face.

'You came back.' She offers a smile which manages to be warm yet cold. 'And you brought a dog.'

'Can we come in?'

She bends to let Kabis sniff her hand. My dog rewards her with a wet kiss. Steph nods and makes room. 'Coffee and a bowl of water?'

'Yes, please.'

'Make yourselves at home. It's good to see you, although you look like you've been through the wars.'

'You look amazing.'

Her eyes shutter and her cheeks glow. 'Thank you.'

Kabis lies across my feet after I make myself comfortable on the sofa. Steph returns with a mug for me and places a bowl of water near the dog's head. I rub Kabis' ears, needing to do something with my hands. Steph looks serene as she sits opposite me, reaches for the remote, and mutes the television. There is an uncomfortable silence, one she expects me to fill.

'I know you were one of *The Friends*. I saw a photo.'

She recrosses her legs, perhaps to distract me from whatever reaction her facial features might reveal. 'Wanda.' The sharpness of Steph's voice elicits a warning growl from Kabis. My name hangs in the air until she speaks again, softer this time. 'So, you haven't moved on. Still, the same obsession, but now a new delusion.'

'Am I talking to Stephanie or the demon?' I ask.

Her lips twist before she reasserts her mask and leans back into the chair. A tiny smile twitches the corners of her mouth. 'I'm going to call Dr Nevill.'

I lean across the table and grab her wrist. 'A psychiatrist, I presume.'

The tears glistening in her eyes, are they borne of sadness or frustration? 'Wanda, you need help. Look at yourself. Have you been living on the streets?'

'Let's cut the bullshit. I've seen the photos, and I know you were in Highgate before the first massacre. What I don't know is whether you or something else controls your body.'

'If you expect me to feed your psychosis, you've got the wrong person.'

I scream at her through clenched teeth, releasing her wrist. Kabis leaps onto the sofa, hackles up, distressed by the sudden change in mood.

Steph divides her focus between my dog and her mobile phone; slowly, she retrieves the latter. Is she afraid Kabis will attack her? She dials, then puts the phone to her ear. I leap off the sofa and tackle the phone from her grasp, flinging it at a wall. Raising her hands to shield her face, she peers between trembling fingers, following my movements, as if waiting for me to strike. I recall the beach, my version at least, when I punched and punched her until she lost consciousness, but I will not hit her now. I don't want to hurt her, only make her listen and accept my reality for the first time. She edges away, and I sense she is trying to reach the front door, but I can't let her leave.

'Don't move,' I say. 'I only want to help you.'

'It's you who needs help, Wanda. Can't you see?'

'Sit down. I won't hurt you. We need to talk.'

She shakes her head but sits down, shoulders touching her ears, while perfect teeth gnaw her bottom lip; her thighs squeeze together, and her hands twitch in her lap. When I lower myself onto the sofa, she refuses to meet my gaze. She is either terrified or acting the part perfectly.

I don't know what to say, or how to calm her, reassure her she is safe. 'When I left, I had nowhere to stay, so yes, I have been wandering, sleeping in shelters and… other places, but I have had time to clear my head and process everything. It's obvious now why you wanted to get far away from the Highgate house and why your aunt warned me not to trust you. You and Melissa made me doubt reality, but it's clear now. Everything that happened to me, everything you keep trying to deny… I don't need a shrink. I need you to tell me the truth at last, and when Harrokabis gets here, he can take that parasite home, and you and I can decide what we want to do.'

I wait for her to contradict me, but she remains silent, trembling, childlike.

'Please leave,' she whispers.

'This is my house too,' I remind her.

'Then let me go. Keep the house if you want.'

'For Christ's sake, Steph, I *want* to help *you*. I've travelled for days, walked for hours, haven't slept or eaten since… well, I honestly can't remember, but it's been a long time. Soon it will all be over, and you'll be free.'

'I'm frightened,' she says.

'Don't be. I'm not going to hurt you, I promise.'

'You're not…' She glances at me then drops her gaze to her lap again.

I pull Onyx's book from my bag, open it to the photographic plates, and pass it to her. 'It's you.'

She pushes it away, and it falls to the floor with a thud.

'Won't you even look at it?' I ask.

A tiny jerk of her head to the left. If Harrokabis doesn't arrive soon, she'll try to make it to the door again. I have no idea how to tackle her demon without him or restrain Steph without hurting her. I feel ridiculous. Although I know I'm right, everything I say, and everything I want to say, sounds insane. Steph may not even sense the creature's presence. She might be sat there, trembling and close to tears, because she believes I'm dangerous, a madwoman. If our roles were reversed, I would think the same. But if it were my photo in the book, me who had been present at the ritual and survived, I would know demons are real. Steph is lying, or her memories have been manipulated to make her forget everything.

'What happened at the first ritual?' I ask.

I study Steph's body language – spring-tight. Silence envelopes us. I don't fill the air with questions or useless platitudes but allow the absence of sound to permeate our pores, hoping Steph will feel compelled to speak, or suppressed memories will tickle the edges of her consciousness until she confronts them and understands. We sit for what seems like hours, but without a clock, I can't be certain how much time passes. Kabis retreats and waits by the front door without breaking the silence.

When Steph's eyes meet mine again, there's a new slyness in her gaze. I force myself not to shudder. She grins, and I clench my fists.

The room plunges into darkness. Voices whisper my name, surrounding me; some are so close they ruffle my hair. It's only a trick. She's trying to frighten me. I stand up, or try to, but the floor is no longer there. I fall through dense blackness, forcing myself to remain calm. It's another illusion.

'Wanda, don't you dare hide from me.' My father's voice. Is Steph's demon rifling through my fears until she finds one that works? I'm bigger and stronger now, and the threat of his violence does not cow me.

Claws dig into my shoulders. I cross my arm over my chest and grab a scaley foot. Rough, wrinkled skin hangs in folds. A bird of prey, is this the monster's true form? I tug the digits, but the grip is too strong. Talons penetrate my skin, making me hiss. Recalling Chow Lee's insistence that demons ripped out her heart, reminds me the pain is in my mind; however real it feels, whatever agonies I endure, it's a lie. An awful thought fills my head. If the pain isn't real, it could last forever.

I hyperventilate. The air is too thin and the pain too intense. I'm powerless against this creature. My only hope is if Steph fights with me. I stroke the foot, trying to reach out to whatever love remains between us. 'Help me, Steph. Push the evil creature out and talk to me, darling.'

A squawking sound, which resembles laughter, slices the air above and behind me.

'It's Wanda, baby. I'm here for you. We can be free, together.'

The room flickers, emerging from the darkness, solidifying around and beneath me. I spin on my heels to face the horror, appalled by the ancient stare and cruel mouth. Hands twitch at my sides then dart upwards. My fingers curl around her throat; her heart hammers against my thumbs as I squeeze, but she doesn't resist. Her eyes communicate sad resignation. Has she always known it would end like this? Her mouth morphs into a tall zero as she struggles to draw breath. The rapid beat beneath my thumbs slows, growing faint. Her eyes roll back in their sockets, communicating nothing. Her jaw slackens, and her weight pulls against my arms as she loses consciousness, but I do not let go. My face is hot with tears, my lips cold and dry when the tip of my tongue glides across them. Steph's tongue is grey when it emerges from her mouth. I gasp, horrified, and release my grip. Her body crumples, bouncing slightly as it hits the carpet. Have I killed her? Dropping to my knees, I caress her ankle – cold. I crawl over her legs and rest my head on her silent chest, my tears and drool darkening her shirt. A lonely wail builds in my chest, echoing through my skull as I release a howl of despair. For a blissful second, I believe the thunderous pounding is her heart kickstarting before I realise someone is hammering on the door. Blue flashes from emergency service lights penetrate the curtains. If I do not flee, I'll be sent to prison for this terrible, senseless crime. I imagine shuffling around C block, tormented by Lily Masterton and her cronies, Humphreys insisting she always knew something was off with me. Alone in my cell, trying to smother myself with an unyielding prison-issue pillow, my mother gloating when she visits, telling me they tried to save me, accepting it all because I deserve this torment. Worthless.

I shrug off the pressure on my shoulder, deserving no human kindness.

'Wanda.' I know that growl, but it can't be him. He is in the woods, entranced by a new companion. 'Wanda, this isn't real.'

I open my eyes. Steph's lap is my pillow. I raise my head and torso, arms shaking beneath me as pain slices across my shoulders. Steph is sitting up now, and the cold intelligence behind her face displays a victorious sneer that energises my arms and makes me want to strangle her again.

Harrokabis shoves me away. The sofa catches me, and I rest

my back against its frame, glaring at my possessed ex. The dog returns to my side, tail tucked between her trembling hind legs.

'Take that thing away from me,' I beg.

Harrokabis nods and wraps his many arms around Steph's sublet form, then everything turns upside down. I tumble and hit the ceiling, watching the battle of wills continue above, no, below. I'm not the only audience. Eyes grow from the carpet like demonic daisies and alien life animates the furniture. The carapace of the coffee table opens to reveal jade wings which it uses to free itself from the tangle of fighters' limbs. It scuttles a few metres, treading on eyes which ooze purple and release an unearthly stench as they burst. Sofa cushions lift and bend to reveal a mouth which chatters in an unknown language. The television screen bulges to accommodate a misshapen nose and stiletto fangs; its daggered mouth opens and closes to emit short bursts of white noise. Pictures leap from the walls to bounce upon the sofa's mouth before armrests bat them away.

My mind cannot process any of this, but my eyes refuse to close. Even when I cover them with my hands, the chattering, clattering, hissing sounds allow no respite for my sanity. Some noises seem dangerously close, and I lash out with my fists, losing my blindfold in the process and allowing the kaleidoscopic scene to slam into my cranium again. Is this real? I hope not, but it is impossible to disbelieve. I focus on the eternal gladiators writhing in each other's arms. Bright auras of red and green twist around each other until they finally merge; gravity corrects itself, and I fall again, slamming into the carpet and knocking my arm out of its socket. The pain makes me vomit, and I bring up bile laced with coffee.

Steph crawls beside me. I yelp when she pats my shoulder.

'Let me fix it,' she says, making me scream as she grabs my limp arm and scrapes it into place.

Pictures litter the now blind carpet, and the sofa cushions form a triangle; the television screen is torn at the centre and puddles of coffee seep into pale carpet fibres.

Kabis slinks out from behind the sofa. 'You're okay.' I rub

her back and nuzzle my face into hers.

Steph clenches her teeth, hissing through them when she asks, 'What did you do?'

After clambering to my feet, I shuffle around the room, hanging pictures on their hooks and straightening furniture until the hot ache in my shoulder is no longer bearable and I collapse on the sofa.

Steph picks up Onyx's book and flicks through a few pages before her eyes settle on an image, the one I tried to show her earlier. A trembling finger caresses the glossy paper.

'A friend introduced me to the group when I was in my first year at uni. It seemed cool in an out-there kind of way…'

I lift Kabis onto my lap and settle back, ready to hear yet another epic tale, while knowing it will not be the definitive version, the one which will explain everything. Nobody's perceptions are perfect, and Steph's retelling will be a cocktail of fact, fiction and speculation. When her story is finished, it will be up to me to decide which parts I believe, and how much I can forgive. Harrokabis may be gone, but I am not alone, and I will survive this too.

THE END

ABOUT THE AUTHOR

CARMILLA VOIEZ is a British horror and fantasy writer living in Scotland.

Her influences include Graham Masterton, Thomas Ligotti, and Clive Barker. She is pansexual and passionate about intersectional feminism and human rights.

Carmilla has a First-Class Bachelor's degree in Creative Writing and Linguistics. Her work includes stories in horror anthologies published by Crystal Lake Publishing, Clash Books and Mocha Memoirs. She co-authored a Southern Gothic Horror novel with Faith Marlow and has self-published two graphic novels with art by Anna Prashkovich.

Graham Masterton described the second book in her Starblood Trilogy as a "compelling story in a hypnotic, distinctive voice that brings her eerie world vividly to life".

Her books are both extraordinarily personal and universally challenging. In the words of Jef Rouner (Houston Press): "You do not read her books, you survive them."

Carmilla is also a freelance editor and mentor who enjoys making language sing.

www.carmillavoiez.com